The Widow of Wakeford

Lynette Rees

LYNETTE REES

Chapter One

Mid-November 1875

Snow had fallen earlier that day in a flurry of flakes on the mountains of Marshfield, settling on the peaks and later capping the mountains so they resembled an iced Christmas cake. And now it was snowing too in the village of Marshfield down below. The red berries on the holly and rowan trees were plentiful this year, heralding a harsh, bitter winter ahead.

Cassandra Bellingham stood amidst the swirling snowflakes that were sent into a merry dance all around her. Her piercing sapphire blue eyes failed to take in the black-hatted men and women who were gathering around her husband's grave to pay their last respects. She wasn't welcome here by any of them at St. Michael's Church—even though she was the chief mourner and it was *her* husband who had just been lowered underground.

Most of the mourners had blanked her throughout the funeral service, though there were one or two where she felt their hard stares bore a hole into her back as searing as a red hot poker. Reverend Hardcastle had given a fitting tribute to Lord Bellingham when he'd spoken about what a fine upstanding member of the community he'd been, though, he failed to mention the Lord's final months when he had tossed his fortune away like someone scattering seeds over fertile land. But of course, then the seeds would take root and yield a possible harvest that surpassed all expectations. However, the Lord's money had fallen on stony ground that much was for certain.

The bitter north-east wind caused Cassandra to shiver as she took in the bleak churchyard with its higgledy-piggledy gravestones covered in ivy and a dusting of snow, she wrapped her cape closely around her shoulders in a vain attempt to keep the severe chill at bay. Some of the gravestones appeared almost as if about to topple over at any given moment as they were that ancient and in a precarious state.

'Ashes to ashes, dust to dust...' the reverend was saying as he scattered earth over the coffin. He offered a small wooden box containing the earth towards her so she might do the same, fighting back the feeling that she didn't want to do so, she just nodded instead through glazed eyes and taking a pinch of earth, scattered it just as he had done. There was no one else to do so. No family, no friends, only the staff from Marshfield Manor, who fairly soon would be out of the place: jobless, penniless and possibly without even homes to go to in some sad circumstances.

By this time next week, they'd all have departed as the new owner, Josiah Samuel Wilkinson moved in. Josiah was the owner of Marshfield Coal Pit, so it would be fitting that he'd now own Marshfield Manor House too. The price paid for the property would be used to pay off the lawyer, the estate agent and the lord's crumbling debts to various people, there would be very little if anything left over.

Cassandra's final trip in his lordship's coach following the service would now be to the little village of Wakeford as another member of staff brought a cartload of her belongings alongside. And Polly Hedge escorted Cassandra's young daughter and poor sighted aunt in another cart behind the cortege.

***

Cassandra glanced around herself. Was this all she had to show for her two-year marriage to Lord Bellingham? A cartful of expensive clothing, a carved beechwood bureau and a silver set of cutlery? But then again, should she be surprised? After all, once upon a time, she'd been his lordship's "guilty secret" when he'd taken her as his mistress whilst Lady Bellingham had still been alive. The truth was that she and his lordship had been crazy about one another when she'd arrived to work as a housekeeper at his vast, rolling estate. Lady Bellingham had been in ill-health at the time and Oliver hadn't wanted to hurt his wife and did his best to keep it a secret, but secrets had a way of getting out and it wasn't long before the staff at the house were chattering amongst themselves about the pair while Lady Bellingham lay on her death bed on the floor above, gradually fading away.

In a vain attempt to keep gossip at bay, the lord had found a small cottage for Cassandra and her young daughter, Emily, in Wakeford, a small village just a couple of miles away, where he'd paid her visits several times over the months. At least then, Cassandra was away from any staff gossip and Lord Bellingham had no need to reprimand any of his staff for salacious slander regarding his good name and that of his mistress.

Once Lady Bellingham had passed away, naively, Cassandra thought the staff at the big house would have forgiven her and been more accepting when Lord Bellingham declared the year after his wife's sad demise, he was to take a new wife and they already knew her.

Indeed, there had been uproar at the house. Cook threatened to walk out and take half of the kitchen staff with her and even a couple of the chambermaids threatened to go along with them. But in the event, it was all talk as all the staff remained where they were on the day of the wedding of Lord Bellingham to Cassandra Browning. But if Cassandra thought it would be plain sailing afterwards, she had another think coming, as the staff at the house did as they were told but refused to engage in any conversation with her. They delivered her meals on time, a maid even assisted her to get dressed in the morning, but by and large, all the staff were cold towards her except for Polly Hedge, her child's nursemaid. Polly was a wise but simple soul who tended to keep herself apart from the other staff. Cassandra felt she didn't even have anything to complain about to her husband, as after all, it wasn't as if the staff weren't carrying out her orders, they just made her feel lonely and unwanted at Marshfield Manor. She was like a square peg in a round hole and the reason for that was because the staff had been devoted to Lady Bellingham, in their eyes she was an angel and her husband, an ogre, to do what he had done, but even so, he was a man and men were weak and could easily be led, but a young brazen hussy who had supposedly seduced a good man, what was she? An outcast, someone to treat with scorn and utter contempt.

'Cassie!' Cassandra heard her aunt call out her name in a raspy voice. She turned to see the woman standing outside the cottage with Emily, Cassandra's five-year-old daughter, and nestled beside them was Polly Hedge holding the child's hand. Cassandra let out a long sigh, this wasn't what she wished for any of them to begin all over again in such a small property. The two-bedroomed cottage itself was at the end of the row of thatched properties. It had white-washed external walls and low windows. There was no garden at the front, only a small one at the rear. It brought back so many memories of the happy times she spent here though with his Lordship when they'd first fallen in love. Not wanting to cry in front of anyone, she sniffed back a sob and then turned to face them all, forcing a smile at the trio. Best to put a brave face on things under the circumstances.

Cassandra bade the coach driver farewell, wishing him all the best for the future as she handed him some small change, she couldn't afford any more than that. He nodded politely at her as if he understood—at least he was one member of staff who didn't appear to have it in for her. Sadly, she huffed out a breath. Her coach riding days were now over for time being at least. Every farthing had to count from now on. She walked towards the trio and she patted her aunt's crepe-like hand. 'Oh Auntie, we're here at last,' she said, and then she fished about in her reticule for the front door key to the cottage. 'It's going to be a tight squeeze with all of us living here,' she added.

'That's 'orright though,' Polly Hedge smiled. 'We'll manage. Now let's get Aunt Bertha inside so she can rest up.'

Cassandra nodded. 'From now on, Polly, just refer to me as Cassie. That was the name I was brought up with, don't want them thinking I have put on airs and graces around here!'

Polly nodded. 'I understand, Lady B— sorry I

mean, Cassie.'

Cassie stooped to kiss her daughter's soft cheek. 'Don't worry, poppet,' she said, tickling the pretty cherubic face beneath her chin, 'We'll soon be inside and shall get a nice fire going.' She inserted the key in the lock, which was stiff to turn, she figured the cold weather had seized the lock up a little, but after some huffing and puffing, the lock turned and she was able to push open the front door.

Only the scene she was faced with wasn't at all how she'd imagined it would be. As well as it being perishing cold inside, there didn't appear to be a stick of furniture in the place! Where was the table and chairs that used to be up against the window? Where was the walnut dresser that had housed a blue and white Staffordshire porcelain crockery set? Where were the two armchairs placed on either side of the hearth? She opened her mouth and closed it again. Her heart sank, everything seemed unfamiliar to her.

'What's wrong?' Asked Polly as she rushed in behind her.

'Everything's gone!' said Cassie, her bottom lip quivering as she fought to hold back the tears. 'Every last stick of furniture I think.' She immediately thought to check out both bedrooms and dashed up the winding stone steps to the upstairs. Then she heaved a sigh of relief to see the double brass bed in the front bedroom was still there, although there were no pillows or bedding of any sort, just the mattress on the bedstead and it was the same in the other bedroom.

'What's happening?' Polly shouted up the stairs.

Cassie appeared at the top of the landing. 'At least we have beds,' she said biting her bottom lip. 'But we're going to have to get some bedding and a couple of chairs from somewhere for time being. Someone's been in here and removed the furniture.' Slowly, she descended the stairs until she stood on the bottom step, and addressing Polly and Aunt Bertha along with Emily, she sniffed, 'Most of the furniture has gone. Maybe we were robbed.'

'I doubt that very much,' clucked Aunt Bertha. 'I reckon the bailiffs have been inside here to take more of what the Lord owed them.'

'Aye, you're probably right an' all,' Polly tutted. 'Ruthless devils they is.'

This was Cassie's worse nightmare, she fought to think about what to do next. She figured that lighting the fire in the grate would make everyone feel better. At least they'd brought some food with them. She'd taken along a sack of potatoes, some carrots and onions—the gardener at the big house had insisted she take them with her as he was sorting everything out before he left for good. She, herself, had taken a jar of oatmeal and a jug of milk and there were a couple of loaves of bread that Polly had scrounged from Cook by pretending they were just for her. Polly hadn't informed the woman she would be moving in with the mistress. Oh, no, that would never do else Cook would never have provided them otherwise. She'd believed Polly's story that now she was on her uppers and forced to seek lodgings elsewhere as her services as a nursemaid were no longer required now the mistress had left Marshfield Manor. Cook had fallen for it all, and to Polly's delight, she'd even packed a fruit cake for her. So they wouldn't starve for a few days at least.

'We'll get a nice roaring fire underway,' Cassie declared with a note of optimism in her voice. 'Now there isn't any furniture here for time being, apart from the beds upstairs, so I suggest we use the wooden packing crates and tea chest to sit on and eat off for time being. I'll just ask the cart driver to bring them in for us.' She disappeared outside for a moment to have a word with the driver, who obliged by hefting the few crates and tea chest inside the house for them, while Polly got down to lighting the fire. Thankfully, they'd had the foresight to bring some kindling and matches with them.

Cassie offered the driver some small change as she had done with the other, but he waved her hand away and smiling said, 'No, no, Lady Bellingham. I reckon you'll be needing it more than me.'

She smiled at him through glazed eyes in disbelief at the kindness of the man. Old Jake was a good sort. 'Thank you,' she whispered. 'Would you like to stay for some refreshment?'

He shook his head. 'Tis very kind of you to think of me but I want to get back to the big house before weather conditions get too bad. Need to pack up me stuff there and make tracks, you see.'

'Where will you be staying?'

'I'll be movin' in with me sister and her husband in Wyefork.'

She nodded at him. 'Thank you for your service this past two years, Jake,' she added.

He smiled and tipping his cap at her, made to leave the house, but then he turned back in her direction. 'You take care now, you hear?' he said with a note of concern in his voice. 'By all accounts, you had it tough at the big house especially after marrying his lordship, and er…in the end, he let you down, like.'

She nodded and now there was a huge lump in her throat as she watched him clamber on top of his cart and gee his horses onwards back to the manor house.

The Lord's death and gambling debts had left a lot of folk in dire straits that much was for certain.

***

The weather was too bad to go out searching for old second-hand furniture at the marketplace right now, but Cassie reckoned, if she rose at first light and made her way there, she'd be able to pick up some pieces quite cheaply. At least she could afford that much, but the funds would run out fast if she didn't secure some sort of a job for herself. The cottage itself she'd been bequeathed in her husband's will. Thankfully, he'd made a new one following Lady Bellingham's death leaving the cottage and the estate to her, though of course, the estate had been swallowed up by his debts, thankfully, the solicitor had informed her, the cottage was legally hers to do with it what she wanted. She guessed she ought to be grateful as most young women of her age didn't own any property at all. In fact, they *were* their husband's property.

She glanced at Emily who was now sitting on the tea chest playing with her rag doll who she had named "Raggy Anne". She seemed happy enough. Aunt Bertha was seated on a wooden crate while Polly attended to the fire. She was on her knees, scrunching up balls of old newspaper that had been left behind by the previous occupant. The lord had been renting it out to a husband and wife who moved out of there a few months previously. Might they have taken the furniture with them? But no, she couldn't imagine the Masons doing that, they were so law-abiding—it must have been the bailiffs.

Aunt Bertha seemed happy enough, though now Cassie worried about the woman's failing eyesight. She used to be a seamstress and a very good one too, people came from miles around asking her to make garments for them: a dress for a daughter's wedding, a pinafore slip for a young girl, a smart waistcoat for a gentleman, a young lad's pair of breeches, but nowadays she struggled to even hem a dress. Her eyesight just wouldn't hold up and it frustrated the woman so.

As Cassie surveyed the scene around her, she went in search of the kettle from one of the storage boxes. Surely tomorrow had to be better than today?

Chapter Two

That night they managed as best as they could – Cassie taking Emily into bed with her. As there were no sheets or pillows, she rolled up some clothing to place beneath their heads and draped her cloak and some other garments of clothing over them to keep warm. And Polly and her aunt did the same thing in the other bedroom next door. At least they could huddle together for some extra warmth.

Cassie rose at the crack of dawn the following morning, she intended to take Polly to the marketplace with her. A pale sun had appeared in the sky as she drew back the bedroom curtains and outside the window, she could see the long row of cottages opposite and beyond that the snow-capped hills and fields of Marshfield, no longer her home.

She roused Polly and they quickly got themselves ready, leaving Aunt Bertha in charge of Emily, but Cassie warned the little girl not to stray too far as Auntie's eyesight was not very good. Emily had nodded as though she understood. Cassie realised even at that tender age, she could put her trust in the little girl. Indeed, the three people she trusted most in the whole wide world were under the same roof as her.

It was a short walk over the icy cobblestones and across a frosted field to reach the market on the common. Already, vendors were setting up their pitches with shouts of 'Get yer fresh fruit and veg here, folks!' and 'The best meat and poultry in Wakeford for sale right here!'

Cassie glanced around nervously, to see if there was anyone she recognised, but so far, there was no one of note. She dipped her hand into her reticule and fished out a shilling. 'See what you can buy with that, Polly!' she said handing the coin to the woman. 'Get some meat, some baking apples, oh, and a couple of eating apples for Emily. And anything else you think suitable that we might require.'

Polly nodded eagerly at her and made her way off to the meat stall while Cassie browsed around a furniture stall. There was a scrubbed pine table without any chairs but that would do nicely, she thought. 'Do you have any suitable chairs to go with it?' she asked the seller.

He was a man of about thirty-years-old with tousled sandy-red hair and green eyes. On his head, he wore a tweed flat cap and around his neck, a navy and white spotted kerchief. His corduroy jacket had seen better days by the look of it and beneath that, he wore a flannel shirt and his trousers looked well-worn too. He grinned. 'Yes, ma'am. Got a few but they're not matching or anything.'

She smiled as he showed her four wooden chairs but even though they weren't matching, they looked sturdy and solid enough.

'Do you deliver?' she asked hopefully.

He smiled broadly as he shook the leather pouch of coins around his waist so that they made a rattling sound. 'Aye, I can do so when I finish here later on. I'll be all done by around midday, where do you live?'

She pointed across the way. 'I've just moved into "Hawthorn Cottage" Over there!'

'Aye, I know of it. Notorious place that is, 'twas said some lord or another kept his fancy bit in it for a time...' and then, as if realising his folly, he swallowed hard and knocked back the peak of his cap with his hand as if to get a better look at her features. 'Sorry...I didn't mean nothing by it. It were talk 'tis all.'

Cassie shrugged. These days she was used to disparaging comments being made about her. 'It's all right. There's plenty of folk who don't like me in these parts, Mr er?'

'Clement, Jem Clement, ma'am.' His face reddened.

'Do you have anything else suitable too, Mr Clement?'

He smiled broadly as if he realised she had forgiven his misdemeanour. 'Aye, I do. Step this way.' He showed her over to another stall where there was all manner of furniture and bric-a-brac. She ended up purchasing a mirror to go over the mantelpiece, a footstool, a small cabinet and a bookcase and all for four shillings. The wardrobes and cupboards for the upstairs could wait for time being, though Jem reckoned he'd have no problem getting some for her shortly and suitable bedding too. He had tried to sell her a dresser but she explained she'd already brought a walnut one with her. If he was surprised then he wasn't saying so.

On the way back home, Cassie took a couple of baskets from Polly, much to the woman's relief as they were heavy. 'You haven't said much about how you're feeling about everything?' Polly remarked. 'Yesterday must have been a difficult day for you with the funeral and then moving out of the manor house?'

Cassie nodded, there was no use in getting maudlin' about things. 'To tell you the truth, Pol, I'm trying not to think about it. In my mind his lordship is still around, I can't even begin to believe he was buried yesterday...' as she said the words she realised they were truer than she thought for it would be still as if he was around to the folk of Wakeford who had long memories and some had short tempers too.

***

Emily was excited on their return. 'Look, Mama!' she shouted as her mother, closely followed by Polly, emerged through the door, stamping the snow from their leather ankle boots as they walked.

'Just a moment, dear,' Cassie smiled and then she huffed out a breath. 'Let me put these heavy baskets down for a while.' She placed the baskets on the flagstone floor in the living room and Polly followed suit. Then Cassie untied the ribbons of her bonnet and hung it on a peg on the wall along with her cape. 'Now then, what is it?'

'Look what I found in the back garden!' Emily enthused.

Cassie knelt to see a tiny ball of grey fur nestled in her daughter's arms. 'Can I keep him, Mama, please?' Emily looked at her mother with pleading eyes.

The puppy looked quite young. 'Oh, I don't know about that, dear. He might belong to someone...'

'I don't think he does, Mama,' she said. 'He was outside all on his own and anything could happen to him.'

'That's perfectly true,' interrupted Aunt Bertha. 'I reckon he's been left to his own devices. Someone's bitch has had a litter of puppies and they can't find a home for them. More mouths to feed I suppose!' She sighed heavily.

As if on cue, the puppy whimpered, causing Cassie's heart to go out to the poor little soul.

Cassie nodded, she guessed both Aunt Bertha and her daughter might have a point. 'Very well, then,' she said. 'But if someone comes to claim him then he's to be given right back to them, understood?' She met her daughter's persistent gaze.

'Yes, Mama,' she nodded.

Polly let out a sigh. 'Your mother's spoiling you again, Emily!' she said in a tone as if she was cross about the situation, but then Cassie caught her winking at the girl, and she smiled.

'We'll have to find a bed for him and something to eat and drink, I suppose.' Cassie looked at Polly.

Polly nodded. 'It's not a problem as there's a small wooden box I brought some of my whatnots in, we can use that with an old shawl of mine that's nearly falling to pieces it's got that many holes in it!'

'Can we feed him, Mama?' Emily asked, her big brown eyes wide and shiny.

'I expect we'll manage something. Polly's going to cook a nice mutton stew later.'

'Yes,' said Polly. 'I'll boil the meat off the bones and he can have the bone and a bit of leftover meat. He'll enjoy that!' she patted the little dog on his furry head. Cassie had no idea what breed he was and guessed he was most likely some sort of crossbreed. He had the black and white colouring of a Collie Sheep Dog but seemed more robust and plumper more like a Labrador, though he did seem to have overly long limbs so maybe there was some other breed involved somewhere in his lineage.

***

By the time Jem had turned up with the furniture and had helped set the table and chairs by the front window, the bookcase set down in the corner and the mirror installed over the mantelpiece, the room was beginning to look homely.

'Oh, there's something else,' said Jem. 'I've got a surprise for you.'

Cassie smiled a little unsure of what was going on.

'I'll just nip out to me cart,' he said. He returned a couple of minutes later with a bunch of yellow and white chrysanthemums and a blue and white pottery vase. 'A little gift for your new house!' he announced. Then his face flushed red as he said, 'the pottery vase were something I picked up when I go around purchasing stuff from folks' houses. It's not new or nothing but I thought maybe you'd like it for your new home.'

A small smile played on Cassie's lips. 'How delightful!' she enthused. She'd forgotten what it was like for someone to treat her nicely after the way the staff at Marshfield Manor had treated her so coldly. 'The kindness of a stranger...' she mumbled to herself.

'Pardon?' Jem quirked a puzzled brow as he squeezed his flat cap between his hands.

'I was just thinking aloud that's all. Would you like to stay for tea?'

He nodded eagerly at her. 'If it's not too much trouble?'

'None at all, Jem!' she reassured.

Polly smiled at them. 'I'll put the kettle on and slice some bread, and there's that slab of fruit cake in the larder.'

Soon they were seated around the table, with Emily perched on a crate and the pup ensconced in his new makeshift basket. Polly had made some cheese and pickle sandwiches and a pot of tea.

Jem savoured it all as he closed his eyes.

'Where do you live then, Jem?' Cassie asked.

'I live at Rose Cottage which is the furthest cottage at the far end of the village,' he replied. 'It were left to me by me father when he passed on a couple of years since.'

'Oh, I'm sorry to hear of his passing,' she said, now unsure of what to say, but he smiled at her.

'It's 'orright. It were a blessing in the end. He were fading away afore me very eyes. He were a good age an' all mind. Me parents had me late in life, see. I were a surprise baby.'

'And your mother?'

'She's not around either. She died in childbirth. There were another after me and she weren't so lucky.'

'Oh, you poor man,' she said suddenly and then she laid a hand of reassurance on his shoulder which surprised even her as she was not usually so tactile with strangers. She paused for a moment to look into his vivid green eyes. 'So your mother and younger sibling died at the same time?'

Jem vigorously shook his head. 'Ah, no, the infant survived and is still alive today. Me younger brother but he ain't right you see.'

She frowned, what on earth did he mean by that? 'How so?'

'There's something not right about him. I mean he looks like a man and sometimes sounds like a man but it's like he's got the mind of a child at times. I worry as people have tried to take advantage of him. He usually helps me on the furniture stall but today he's been invited to our aunt's house in Hocklea. She sometimes takes care of him, she's me mother's sister.'

'What's your brother's name?' asked Cassie, dropping her hand to her side.

'Clitheroe,' he sniffed. 'Clithoroe Clement. But he goes mostly by the name of Clyde. Clitheroe Clement is a bit of a mouthful, you see...'

Cassie nodded. 'I do. One afternoon you'll have to bring Clyde here for tea. I'm sure he'd love to see Emily's new pup.'

Jem nodded eagerly. 'Aye, he would an' all. He loves animals even though he's sometimes wary of people.' Cassie thought she could detect a level of pain behind Jem's now watery looking eyes and then he looked away as if clearing his thoughts. He turned back to face her. 'But I'm sure once he'll get to know you he'll be fine.'

She nodded and smiled at him but said no more about it for time being, it seemed a sensitive topic for the man.

When Jem had departed and Polly and her aunt were sitting comfortably at the table chatting with one another with Emily lying on the rug in front of the fire with the little dog, Cassie excused herself and lay down on her bed upstairs. It was the first chance since yesterday's funeral for her to be alone, take stock and weep for the only man she'd ever truly loved and she hoped no one heard her downstairs as her entire body was wracked with grief. That night, she slept better than she had in weeks.

**

The following morning, Cassie walked along the cobbled streets, passing the rows of small cottages and one or two farmhouses along the way to get to the neighbouring village of Drisdale to seek work. Drisdale was separated from Wakeford by a fast-flowing river and to get there she had to cross a very old stone bridge. She wasn't as well-known there and figured she might get a position working in a shop as an assistant of some sort or even employment at the wool mill, it might be something to help to support them all. But everywhere she went, doors were closed in her face as no one needed any new workers. Even at the mill, the manager said he wasn't taking anyone new on right now and in any case, as he put it, 'I have a list as long as my arm of people trying to get work here.'

Jobs are in high demand in Drisdale. I'm unlikely

to get one here as an outsider! She shook her head sadly.

There were few shops in Wakeford which included a butcher, poulterer, grocer shop and a post office, so she didn't much fancy her chances and there was the added factor that most folk knew who she was and wouldn't employ her anyhow due to her associations with the lord—she was a marked woman. The only reason Jem hadn't initially realised she was the Widow of Wakeford was because he lived at the far end of the village, and even then, he had evidently heard the local gossip about her. She supposed she might put the cottage up for sale and they could all move elsewhere, but what bother that would cause. Having to look for a new house, then there would be transport costs and the fact it would be very unsettling for everyone to be uprooted once again. She estimated she'd have to move about ten miles out of the area for people not to realise who she was.

Oliver had been so good to her when she'd first arrived at Marshfield Manor. He'd been so warm and welcoming and back then, so had the other staff, before they'd discovered the love affair that had been blossoming right beneath their very noses. The staff had even taken orders from her as housekeeper in those days as she had an air of authority about her as she instructed Cook what she was to prepare for dinner that evening, or she instructed a parlour maid to light a fire in the drawing-room, or a footman to be prepared as guests were arriving that evening. She had loved her job too. Aunt Bertha's eyesight was better back in those days and she still worked as a seamstress in her small tithed cottage in Drisdale so that she could also take care of Emily who was a baby back then. Cassie's first husband, Albert Browning, had been a cruel sort, who had been seemingly good to her until they wed. It was on the night of their wedding that he'd taken his fists to her when he'd demanded his conjugal rights with recourse. She had declined as she was feeling unwell at the time, but he'd insisted, telling her, 'Woman, from now on yer my property! And when I wants me rights, I gets them!' And so she had complied and taken part in a love act where there was not a hint of compassion nor love and the next morning, her body was covered in bruises where he'd pinned her down and she was sore between her legs. And as she'd washed him away from her skin in a tin bath with water as hot as she could possibly stand, she'd wept. Even though she could scrub his smell away which she'd felt tainted her, she hadn't managed to wash away his seed which had implanted inside of her.

The strange thing was, after that night, he never went near her for sex ever again, although he still raised his fists a time or two. It had puzzled her why he no longer wished to satisfy his lustful urges, but the mystery was over when she bumped into a village gossip who delighted in telling her that her husband was having it away with a buxom young barmaid from The Crown and Feathers. She should have been upset by that but she wasn't as she realised the young woman was doing her a mighty favour. But her elation turned to despair when she realised she was pregnant by Albert and it must have occurred that night when he'd beaten and abused her for there was no other time when their bodies had been in union with one another.

She hid the pregnancy from him for as long as she could muster and was surprised to discover he was over the moon about it. 'A son for me at last!' he'd declared, for he was a lot older than her. She worried then that if it was not a boy she carried in her womb but a baby girl, would he get angry and lash out at her? But she needn't have worried as exactly one month later, Albert was dead, collapsed in the arms of the young woman at the pub. Buried within five days and lying beneath the earth in consecrated ground at St. Andrew's Church in Drisdale. His heart appeared to have given out, which she thought of as ironic when he didn't appear to have one. It was then she'd decided that she needed to get a job to support herself and the baby and that was when Aunt Bertha had stepped in to take care of the infant. To begin with, Cassie started working as a parlour maid at Marshfield Manor and within eighteen months had been promoted to housekeeper and all had been well until she'd succumbed to the charms of Lord Bellingham.

But as she shook herself out of her memory of that time, she realised, it was like history repeating itself: she was widowed once again and needed a job, badly.

***

It was while she was on her way to Jem's cottage to pay a visit with a plate of seed cake that Polly had baked especially for him, in her wicker basket, that Cassie noticed an empty shop at the top of Rowan Road. The shop was one she had remembered last year as being owned by a milliner called Madame Claudette. The woman had appeared to be French but Cassie knew she wasn't as when she'd gone there to be fitted for a selection of new hats, she'd heard the woman slip into her usual accent when she was unaware that Cassie was seated behind a curtain as Lady Bellingham back then. The woman's accent was definitely Northern by Cassie's estimation, more Northern than Normandy as where she claimed to be from.

What had occurred for the shop to close down, she wondered? On closer inspection, she noticed a card in the window written in elegant copperplate handwriting which read, 'Shop to let, enquire at number 5 Meadowcroft Cottages, Ravensdale.' She quirked an interested brow. Ravensdale was about six miles away. Could she afford to rent the shop? And if so, what could she possibly sell? Wakeford had a small selection of shops already and she was no milliner herself to make hats to carry on that tradition, yet, that shop and business would have the goodwill of the affluent and even less affluent folk in the area.

Shaking her head, she dismissed the idea as being pie in the sky and carried on with her walk towards Jem's cottage. As she turned the corner at the top of the hill, to turn right in the direction of the path that would take her towards the outlying cottages, she noticed two women heading towards her. Oh no, Mrs Hewitt and Mrs Peterson. Two older ladies who thought they were amongst the elite of Wakeford. What should she do? Turn around and retreat to avoid a confrontation or carry on? But they had already seen her as both had stopped chatting to one another as their eyes were fixed on her. Mrs Hewitt was smartly dressed in a dark brown Cambrian cloth dress with a checked beige and brown shawl around her shoulders. Her brown bonnet matched her outfit, but Mrs Peterson, who was the smaller of the two, wore a bright flowered dress and a cream shawl with a pretty frilled bonnet. Their outfits seemed to match their personalities: Mrs Hewitt being brown and boring and Mrs Peterson's light and gay.

As the women drew close all three of them stood in their tracks. Mrs Peterson's eyes reminded Cassie of a timid little bird but Mrs Hewitt's eyes were sharp and accusatory.

'Mrs Hewitt, Mrs Peterson, good day to you both!' Cassie greeted with a smile of uncertainty on her face.

'Good day, Lady Bellingham,' Mrs Peterson greeted, but then seeing the look on the face of her companion, said no more.

'Why are you referring to her as Lady?' Mrs Hewitt said sharply as Mrs Peterson looked down at the ground as if she feared she had done the wrong thing in replying to Cassie.

'You're perfectly correct, Mrs Hewitt,' Cassie said, 'I am no longer the Lady of Marshfield Manor. I've returned to live here once again in the cottage.'

Mrs Hewitt sniffed loudly. 'If I had my way you wouldn't be back here at all after all those fine goings-on under that roof. It was like a hot bed of sin! You should be ashamed of yourself!' She placed one hand over the other and pursed her lips in a prudish manner.

Cassie noticed that Mrs Peterson's face had flushed red.

'I...I don't know what to say,' Cassie stammered. 'All I can tell you, I suppose, is that I loved his lordship and he loved me. What more is there to say?'

Mrs Hewitt harrumphed and then addressing her companion said, 'And all the while she and the lord were carrying on in a fine fashion at that cottage, poor Lady Bellingham was on her death bed...'

'It wasn't quite like that,' Cassie protested. The truth of it had been that, yes, they had both fallen in love with one another and, yes, Lady Bellingham was dying at that time, but what no one knew was that the Lady herself had permitted her husband to conduct a relationship with her. She had even told him to marry Cassie as she approved of her. In essence, she'd been looking for someone for her husband before she departed this world but she could hardly tell Mrs Hewitt that, she just wouldn't understand.

'Then what was it like?' Mrs Hewitt stepped forward, invading Cassie's space.

Cassie took a step back. 'The lord wasn't as callous as you might think and neither was I. If people were to know the truth then maybe they wouldn't be so quick to judge us.'

'Judge you both? The lord was a man, he can be excused for his behaviour but you've behaved no better than a wanton, cheap hussy!' Mrs Hewitt's nostrils flared and then she raised the palm of her hand and then Cassie felt it, a searing sting across her cheek as she rebounded backwards from the force of the blow.

'Come on now, Edna,' Mrs Peterson pleaded with her. 'This isn't helping anyone...' she looked at Cassie with sympathy in her eyes.

Cassie's eyes glazed with tears. This was so unfair after all she'd been through lately. There was a lump in her throat and she didn't want to break down in tears in front of the woman. 'All I'll say to you, Mrs Hewitt, is you'd better keep out of my way in future or I'll be slapping you one back!' she said angrily. Then she pushed roughly past the women, elbowing Mrs Hewitt out of her way.

'Well!' she heard the woman say, 'Can you believe that, Maisie?'

A small smile played on Cassie's lips as she walked away, she might not have won the battle but she'd certainly left her mark when she'd stood up to the old crone. From now on she was determined to fight fire with fire and stand up for herself against anyone who crossed her in the village not as she'd previously done in the past when she was the lord's mistress and had to bite her tongue for fear of recrimination.

***

The path Cassie had to take to get to Rose Cottage was unfamiliar to her. She'd never walked this way before. After leaving behind the smoking chimneys of cottages in the row behind her, she was now faced with a steep mountain pass from where, far in the distance, she spotted several cottages dotted across the bottom of the mountainside, but which one could it be? She remembered Jem had said it was the furthest away. The road was a rocky pass that was for sure, but fields and hedgerows as she passed by were pleasant with their green and red holly and berries dusted with snow. The first couple of cottages were obviously not Jem's as the first had a sign outside which read, "Dunraven Cottage" and the second had children playing in the garden outside, but the furthest in the distance had a cart outside which she recognised as Jem's from when he'd transported that furniture to her place.

Stood outside was a young man, head bent and she wondered what he was doing. Then she noticed he was whittling some wood. Was this Clitheroe or Clyde as he was known? Initially, he didn't seem to notice her approach as she opened the wooden gate but then there was a loud clatter which she hadn't expected as it slammed shut behind her. It had some sort of spring attached to it to ensure it shut behind folk.

The young man looked up and immediately his eyes as they met hers were guarded. He was wearing a rough white shirt, tweed waistcoat and green corduroy trousers. He was quite a handsome young man, but he looked petrified as he ran towards the house shouting out, 'Jem! Jem! There's s...s...someone here!'

Jem emerged through the front door and grinned when he saw who his visitor was. 'It's all right, Clyde,' he reassured as he patted his brother's arm. It's the lady I were telling you about, Lady Cassandra Bellingham.'

Clyde smiled nervously and followed in his brother's wake as he approached her.

'This is a nice surprise!' Jem greeted. 'What brings you here this afternoon?'

'You, of course,' Cassie returned his smile. 'I've brought a seed cake that Polly made for you and Clyde.'

'Now that's most kind of you, Lady Bellingham.'

'Please, call me Cassie. I'm no longer lady of the manor.'

He nodded. 'Whatever you wish. Won't you come inside?'

Cassie followed Jem inside the house with Clyde shyly shuffling behind them, dragging his feet. The first thing she noticed once inside the house was just how cluttered it was. There was hardly a space available as items of furniture were stacked against the walls and piles of bric-a-brac lined every available shelf and windowsill. Jem removed a wooden box from the armchair and offered her a seat. Then he drew a dining chair from the table and sat himself down. 'Please excuse the mess,' he said shaking his head. 'This house lacks a woman's touch.'

Cassie held up her vertical palm. 'Please, there's no need to apologise. I perfectly understand. She dipped her hand into her wicker basket on her lap and handed him the plate of cake which had a tray cloth covering it.

'Thank you,' he said, taking it and placing it on the table beside himself.

On seeing the cake, Clyde began to look interested and slowly brought himself into the room. 'So, you're Clyde then?' Cassie smiled at him.

He returned the smile as he slowly approached. 'You like cake then, do you?'

He nodded eagerly and grinned. 'Yes...Y...yes I do. I like cake I do...'

It was strange as Clyde did have the look of a man but the demeanour and mannerisms of a child. 'I was telling Jem that he'll have to bring you over to our house one day for your tea. You'll be able to see our puppy dog then.'

Clyde's eyebrows shot up with interest. 'Wh... what's his name?'

'Do you know, we haven't named him as yet. He's Emily's puppy, she found him. I suppose we will have to think of a name.'

'Wh...who's Emily?'

'She's my daughter, Clyde. You'll get to meet her soon.'

He seemed satisfied with that answer.

Jem looked at him. 'Put t'kettle on t'boil, Clyde,' he said.

Clyde nodded and went off to do so.

'Is he safe handling a kettle of boiling water?'

'Oh, aye,' Jem said. 'But usually, he just puts it on the hob to boil and I take care of the rest.'

Suddenly remembering the shop, Cassie told Jem that she'd noticed the hat shop was for sale.

Jem scratched his chin as if in contemplation. 'Oh, yes. I heard that *Madame What's Her Name* has moved out of the area. She's opening a new shop in Ravensdale. Why do you ask?'

'I'm interested in renting it but I've no idea

what to sell.' She had an immediate thought. 'Look, I've just had an idea. You have all this furniture, how would you like to become a partner with me and we could open the shop to sell furniture and bits and pieces. It would be better than you standing out in all weathers in the marketplace.'

He nodded as if thinking about things. 'I suppose it's an idea, though I've not got a lot of capital to invest.'

'You wouldn't need to really. As long as we could cover the weekly shop rent any profit we make, we could split between us. I've been inside that shop several times, and there are two shop fronts. On one side we could sell the furniture and on the other side maybe we could create some sort of tea room. Polly is a dab hand with baking. I never realised it before as Cook did all the baking at the big house but since I've been at the cottage, she's baked some delicious cakes.'

'Is that kettle boiled yet?' Jem shouted toward the scullery door.

Clyde emerged through it with a big smile on his face. 'Yes, Jem. It's b...b...boiled. He grinned and winked at Cassie.

Jem chuckled. 'That wink means he likes and accepts you!'

Cassie smiled, she was so glad of that.

***

Days settled down into a pattern of Polly Hedge taking care of Emily, whilst Aunt Bertha did the best she could to help out at the cottage but her eyes were failing her dreadfully. Cassie had made enquiries about the shop that was up for rent, she worked out she had enough money to scrape together a couple of months' rent if Jem could chip in with his half. He certainly had enough furniture and bric-a-brac to fill one side of the shop languishing back at his cottage. She told him they'd need a few small tables and chairs and a counter for the tea room. He'd assured her that was no problem and he could get that all installed for her, even offering to construct the counter himself—he was a handy person to know who it seemed could turn his hand to almost anything. So she set about giving the place a good clean up with Polly's help as Bertha remained at the cottage with Emily. They washed the window panes until they sparkled, scrubbed the flagstone floors and polished the furniture Jem had supplied with beeswax and lavender polish. Polly had even sewn some blue and white gingham curtains to adorn the windows and the lower insets of the front bay windows were covered in lace. Each table was laid with a pristine white table cloth and a small vase of flowers placed at its centre.

It was the beginning of December and the shop was ready to open, over the door a sign had been constructed by Jem himself which read, 'Jem's Furniture Emporium and Tea Room'. Cassie had decided to leave her name off the sign even though the tea room would be hers as her name seemed to be mud in the village and she didn't want folk reminding that Lord Bellingham's Widow was lying in waiting for them—all she wanted was for them to try out the tea room as there hadn't been one in Wakeford for years, people had needed to travel to Drisdale for the chance of a pot of tea and some fancies as a treat.

So, on a Monday morning at the beginning of the Christmas season, Cassie and Polly waited anxiously for customers to arrive. The tea urn had boiled, there was a selection of cakes and fancies at the counter and Jem waited in his side of the shop too with Clyde at his side, but no one came. Not one person set foot over the threshold to peruse the furniture nor the tea room.

'Give it a bit o' time, gal!' Polly encouraged when they'd waited a whole hour for even a sniff of a customer to arrive.

Cassie folded her arms and let out a long sigh. 'It's me, Polly. Folk haven't forgiven me for taking away their precious lord and as well as being blamed for the death of Lady Bellingham, I'm sure they think I'm somehow responsible for his death too!'

'Stuff and nonsense, gal!' Polly said forcefully as her chin jutted out in defiance. Out of all the staff employed at the house, Polly was the only one who would have dared referred to her as 'gal' as if she were one of her own kind, but of course, she was one even though folk wouldn't forget what had happened. She'd been born working-class and working-class she was destined to die and all.

'How else do you explain it?' Cassie shook her head sadly, trying not to give in to tears.

'It's early days and it ain't even half-past ten yet. I reckon you ought to put a small sign in the window to tempt them in.'

Cassie frowned and then chewed on her bottom lip. 'How'd you mean?'

'Tell it like it is. What we 'ave to offer here,' Polly said with a smile.

'You mean like "Pot of tea for two with sandwiches and a selection of cakes for such and such a price?"'

'Aye, something like that. To tempt them across the threshold. Or maybe offer special prices for the first day.'

'That's a terrific idea!' Cassie said, suddenly brightening up. 'I'll ask Jem if he has a piece of wood left from building that counter and ask him to make a small placard to go outside. On one side he could paint, "Early morning special offers. Tea for two and a selection of pastries and fancies" and the other side something like, "Open all day. Friendly service." After the morning special offers, we can turn the placard to the open all day side.'

'That's sorted out then!' said Polly with a smile. 'People will know we're open when they see the placard outside. That way there'll be no confusion.'

Cassie stepped over to Jem's side of the shop to put her request to him. He smiled. 'That's a good idea.' Then glancing at Clyde he asked, 'Can you find that piece of wood leftover from when we made the counter, it's out t'back somewhere. And there's a pot of black paint and a paintbrush, can you fetch those, please?'

Clyde nodded. He shuffled off to fetch the implements to his brother, seeming pleased to be of assistance to them both. That cheered Cassie. Clyde though, she realised, was a tall man, well-built too, towering a good four inches over Jem, who was of average height. If he wasn't so affable, she realised he might frighten folk but as it was, he appeared to be a gentle sort of giant.

Quite soon, Jem had constructed the placard to place outside of the shop. Cassie stood back and smiled, folding her arms as she took in the sign and its placement. She had to admit, it was rather eye-catching. If this didn't get the customers in, then nothing would. She glanced at Jem, who looked quite proud of his handiwork, and then he returned a smile and patting her on the shoulder said, 'Don't worry none, Cassie, it will take time to build up custom. People are probably busy with it's coming up to Christmas. Things to do and places to be and all that.'

She nodded. Maybe they were otherwise occupied.

Polly was proved right though as about twenty

minutes later, a large framed lady turned up with her husband. He looked quite diminutive beside her, being a thin and wiry sort and a good four inches shorter than she. Cassie watched as the pair studied the placard and the inside of the shop, then they exchanged comments with one another, nodding as they did so.

Polly rushed to the door to open it for them, 'Good morning, both!' she greeted. 'How would you like to step inside of Wakeford's newest tea room? We have a special offer on in the mornings, tea for two and a selection of pastries and fancies.'

The gentleman, who must have been around middle age, Cassie reckoned, removed his top hat to reveal an almost bald pate but what he lacked for on the top of his head, he more than made up for with his bushy brown sideburns. He smiled generously and looking up at his wife asked, 'Shall we step inside, Martha?'

The woman smiled at him. 'Yes, George. Let's try it.' Her smile seemed to lighten up her entire face as her chubby rosy cheeks wobbled as the pair stepped over the threshold, holding hands with one another. George held his wife in great esteem.

Cassie watched, her heart racing as Polly showed them to a window seat, drawing out two chairs for them. She so wanted this first sale to go well. Polly didn't seem as concerned about the first day as she did as Polly Hedge was the sort who always took most things in her stride. She hadn't even got her bloomers in a knot when she'd been informed that all the staff had to leave Marshfield Manor, she'd just sort of accepted it, saying to Cassie. 'I believe there's a cycle to everything in life. If it's to end here, it's to end.'

Cassie's mouth was dry with anticipation as she waited at the counter for Polly to take the couple's order, drumming her fingers on the wooden top as she waited impatiently. Then she walked over to the table to introduce herself. 'Good morning, both,' she said with a big smile on her face. 'So pleased you've decided to call in. I'm the proprietor.'

'And we're Mr and Mrs Moody,' said the man. 'We're from Dykingdale Farm over yonder.' He pointed, but where he was pointing to, Cassie did not have a clue for in that direction was a line of cottages called Mulberry Row. So they were a farmer and a farmer's wife. Maybe that explained the way his wife looked so robust, they had plenty of good food to hand, no doubt. Not rich by any means but not badly off either. She figured they might be handy sorts to know if they sold their produce locally.

'I used to call to this shop for my hats,' explained Mrs Moody. 'Do you remember it when it was a hat shop which was run by a French lady called Madame Claudette, she managed to bring in the finest materials from Paris...'

Cassie felt like smiling. French indeed! *Ma-*

dame Claudette was no more French than she was and she guessed she obtained her finest materials to adorn her couture hats from the market stall at Drisdale. But instead of smirking or rolling her eyes, she listened intently to the lady as she jabbered on and on. It was as if living on that farm had starved Mrs Moody of sociable company and now she was telling all to Cassie, the woman didn't even pause to draw a breath. So, she was quite relieved when Polly showed up at the table with a tray containing a pot of tea for two and a plate of pastries between the pair.

Mrs Moody's eyes enlarged when she saw the generously sized pastry slices that were oozing with thick yellow custard and slathered in white icing, and the miniature pastry nests inset with cooked egg, cheese and chives. Cassie made her excuses to leave the pair to it and she returned behind the counter at Polly's side. 'See, I told you it were early days,' Polly said sagely, and with arms folded she gave a knowing nod and said, 'you ain't got a lot to be worried about, lass.'

***

But Cassie did have something to worry about because although the day had gone well enough at the tea room, as later it began to fill up and customers drifted back and forth between the tea room and the furniture shop, she had noticed Mrs Hewitt had come to stand outside the shop a time or two and had glared through the window at her. What was all that about? She wondered.

In fact, it is I who should be glaring at her the way she confronted me recently and slapped my face!

When it had happened for the fourth time that day and the woman was standing there giving her the evil eye over the top of the half lace curtains, she decided to do something about it.

'I can't stand this anymore,' Cassie clenched her teeth. 'That woman has been goading me all day.'

'Now hang on a moment,' Polly touched her shoulder and looking into her eyes said, 'don't let the likes of her ruin it for you. If she knows she's getting to you, she will persist, but if you let things lie, she will soon get fed up.'

Maybe Polly was right but why on earth should the likes of Mrs Hewitt ruin her first day? 'She's putting off the customers too as they're eating though!' Cassie moaned as she noticed one lady shake her head and turn her chair around so she no longer had to see Mrs Hewitt staring through the window at her as she nibbled on a currant bun. Finally, the woman stood and left her half-eaten bun behind as the tea room doorbell jangled behind her.

'That's it! I've had enough!' Cassie declared as she marched out towards the door with Polly in pursuit. Heads were now turning towards the commotion.

Chapter Three

'Mrs Hewitt,' Cassie began as she stood on the pavement facing the woman. She was about to have a go at her as she felt angry she was trying to put off her trade and knock her off her stride into the bargain when Cassie smiled sweetly and said, 'I can see you've been fancying trying out some of our delicious concoctions. As you've stood outside so long, I can only conclude you're a little shy to step over the threshold or else, don't have the money to do so, so won't you come in and be my guest? You can try a nice sticky bun with a cup of tea or a pot of coffee and as it's the first day, it will be on the house especially for you.' Cassie stepped forward and taking the woman's elbow attempted to steer her inside the establishment.

Mrs Hewitt, not knowing how to react to this perceived offer of generosity, pulled her arm away from Cassie and with chin jutting out in defiance said, 'I most certainly do have enough money to pay for anything at all in your blessed tea room but I do not wish to step one foot over that door.' She pursed her lips and narrowed her gaze in Cassie's direction.

A smile played on Cassie's lips. 'Oh, dear! That is such a shame. I can only conclude then you are waiting for someone as you've been loitering for such a long time outside the tea room, and as you do not see fit to enter the premises, may I suggest you wait elsewhere or I shall be forced whenever I see you to go outside and sweep up anything that shouldn't be on the pavement with a very large broom!'

Mrs Hewitt harrumphed loudly and when she had noticed that Cassie had gone back inside the tea room, she stood there with a smug look upon her face until Cassie returned with the broom. Then a look of horror swept over Mrs Hewitt's face as Cassie came at her with the broom like a whirling dervish as she brushed the pavement hard and fast so that the woman had to step out of the way. It was not a few seconds then before the woman turned on her heel and walked off at a fine pace in the direction of Mulberry Row.

Cassie smirked to herself as she entered the shop with the broom in her hand and Polly stood behind the counter chuckling to hold back her mirth as she brought the apron of her pinafore to her face not for the customers to see her laughter, but oh it did feel good giving Mrs Hewitt her comeuppance that particular day.

***

There were no further problems from Edna Hewitt that week and Cassie reckoned, for now, the woman had gone to ground, but being the sort she was, she didn't reckon it would be the last she'd see of her. Wakeford was a small village and it was easy to bump into folk when least expected. Still, business was slowly picking up as people got to hear about the tea room and its excellent reports. Customers were even coming in to order special cakes to take away with them. Polly baked these at home in the evenings while Emily was fast asleep in her bed and Aunt Bertha was napping by the fireside. It was such a contented scene back at the cottage that Cassie realised she was fortunate in that her daughter was a well-behaved child, else her great aunt would never cope with her great-niece all day when she was out working!

It was while Polly had her hands in the large pottery mixing bowl that the topic of the child's education arose.

Cassie chewed on her bottom lip. 'I suppose in light of everything that's happened and it being near Christmas and all, I hadn't paid it much attention. I mean her governess was all that was needed back at the big house and other times you took over...' She looked at Polly to gauge her reaction.

Polly shook her head and tossed a handful of currants into the bowl, slowly mixing them in with a wooden spoon. 'Trouble is, she has neither a governess nor a nursemaid at the moment as I'm too busy with the tea room...' she huffed out a breath.

Cassie drew nearer the woman. 'I am sorry,' she said, 'it's only until I get on my feet. I don't have the baking skills that you do.'

Polly sniffed loudly. 'It ain't that. I enjoy working at the tea room, in fact, I love it.' She stopped stirring the ingredients for a moment and added a few large spoonful's of sugar from a glass jar, then looked at Cassie. 'I just think you ought to now make other arrangements for Emily. She's as bright as any boy, so intelligent for her age, might I say. I've looked after a fair few children in my time and let me tell you none of them were as bright as your Emily for their age.'

Cassie beamed with pride. She was about to say something when Aunt Bertha stirred by the hearth, opening one eye and then the other. 'Emily? You say,' she grunted. 'I agree with Polly. How about sending her to a private tutor then?'

Cassie frowned. 'The trouble is every farthing has to count at the moment, we need to get this business going, maybe next summer we'll have made enough to pay a tutor.'

'I was listening to two customers in the shop today,' Polly said knowingly, 'anyhow, this is what I'm coming to. There's a school starting in the church hall in January. It won't cost anything either as it will be funded by some kindly benefactor. Apparently, no one knows who he or she is.'

Aunt Bertha sniffed loudly. 'Curious! So, they're anonymous then! I wonder why?'

Polly shrugged. 'No idea, but if you could have a word with the vicar, Cassie, they might take your Emily on, especially if you explain the circumstances to him.'

Cassie felt dubious and she chewed her lip. 'Maybe, but as soon as they find out who I am I bet they'll turn my request down.'

'Not necessarily so!' Aunt Bertha wagged her index finger in her niece's direction. 'If the vicar is as God-fearing as all that he won't pass judgement.'

Polly nodded enthusiastically. 'It has to be worth a try, hasn't it?'

Cassie nodded but she knew from experience how judgemental folk were likely to be in her direction.

**

The following morning, Cassie stood with Emily by her side outside The Vicarage. A brass doorplate to the side of the front door read, 'Reverend John Ainsworth'. She wondered for a moment if she should use the back entrance to the house, but being indecisive would get her nowhere. So, she stepped forward to lift the brass knocker and rapped on it three times. Then she stepped back and appraised her daughter's appearance. My, she did look smart in her dark green velvet cape and matching bonnet, around her neck hung a fur muff which both of her little hands were plunged into to keep out the cold. Cassie, herself, had worn her navy cape and a plain bonnet to match. She waited impatiently, all the while wondering why she felt so nervous. She was about to rap on the knocker once again when the door swung open. A middle-aged woman in a long black dress and white pinafore and mobcap answered. 'Can I help you?'

The woman looked a friendly sort, she had rounded cheeks and a big smile and twinkling blue eyes. Cassie thought she looked around the same age as Polly.

'Yes, please. My name is Cassie Bellingham, I've recently moved back into the village with my daughter and I've heard that there are places going at the new school being set up at the church hall?' she asked hopefully, all the while worrying that the woman would pass judgement as soon as she heard the name Bellingham as everyone knew that name around these parts and would link her with the lord. But she was relieved when the woman answered as if the name was of no consequence whatsoever.

'I'll just go and ask Reverend Ainsworth,' she said politely. 'Quite a few parents have already enrolled their children at the school so I'm not too sure if there are any places left. Are you regular members of the church? I can't say I've ever seen you there before?'

'Er, no.' Cassie was feeling a little uncomfortable now as the woman might think she didn't attend church at all. 'We used to attend St. Michael's until we moved back here of course.'

'Very well, I'll go and ask for you.' The woman turned, leaving the door ajar.

Cassie honestly hadn't thought they'd need to be church members but of course, it would make sense for those children who attended Sunday School there that should be in line for enrolment.

The maid returned a couple of minutes later with a smile on her face. 'Reverend Ainsworth would like to see you in his study,' she said knowingly, which made Cassie wonder if it was good news, especially on seeing the woman smile like that.

She led Cassie and Emily into the hallway and along the parquet floor to a room with a big heavy black oakwood door which she drew open and invited them to step inside.

The Reverend Ainsworth was stood gazing out of the large bay fronted window, hands behind his back as if deep in thought. On hearing the door open, he turned and smiled warmly at them, his arms now in front of him in an open, welcoming gesture. Cassie noticed he looked middle-aged too, his dark hair was thinning on top and he had a hooked nose and rather shrewd looking eyes beneath his gold-rimmed spectacles, but his smile was definitely one of warmth as he stepped forward to greet them both. His black cassock rustled as he walked towards them.

'Good morning, both!' he said, encouraging them to enter further into his study which was adorned wall to ceiling in bookcases; a large walnut desk and chair sat against one wall and a matching dresser against the other.

He invited them to take a seat on the settle beside one another while he sat in a large winged armchair opposite them as a roaring fire blazed in the hearth. Cassie gazed around and imagined the man loved this room and she thought she detected the faint aroma of pipe tobacco which reminded her of her father when he was alive. She found it comforting somehow.

'Good morning, Reverend,' Cassie said when they were all seated.

The vicar raised a curious straggly brow. 'I understand that you'd like to enrol your daughter into our new school, is that correct?'

'Yes, please.'

'And how old is the child? I'm assuming the child with you is the child in question?'

'Yes, she's five years old but very bright for her age.'

'I only have a couple of places left but those were intended for older children, those who already have a basic education in the three Rs. You see, the younger class is already full up.' He steepled his fingers then brought his hands together beneath his chin, almost as though in prayer.

'Oh, there's no problem there,' explained Cassie, 'Emily can already read and write.'

'Can she indeed!' said the vicar as his hands

were now splayed wide open, palms up as if surprised by this nugget of information.

'Yes, and she can also add and subtract some simple sums.' Emily beamed beside her as her mother discussed her progress.

'But how is that?' The vicar rubbed his chin.

'Because she used to have a private governess when we lived at the big house.'

'Ah, I see,' he said with some recognition now, 'So you are Lady Bellingham? I recognised the name of course as soon as the maid told me, I just wanted to be sure.'

Suddenly, she felt shame at the mention of the name. 'Was,' she said with some sadness. 'I'm sure you will have heard that my husband recently passed away, leaving me practically penniless apart from an old cottage in Wakeford.'

'I have to admit, I had heard, my dear. But that is of no consequence now as Emily will be eligible for enrolment if she can read and write as well as you suggest. There is no payment for lessons as they will be paid for by a benefactor and also meals provided shall be free of charge.'

'So, you'll accept her into the school, then?' Cassie asked hopefully.

'Yes, of course. Provided you both begin attending regular services at the church.' The vicar beamed at her. 'Now then, young Emily, would you like a glass of ginger beer?'

'Yes, please,' said Emily, who up until now, had been sitting shyly throughout until the mention of the beverage.

'Yes, we would be both more than happy to attend your church, Reverend Ainsworth. I think my aunt and Polly, who was my daughter's nurse-maid, would like to attend also. They both had to leave the house when I did too and now live with Emily and myself at the cottage.'

'Splendid!' said the vicar. 'I'll ask the maid to bring us a pot of tea while I find out more about you all.'

Cassie smiled, secretly delighted that at least someone in Wakeford was pleased that she was here and she figured church attendance would be a good way to ingratiate herself within the local community as there was a small segment, thanks to Mrs Hewitt, who would not want to set a foot over the tea room door.

***

'H...h...have you thought of a name for him yet?' Clyde was sitting on the rug beside Emily as she held the puppy towards him.

'Not yet,' said Emily. 'Do you have an idea of a good name for him?'

Clyde took the little dog from her hands and nestled him into his chest as gently as if he were a precious piece of porcelain. 'He l...l...looks like a Sammy to me...'

'Why do you say that?' Emily looked up at him wide-eyed with interest.

'Well, see, he looks like he might be strong like Samson in the bible and I think Sammy could be his nickname like me, see. I...I...was born a Clitheroe but that's too...too...much of a mouthful so Jem calls me Clyde instead. 'Cept when he's angry with me like when I burnt the bread in the oven once and then he shouted, "Flippin' Clitheroe, you clumsy clot!"'

Emily burst into laughter. 'Yes, I like the name Sammy, I'll call him that!'

Cassie and Polly were watching the scene before them at a distance from the scullery where Polly was rolling out some dough to make biscuits for the tea room. 'They seem to be getting on tremendously with one another!' Polly remarked.

'Yes,' Cassie smiled. 'Between you and I though, Jem says Clyde is like a child trapped in a man's body. He's never grown up so no doubt he feels more at home with Emily than either of us.'

'True!' sighed Polly then she spoke in hushed tones not for him to hear. 'I mean he does look like a man until he speaks and then he stammers over his words and says things I could imagine a child saying. There's no harm in him though, is there?' She set down her rolling pin and glanced at Cassie.

'Oh, none whatsoever. We can trust him entirely. He was asking earlier if he might take both Emily and the pup out for a walk.'

'If they're going they'd best be fast about it,' Aunt Bertha said entering the kitchen and feeling her way along the counter as she went. Cassie so wished that something could be done about her aunt's eyesight.

'You're right,' said Cassie decisively. 'I'll go and tell them both to go now and be back before dark.'

Emily's eyes shone with delight when her mother told her she could go with Clyde to take the puppy for a walk. 'Hold on tightly to Clyde's hand, mind you,' her mother warned. 'And don't stray too far.' Then looking at Clyde she said, 'Only go out for about half an hour as it will be dark soon.'

'Right, missus, understood,' Clyde said. 'An' I'll hold Emily's hand and shan't let Sammy out of our sight neither.'

'Good lad,' shouted Polly from the other room. The woman had grown very fond of Clyde of late and Cassie realised it was because when she was married and widowed young that it was because she'd never had a child to call her own. She'd once told Cassie she'd love to have had a son.

Clyde and Emily left the cottage with Sammy snuggled in Emily's arms. Clyde had an old coil of string in his jacket pocket he said they could use as a lead for the little dog. Emily seemed to like and trust Clyde and that was enough for her mother who ensured she was togged up in warm clothing before they left. It hadn't snowed for a few days but although it was comfortable and cosy in the cottage, it was bitter cold outside.

'Aye, it warms the cockles of me heart,' said

Polly as she stood wistfully staring into the flames of the fire from a rocking chair Jem had presented them with, 'to see those two get on like a house on fire. Seems to me the lad is quite lonely, don't think he has any friends as such.'

'If you ask me,' said Aunt Bertha who was seated opposite in an armchair, 'I think folk around here are fearful of Clyde. I can't see him too well myself as you know my sight is failing but I can make out what a large frame he has.'

'That's true,' Cassie said as she emerged from the scullery with a tray that contained three cups of cocoa for them. 'He's harmless enough. Wouldn't hurt a fly, Jem told me and I believe him. I think people are afraid of him, Auntie. I would think he could hold his own if it came to it in a fight.'

'Aye, maybe,' Polly nodded. 'But we mustn't forget the man has the mind of a child and sometimes needs to be treated as such.

Chapter Four

Darkness had descended. The flickering candle on the mantel shelf had shrunk and now, Cassie was beginning to feel uneasy. She bit on her bottom lip. 'I thought they'd have been back by now?'

'They'll have got carried away with tending to that new puppy I suppose,' Polly said brightly, but Cassie could tell it was an enforced cheerfulness on the woman's part not to alarm them all. 'Give them a few more minutes, they'll return, you'll see.'

But a quarter of an hour later when they had failed to show up, Cassie made her way tentatively in the semi-darkness to the front door and yelled, 'Oh, no! It's coming down heavily outside! It's snowing!' Thick snowflakes were falling from the heavens fast and furiously so that she could barely see the row of cottages opposite.

Polly's mouth popped open. 'We'd better go and search for them I think then. You go and check to see if Jem is still at the store, Cassie, he said he was going to work there late tonight repairing some furniture for a customer. He'll help us. Meanwhile, I search the surrounding streets.'

Cassie nodded feeling unable to utter a word. She dragged her shawl from the peg on the wall and lit a lantern to help her see her way. For some reason, the gas lights hadn't ignited in the street outside which made her wonder if the gas-lighter hadn't made it in these conditions. There were only two lamps anyhow, one either end of the very long row of cottages. Finally, finding her voice she turned to her Aunt who was also grabbing her own shawl from the back of her chair. 'No, Auntie,' she said firmly. 'You stay here in case they return. It's too dangerous for you to go outside in the dark and with the eyesight you have, you might slip and have a bad fall.'

'All right then, love,' she agreed. 'I'll put the kettle on the fire to boil though in case they return and need a hot drink. I can manage that much to help.'

Cassie frowned. 'Very well, just be careful though, don't fill it too full in case you tip it and end up scalding yourself.'

Auntie shook her head. 'No problem, I'll take care. Now you hurry off and go and fetch them both back here quickly.'

Cassie nodded as she left the cottage with an extra shawl wrapped around her head as she stood beneath a swirl of snowflakes, fearful for the whereabouts of her only child that she hardly noticed the bite of the chill wind.

***

'L...look, Emily!' Clyde pointed.

'Where?' Emily snuggled Sammy in beneath her shawl towards her chest, the poor little dog was shivering despite his fur coat and hadn't been able to walk another step, so the child had scooped him up in her arms. Snowflakes were now landing on Emily's eyelashes and she quickly blinked them away, darkness had descended like a black cloak that enveloped them as they made their way back to the cottage.

'Up there in the sky!' He puffed out a cloud of steam. 'But you'll have to look quickly as it's starting to snow, s...soon it will disappear from v...view.'

She glanced upwards to see a large glowing star in the sky. 'I see it!'

'That's the pole star. It's the biggest and brightest in the sky.' He was about to tell her more about the star when a gang of lads appeared and stood in front of them. Emily shivered and moved nearer to Clyde. The boys frightened her as she could sense they were out to cause trouble as they swaggered towards them.

'What yer up to then, *Snide Clyde*?' Sneered a lad in a peaked cap as his mates egged him on as they dug their hands in the pockets of their trousers and leaned back to laugh in unison, throwing back their heads in merriment. The lad who had spoken began to push Clyde with the palms of his hands, and when he couldn't budge him as he towered above them with his large frame, the others surged forward and began pummelling at him with their fists and aiming kicks at his shins with their leather hobnail boots.

Emily watched as Clyde's eyes grew large and he let out a loud groan which caused the lads to step back in fear. To Emily he sounded like the big bull that had been kept on land at Marshfield Manor, he's made noises like that which had scared the little girl. Then suddenly, pushing his tormentors away, Clyde rounded on the lad with the peaked cap who had first started the fracas, and without a single word, grabbed him by the lapels of his jacket and pulled him up off his feet so the tips of his boots were inches from the ground, then he swung him around faster and faster as the lad's friends stepped back for fear of being in the firing line and they stood watching, open-mouthed in disbelief. Finally, Clyde released him and the lad came crashing down heavily on the cobbled ground, badly hurting himself.

'Yikes!' shouted one of them, 'let's get out of here before he gets us next! He's a madman!'

'Never seen him get riled up like that before!' One lad yelled, for they were used to teasing and taunting Clyde, it had been going on for many a year and all the while Clyde had acted like a gentle giant towards them, heeding Jem's advice to walk away from any trouble, but this was different; now he had young Emily and that little pup in his care so he needed to show them he meant business. Aye, that he did and all.

'Mammy!' shouted another as Clyde stepped towards him displaying a clenched fist, and they fled leaving their friend battered and bruised in a heap on the cobbles. Emily watched the lad rise tentatively to his feet with tears in his eyes, then glaring at Clyde he stood and brushing himself down yelled, 'Yer'll pay for this, you ruddy great lump!' he shouted, and then as if fearful of any recrimination, made off after his mates like a fox being hunted by a pack of hounds. Only the lads had been the hounds really and Clyde the fox in this case, maybe *Snide Clyde* had lived up to his name for once.

Emily stood silent for a while as she snuggled Sammy closer to her chest but Clyde just smiled as if nothing at all had happened, for he was used to that sort of thing, though it was the first time he had actually hurt anyone. Usually, he ignored the comments and insults, putting it down to ignorance. Jem had told him often enough that sort of thing was best ignored. 'Walk away from any violence!' his brother had said.

Tenderly, he looked at Emily. 'S...sorry about that.'

Emily smiled at him and taking his hand, she walked along the street with him, feeling quite protected. Clyde felt like the big brother she'd never had.

***

Breathless, after rushing up the hill towards the shop, a sense of relief washed over Cassie

—Jem was still there, working late. There was a lantern on in the window on his side of the shop but the tea room side was all in darkness as she'd locked up a couple of hours since. The bell jangled overhead as she entered the shop to find Jem bent over the piece of furniture he was in the middle of varnishing. It was a small bookcase he'd managed to get from a set he'd purchased from an old cottage where an elderly man had recently passed away. His daughter and son-in-law were in the process of selling his home and its contents, so he'd cut a deal with them for an oakwood dresser, table and a bookcase as well as a couple of wardrobes he'd acquired for Cassie's cottage. He'd been feeling right pleased with himself as he'd brushed the varnish over the bookcase, realising he could make some decent money from the findings at that house if he renovated and polished the pieces—there was some good stuff there.

Jem looked up as Cassie approached. 'Oh, aye, what's going on here then,' he said with a grin, as now he stood to face her. 'Come to work in the tea room or something?' He screwed up his eyes as if baffled by her appearance.

'No, nothing like that.' She huffed out a breath. 'It's Emily and your Clyde, they went for a walk. They've not come back yet. I wondered if maybe they'd called in here or you'd spied them passing the window?'

'No, I've not,' he said, then he wiped the perspiration from his brow with a handkerchief. 'To be truthful I've had my hands full here, it's been head down and hands to the grindstone this past couple of hours as I want this varnish dry by tomorrow evening so I can apply another coat. But surely they can't have gone far, it's dark now?' He frowned.

She shook her head. 'Hopefully not. Emily wanted to walk the puppy and I encouraged Clyde to go with her as long as they were back before nightfall. Any idea where they might have gone to? Does he have any favourite places to walk to?'

'Around these parts?'

'Yes.'

'Not really as his favourite place to walk is on the moors, not around here.' He looked into her eyes then shook his head vehemently. 'But don't go worrying, he won't have led her there. He's a sensible lad.'

Cassie bit her bottom lip, tears were close at hand. Emily was the sort of child she'd not had to worry about until now. At the big house, all her needs were taken care of, she'd had a governess and a nursemaid and if those weren't around there were plenty of members of staff who could look out for her. Maybe she'd been foolish allowing the little girl to go off with Clyde like that.

Seeing her distress, Jem wiped his hands on a cloth and grabbed his jacket from the back of the chair. 'I'll come with you to look for them,' he said, 'the varnishing can wait a while longer.'

***

Artie Crabtree rubbed his swollen arm. That ruddy great brute had knocked the stuffing out of him, he hadn't realised the idiot would respond as he did. He never had in the past, he and his friends could pummel the hell out of him with their fists all they liked and kick him too, often without him even uttering a word. He just walked away as they taunted him with names like, "Snide Clyde" and "Village Idiot". It was like a sport to them but this time they'd rattled the lion's cage once too often and he'd roared at them. As well as having a bruised body, Artie realised his pride was bruised too as the fool had made him appear a laughing stock in front of his mates by lifting him off his feet like that and swinging him around so fast he'd felt like throwing up the contents of his stomach. And now, his friends were laughing at him—regaling tales to others of how Clyde had swung him around like a rag doll, they'd been wetting themselves as this time they mocked him and not that big brute. Now they were away from any danger themselves they found it all hilarious. They hadn't found it so comical at the time as they'd been as scared as he was and wanted to wet themselves too. Now they were acting as if they were big and brave, it just wasn't fair. None of the other lads had seen just how petrified they'd been as they'd run hell for leather down the road screaming like little girls.

Oh, he was going to get his comeuppance that ruddy great giant of a man. Revenge was sweet and sweetest of all when he'd get the villagers to turn against him. He'd tell them an enormous great lie that would ensure that no one would forgive the bloody big fool ever again. He'd be a total outcast of the village of Wakeford.

Just you wait and see Snide Clyde, I'm coming for you!

***

Cassie glanced around herself in total despair, the snowfall was getting even worse and now visibility was poor, they could barely see a yard or two in the distance. 'Here,' Jem offered, 'take my arm in case you slip, these cobbles are treacherous.' He was right as no sooner had she reached out to take his arm, she started sliding across them. He steadied her and patted her hand saying, 'Stay close to me.'

She'd never seen this side of him before, the strong protective side. She'd never had that from either of her husbands: the first one had harmed her when she should have been protected by him, and the second, although a great charmer, had abandoned her a lot of the time while staying out all night gambling, not just at night but sometimes heading off to London for days at a time. Had she really known either of them?

Her breathing was becoming ragged now as she felt the cold wind rob her of her breath. 'I...

couldn't bear it if anything happened to her...' Cassie said as tears pricked her eyes.

'Now, don't you worry, she'll be quite safe with Clyde. He wouldn't harm a fly.'

Cassie nodded, Jem seemed a man of his word so she figured she ought to listen to him and try to stop becoming so anxious, it would be of no help whatsoever. *Trust,* she whispered inside herself. *Trust.*

The streets seemed deserted to even ask anyone if they'd seen her daughter but at the end of the row was an inn called, "The Ploughman's Arms" where many of the men in the village liked to sup the ale, there was another establishment on the edge of Wakeford but that relied more on passing trade from stagecoaches and those passing through on their way elsewhere. 'Come on,' said Jem intruding into her thoughts, 'we'll go inside here and ask around—someone may know something.'

She could see the inn was lit up from outside the window and there was some form of life inside: several men of varying ages stood with tankards in their hands, one or two seemed to be in deep conversation, others chuckling and one or two stood alone, cutting lonely figures, just content to be with their pints of ale. The sign above them swung back and forth and creaked loudly. There was a blizzard on the way, of that Cassie had no doubt.

Taking a deep breath, Cassie entered the inn

behind Jem. When he presented himself before the clientele, eyes were drawn towards him and there were smiles and nods, it was evident Jem was welcome and well-liked, but when they laid their eyes upon her, the men's expressions changed.

What are they thinking? That no respectable woman should be seen dead in here? Or are they looking at me in disgust for once being The Lord's mistress?

One young man dressed in a leather waistcoat and with a muffler around his neck appeared to be sizing her up as if she were a piece of meat on the rack. She drew her shawl closely around her shoulders as if to protect herself from his gaze. Her cheeks blazed, she hated being appraised like this. He obviously viewed her as a piece of meat, yet one or two other men narrowed their eyes in suspicion of her.

But before she had a chance to think on further, Jem yelled, 'Any of you see our Clyde around? He has a young girl with him?'

There were mutterings and most shook their heads. 'No!' shouted an elderly man who was seated in a window seat in the corner. As Cassie's gaze was drawn towards him she noticed something odd about him. He had a wooden leg without a shoe and his trouser leg was rolled up. It was the type of leg someone had once referred to as a "peg leg". She wondered how he had lost it. 'No, ain't seen your Clyde since early this afternoon!'

Jem thanked them all and before leaving said, 'Well if any of you do see him, tell him he's wanted back at the cottage.'

The men stared at him blankly.

'My cottage,' explained Cassie. She swallowed hard. 'I'm assuming you all know where that is since it was owned by the Lord and there's been enough gossip in this village with all sorts of folks poking their noses into my business!' Her chin jutted out in defiance.

The landlord, who had mutton-chop whiskers, a ruddy complexion and full rounded cheeks, approached and said, 'Aye, missus. We knew the lord and a lot of us here had a great deal of respect for him whilst he was alive, he was very fair to us, so in keeping with his memory we'll do as asked. If we see Clyde we'll send him straight to your cottage.'

'Or love nest!' the young man who had been appraising her shouted which caused one or two beside him to chuckle.

'This is a serious situation, my five-year-old daughter is missing!' she said, desperately trying to hold back the tears.

'Come on now, Cassie,' Jem said guiding her by the arm. 'The landlord has promised if he sees Clyde, he'll send him to the cottage. Let's get out of here.'

Relieved, she allowed him to guide her out into the street where she promptly broke down in tears.

'Whatever's the matter?' Jem asked. 'It wasn't that bad in there, was it?'

Choking back a sob she lifted her head to look at him beneath the street lamp. 'It was the way some of those men were looking at me in there. You couldn't see as they were stood slightly behind you.'

'How'd you mean?'

'The young one was looking me up and down as if I were a piece of meat on the hook at the market and one or two were eyeing me with suspicion. They've never forgiven me for getting involved with Lord Bellingham when he was a married man.'

Jem took her hand. 'I don't think it's that, to be honest...'

'What do you think it is, then?'

'I think it's more likely because you're a woman with your own business. They're too narrow-minded, now I can't say the same for the ladies around here, that Mrs Hewitt for instance, she along with some of her cronies, don't like the fact you were involved with a married man. You see, now you're back in Wakeford they're afraid.'

'Afraid?' she gazed at him as she quirked a puzzled brow. 'Why on earth should they feel fearful of me?'

'Because...because my dear, you are a very attractive woman. They probably fear losing their menfolk to you.'

Cassie tossed back her head and laughed. 'But that's preposterous!'

'Aye, I know it is,' chuckled Jem. 'It just goes to show though how insecure their sort are!'

Good old Jem had cheered her up and for a moment, she'd almost forgotten why she was here in the first place, but not quite. 'I do hope nothing serious has happened to Emily and Clyde.'

Jem shook his head. 'Have no fear they will be all right. Emily will be well-protected by my brother.'

Cassie was about to say something when she heard a voice call out: 'Cassie! It's all right they're both back at the cottage safe and sound!'

Cassie whipped her head around to see where the voice was coming from. It was Polly on the opposite side of the street waving to them. Relief flooded through every pore in Cassie's body—she almost fainted there and then as she felt light-headed out in the cold.

'Come along now,' said Jem sensibly as if he understood, 'let's get you back inside and warm you up. You've had a bit of a nasty shock.'

***

Cassie couldn't remember returning to the cottage but now she was seated by the fireside and Polly was passing her a glass of sherry to warm her up. 'Just a few sips to get your blood circulating,' she comforted.

Emily was seated on the rug in front of the fire with Sammy on her lap, seemingly blissfully unaware of the panic that had ensued since their departure. Clyde was seated at the table with a cup of tea in front of him.

'What happened, Clyde?' Jem demanded.

Before he had a chance to utter a word, Emily butted in. 'Some lads were annoying him. We were on our way home and they stopped him.'

Jem stared hard at his brother as if fearing the worst. 'You didn't hurt any of them, did you, Clyde?'

'N...n...not really.' He lowered his head.

'What do you mean, not really?'

'They were p...punching and kicking me. I... I...was scared for Miss Emily and I wanted them gone, gone, gone! So I pushed them all away but one of them, the one who started it all, that Artie one, h...he...he wouldn't stop so I lifted him up off his feet and swung him around and dropped him like a stone on the ground!'

Jem's mouth opened and closed again. 'Clitheroe, you know what I've always told you, you must walk away from any trouble.'

Clyde looked at Cassie. 'N...now I know I'm in t...trouble, he just called me "Clitheroe"!' He smiled.

Cassie returned the smile but, deep down she was mortified that the lads had done that to him in the first place. The dear gentle giant of a man who Emily liked so much and it must have been an ordeal for her daughter too, even though they'd spared her. She decided she would speak to her about the incident later when Jem and Clyde had gone home.

'I'm not really angry *at* you,' said Jem, softening his tone now, 'I'm angry *for* you. But promise me that you'll be more careful in future?' He looked at Clyde.

Clyde lifted his head and gazed at his brother with big sorrowful eyes. 'I promise,' he said in a tone more befitting five-year-old Emily.

Cassie was about to take another sip of her sherry when her stomach lurched. She felt nauseous and rushed from the room to go to the outside privy. It must have been the alcohol upsetting her stomach in combination with being out in the cold and feeling so upset earlier. No sooner had she got there than she expelled the contents of her stomach in the pan, it was all over so quickly and she felt better afterwards. Strange. If she had a stomach upset it normally seemed to go on for some time but now all of a sudden, it felt settled once again and she even felt ravenous. The only time she'd ever felt that way before was when she was pregnant with Emily.

Cassie's hands flew to her face. Heavens above? She wasn't pregnant again, was she?

Chapter Five

It soon became evident that Cassie was pregnant as the nausea returned the following morning and the morning after that.

In the corner of the living room, Polly was seated on a wooden stool darning one of her pinafores to wear at the shop later that morning. She stopped what she was doing for a while and gazed at Cassie thoughtfully. 'What's the matter with you, Cass? You ain't eaten much breakfast and been looking a bit peaky these past few days.'

Cassie set down the tray containing all the breakfast things on the pine table. Emily was out in the garden playing with Sam in the snow and Aunt Bertha was upstairs getting dressed for the day, so it was an ideal opportunity to confide her fears in Polly. 'I think I'm pregnant,' she said, and then she bit her bottom lip.

'Oh heck!' Polly laid aside her darning on the stool and approached Cassie, wrapping a comforting arm around her shoulders. 'I'm guessing this is something you could do without right now?'

Cassie fought to hold the tears back, she couldn't break down, not right now as she wanted to maintain the strong exterior she always did in front of everyone. Only Jem had witnessed her breaking down and that's how she intended it should remain. 'No, it is definitely something I could do without.' She sniffed loudly. 'Another mouth to feed is all I need right now.'

'Leave the dishes,' Polly said softly. 'Sit yourself down at the table. There's some tea left in the pot, I'll pour some for you and top it up with hot water from the kettle. A spoonful or two of sugar wouldn't harm none either.'

Cassie nodded gratefully as she watched Polly busying herself preparing the tea for her to sip. Polly placed the cup in front of her and she looked up at the woman through misted eyes and then Polly took the seat opposite. 'Don't worry too much, these things have a way of working themselves out. You've got me and your Aunt to help you out.'

Cassie nodded. 'I am most grateful to you both but it's happening at a bad time with the business and all.'

'True enough,' Polly said stoically, 'but in the worst case you could always employ a young girl to work for you at the shop whilst you're in confinement and I could step into your shoes actually running the tea room. I should know what to do by now.'

'I don't like to think that far ahead to be honest with you.' Cassie put her head in her hands in desperation for a moment and then shaking herself out of her despair, she took a sip of the strong sweet brew. Her stomach had now probably settled for the rest of the day until the evening maybe, so she'd be able to cope for a few hours at least. After Christmas Emily would begin as a pupil at the new school at the church so that would help a little at least. The truth was she didn't know how she really felt, she'd lost her husband whom she'd had mixed feelings about in the end, feeling almost as though she never really knew him at all. He had frittered away a fortune and turfed everyone out of his property from his death bed in essence. All the staff who had thought so highly of him would now hit upon hard times due to his excessive wanton behaviour. In her mind, he'd been selfish to do what he had wasting his money on gambling and leaving all that debt in his wake and who knew what else he'd been spending his money on. Her father, if he was still alive, would turn in his grave to realise his son-in-law had wasted an entire fortune when he, himself, had had to toil at the Marshfield coal pit for twelve hours a day since he'd been a young lad.

'It's been a shock for you I expect,' said Polly intruding into her thoughts.

Cassie nodded. 'You can say that again...'

***

Clyde was feeling quite pleased with himself, Jem had offered to loan him the cart to go off to

Drisdale to pick up some furniture they could sell in the shop. There were some good pieces to be had there from someone who was selling up to move overseas, America Jem had informed him and so the family wanted rid of anything they couldn't take with them. The reason Clyde was feeling so pleased was that his brother trusted him enough to allow him to do this. He had a letter in his pocket written by his Aunt Dorothea to explain to the seller who he was and that he had the money in an envelope in his other pocket to pay him for such items he wished to sell. Not having much schooling as young lads, neither Clyde nor Jem were very literate. Jem had already sealed the deal with the seller so all Clyde had to do was turn up at the house and load the furniture on the cart himself and pay the owner.

He had feared after that night he was late returning with Emily that everyone would have turned against him but it was quite the opposite, they'd all praised him for being so protective towards the little girl. Yes, he was right pleased with himself.

As he left Wakeford, he steered the horse and cart down the steep hill that led to the stone bridge over the river and looked across in the distance at the village of Drisdale. It was looking particularly nice today. The snow had melted and the sun was out without a cloud in the sky. If it wasn't that the trees were so bare it could almost be a spring or even early summer's day, it was unseasonably warm.

Nothing or no one could get him down today.

***

Artie Crabtree hadn't been able to get that incident out of his mind from when that big lummox had humiliated him in front of his mates. He'd been sore for ages afterwards and it had been days until the bruises faded away altogether. He'd fought hard in his mind to think of a way to get Snide Clyde back for his so-called dirty deed and he reckoned he'd had the best idea yet.

There was a young woman in the village known as May Malone, nicknamed by the locals as "Scabby May" due to her bad behaviour. Her family came over from Ireland a few years ago and the girl herself spoke with a Southern Irish accent which Artie found appealing, to say the least. The family were quite poor and often May would stand outside one of the pubs begging for money. She was so pretty and charming that often an inebriated young fellow or an old one for that matter would drop a few farthings into her outstretched grubby palm.

Artie found himself the previous day telling May how she could earn some easy money by doing something for him. If May had been shocked by his suggestion to set Clyde up, she wasn't saying so and had eagerly nodded at the idea of earning some dough to add to the family's coffers. Artie's family weren't well-off by any means but he'd earned some money for himself the other day by being taken on at the mill to do some casual work and this would be worth every penny to see that big lummox get his comeuppance fine and proper.

He'd hidden behind a wall outside Rose Cottage listening to the plans for Clyde to go over to Drisdale to pick up some furniture so Artie had arranged for May to hide by the bridge when he approached and lie on the road as if she'd had an accident forcing him to abandon his horse and cart.

***

What was that in the distance? Clyde shielded his eyes from the sun's dazzling glare. Was it an injured animal or something lying in the road? He couldn't bear the thought of anyone harming an animal. Maybe it had been run over by another cart or a coach even. As he drew near, he noticed the skirts of a female. This was no animal it was a young woman and she wasn't moving. He pulled on the horse's reins bringing the cart to a standstill and jumped down, then rushed to the woman's side.

As he looked down on her he thought she looked vaguely familiar, he'd seen her before somewhere. 'M...Miss?' he said, 'Miss? Are you all right?'

May groaned.

'Have you hurt y...you...yourself?'

There was no answer so he knelt by her side and then spontaneously, he stroked her cheek.

'Are you all a…all …r…right?'

May opened one eye and spotting Artie approaching behind Clyde, she quickly grabbed hold of Clyde's hand from her cheek and placed it on her breast and yelled, 'Help! Help me, someone! He's trying to have his way with me!'

'N…no!' shouted Clyde as he wrestled his hand away and he pulled himself up onto his feet, his eyes wide with horror and then he turned to see Artie standing behind him with a look of contempt on his face.

'I saw what you did there!' he said pointing a finger at him.

'B…but I didn't do anything!' Clyde shook his head.

'Yes, he did!' May was now on her feet brushing her dress down and she stood beside Artie as if joining forces with him.

'What happened?' Artie asked.

'That brute saw me walking across the bridge and he pushed me to the ground, got on top of me and placed his hand on my breast. He was trying to have his way with me. Thank goodness you came along when you did to save me.'

'You bloody swine!' Artie shouted at the baffled Clyde. 'You haven't heard the last of this!' Then he put a protective arm around May's shoulder and she wept as he led her away.

To Clyde's dismay, as he scratched his head in puzzlement, he noticed a couple of men heading towards them. The four of them stopped to chat for a moment and then the men removed their jackets and rolled up their sleeves, then they headed purposely towards Clyde. Sensing he was in danger, he hopped on board the cart to head off as quickly as possible.

***

Clyde was taking his time to return from Drisdale. Jem frowned. His brother should have been back by now to unload the furniture at the shop. Maybe he'd made a huge mistake in sending him off to purchase the furniture in the first place, but he'd wanted to put his trust in him. He watched Cassie and Polly from his side of the building, who were now busy clearing up the tea room, the last of the stragglers in there recently departed. Cassie flipped the sign in the window over to "Closed" and then went over to the counter. He walked through to the tea room and stood at the counter, absently jangling the loose change in his pocket until she turned from the sink to face him.

'What's wrong?' She had a look of concern on her face.

Jem sighed. 'I dunno. It's Clyde, he should have been here by now.'

'Just give the lad a little longer,' Polly said sagely. She lifted a tray of used crockery and hefted it over to the counter.

'Aye, I know. I have little choice I suppose. It's just that I wanted to give him a chance to prove himself and he's let me down.'

Cassie went over to Jem and gently patted his forearm, knowing what it was like to feel distressed about family. She worried often enough herself; if it wasn't Aunt Bertha's failing eyesight that concerned her then it was Emily and how she'd settle down living in Wakeford instead of her old home. 'It'll be all right,' she whispered.

But by the time the tea shop had been cleared up in preparation for tomorrow's trade, it was evident that something was wrong.

'I'll have to return to the cottage,' Polly said, 'I need to start cooking our evening meal for us all and then there's the baking to do for tomorrow. Sorry, I can't stay and wait for Clyde with you,' she said glancing uneasily at Jem.

Jem nodded. 'You go ahead.'

'It's all right, Polly. I'll stay here. You get off home. Just check Aunt Bertha and Emily are settled and make sure Sammy's been outside. I don't want to come back to a wet rug again.'

Polly smiled. 'I think the dog is getting so much better now and is almost housetrained. Only the odd slip up if he gets excited.'

Although Cassie returned the smile and then she watched Polly drape her shawl around her shoulders, tie up her bonnet and leave the shop with her wicker basket of left-overs over the crook of her arm, she had an uneasy feeling that all was not right with Clyde.

***

'B...but I didna do anything!' Clyde protested

as the two men approached the cart and ordered him down from it. He complied with their request and stood facing them. Neither was quite as tall as he but both were well-built.

'Those pair say different,' said the one with the moustache. Clyde noted he had steely grey eyes, he was the sort that people wouldn't want to tangle with and the other who was slightly shorter with chubby cheeks, seemed almost as though he were his lapdog taking orders from him. The shorter of the two didn't bother him, he was the sort that Clyde might push past to get to the bar in the local pub without any recriminations, but the one with the moustache, he just had a feeling if he accidentally bumped into him there would be repercussions.

Clyde just didn't have the words to express himself properly. He wanted to explain how the young woman and Artie had set him up but the words wouldn't come. He had difficulty speaking anyhow with his stammer but when he was provoked or upset it was as if no words would be forthcoming.

'Go and fetch the Cavalry,' the moustached one said to his friend.

The other man nodded as Clyde had a sinking feeling in the pit of his stomach. Cavalry? What did the man mean? All he knew about that term was something about soldiers and there were none in these parts.

When his friend had gone to walk back up

the hill the man looked at Artie and the young woman. 'So, you're telling me that if no one had come to the young woman's rescue this big brute here would have had his way with her?'

Clyde noticed now the woman couldn't look him in the eye and appeared nervous and he guessed that was because she'd been lying. Maybe now she felt bad about it. Artie had his arm tightly around her shoulder and had pulled her close to his chest as if he was protecting her. 'Oh, aye.' He nodded gravely. 'Goodness knows what would have happened if I hadn't stumbled along.'

The moustached man glared at Clyde and then his eyes were drawn back to the woman. 'And you're saying the same thing, are you?'

The young woman nodded but did not say a word.

'You do understand of course,' said the man, 'that I have to be sure before the men get here. We can't go pasting an innocent man.'

'I quite understand,' said Artie. 'But it's the truth.'

'Very well then,' said the man as if satisfied with the answer. 'He shall get his just desserts and make no mistake but I'd escort the young lady back home, she doesn't need to see this on top of the ordeal she's just been through.'

***

Artie's face fell. That would mean of course he wouldn't get to see *Snide Clyde* getting the pasting of his life, he'd intended joining in too to get his own back on the man after the way he'd recently humiliated him.

As if noticing he looked taken aback the man with the moustache said, 'All right then. The little lady can turn away as you take the first swipe at him but after that, you're to both walk away without looking back, understood? It's not going to be a pretty sight. We ought to hand him over to the authorities by rights but the men of Drisdale and the surrounding areas like to mete out their own form of justice from time to time and this is one of them times.'

Artie noticed Clyde gulp as the man rolled up his shirt sleeves and Artie followed suit.

Oh, this was going to be such fun. A gang of men had been rounded up from The Farrier's Arms and were now marching down the hill. Artie shielded his eyes from the sun's rays. There appeared to be five in all along with the two men and himself, so that would make eight altogether. Sixteen fists to pound away at Clyde. He glanced over at him expecting him to be shivering in his shoes but to his dismay, he wasn't. He was standing tall and proud.

Then Clyde looked at the trio as he forced out the words. 'I...I...am t...telling you that I am an in...innocent man.'

The man with the moustache looked at him and raised his brows just as the men approached. One with ginger hair and sideburns shouted,

'That's Clyde! I know him he's Jem's brother who sells the furniture. He's harmless!' His gaze was drawn towards Artie and May. 'I might have known,' he said throwing down the pitchfork he had in his hand. 'Artie and Scabby May, two dodgy dealers if ever there was!'

'Whatcha mean?' The moustached man growled.

'Matt, them pair have been up to all sorts. May hangs around The Ploughman's Arms trying to procure men for their money and Artie runs around with a load of ruffians in Wakeford who cause trouble wherever they go.'

Matt glared at the pair of them. 'If that's the case, run the pair out of the village, the lot of you!'

The men mumbled and nodded and with all the various weaponry they had to hand, pitch-forks, shovels and the like they rounded on May and Artie. Artie began to tremble. 'It's all an honest mistake!' he said showing the vertical palms of his hands. 'No harm was meant, honestly!'

But it was too late, the men were angry at having been disturbed when they were on their break from work at The Farrier's Arms and they began to rush at them. Artie's stomach flipped over and no longer caring about May, he made off like a whippet up the hill with the breeze behind his back feeling as though it were propelling him forward. He had both youth and vigour on his side. May managed to keep up with him but in truth, the men would not have hurt her as it was Artie they were after.

This had taught him a valuable lesson for time being, he thought to himself when they had lost the men.

'Artie,' panted May, 'I think we should...'

'Shurrup!' he huffed as he bent over with his hands on his knees trying to get his breath back. 'Give me time to think.'

***

It was two hours later when Clyde finally arrived back at the shop staggering and slurring his words. 'Oh my goodness,' said Cassie with a note of alarm in her voice as she unlocked the door to allow him across the threshold. His eyes were glazed but he had a big smile on his face.

'Where on earth have you been?' demanded Jem walking towards him with a frown on his face.

'M...made s...some new friends at D...D...Drisdale...' Clyde collapsed onto one of the seats that hadn't been put back under its table.

'You're drunk!' said Jem angrily.

'Only a little *bish*...' Clyde mumbled. He was now slumped heavily over the table resting his head on his folded arms. He opened one eye and closed it again.

'I'll put some coffee on,' Cassie said sagely.

It was a while after they'd all had a cup of coffee that Clyde was able to explain what had happened to him that day.

'Well, I'll be blowed!' said Jem. 'So Artie and May tried to set you up and you almost got the pasting of your life until some man recognised who you were?'

'Yes,' said Clyde. 'They were men who drink in The F...Farrier's Arms.'

'What did he look like?

'G...ginger hair and sideburns.'

'Was he about my age?'

'I think s...so.'

'That would be Jack Crayson. He's a good sort. Him and his old fella are very fair-minded individuals. Thank goodness he recognised who you were and who Artie and May were an' all.' He turned to Cassie to explain. 'The Crayson family used to live in Wakeford but they relocated to Drisdale when his father was left a farm there by his brother when he passed away.'

'I see,' said Cassie, then she whispered in Jem's ear. 'But how come he's so drunk, then?'

'I can hazard a fair guess.' Jem's gaze settled on his brother. 'So the men took you back to the pub with them and bought you a few pints?'

'Yes. Y...you're not angry at me are you, our Jem?'

Jem smiled and ruffled his brother's hair. 'No, lad. As long as those men were kind to you in the end. You have been through some ordeal today.'

'S...sorry about not picking up the furniture,' Clyde said.

'Don't worry. I'll head out that way tomorrow

and sort it all out. I had told the house owner if we weren't able to do it today we'd do it tomorrow anyhow. I'll go on my own though as early tomorrow morning you are going to be dead to the world, he glanced out the window. Thank goodness the horse knew the way back here and Clyde stayed awake long enough to somehow steer him here.' He looked at Cassie and smiled. 'Can you keep an eye on the shop for me?'

'Yes, of course, I will. If anyone wants to purchase any furniture I'll allow them to take a look around and explain you'll be back later to attend to them.'

Jem nodded gratefully. She hated to see how upset he'd been earlier when Clyde had gone missing yet again. He was more like a father to him at times than an elder brother and it seemed that Clyde was just not used to the perils of alcohol.

Cassie poured Clyde another strong cup of coffee before preparing to leave the shop. 'He'll be all right after he's had a good sleep,' she said securing the ribbons of her bonnet and then she turned with her hand on the door handle to look at the pair. 'Good night, both.'

Jem nodded at her. There was no more to be said. Clyde had had a lucky escape that was for sure. As she closed the door behind her she wondered what tomorrow would bring.

***

'Pregnant?' said Aunt Bertha as she looked up

from the armchair nearest the hearth with both hands firmly cupped on the armrests as if clinging on for dear life. 'But how can that be?' The woman hadn't long risen from her bed to begin the day and Cassie had toyed with telling her later but figured now was as good a time as any.

'It happened the usual way I expect,' chuckled Polly.

Cassie cast her a stern glance. She'd wanted to tell her aunt tactfully and didn't want merriment made of it.

'Sorry,' Polly bit her bottom lip.

'Yes, Aunt Bertha. Unfortunately, it's true. Although Oliver and I had little relationship with one another in our final months together as he was more interested in gambling amongst other things...' she shook her head, 'there was one evening I can cast my mind back to when it must have happened.'

'I see,' said Aunt Bertha steepling her fingers on her lap. She sniffed loudly and Cassie wondered what she might be thinking but then she said, 'Then we shall just have to make the best of it. Have you any plans?'

Cassie gulped then nodded. 'Yes. I plan to employ a young girl at the tea shop and Polly will take my place running it whilst I'm in confinement.'

'Very well,' said Aunt Bertha. 'What about Emily? She doesn't know as yet?'

'No, of course not. I decided to inform you and

Polly first.'

Aunt Bertha looked up at her with kindly eyes. 'The child has a right to be told though.'

'Yes, and she will be told in due course but let's get Christmas out of the way first...' Cassie didn't wait for her Aunt's response, she turned her back and began to clear away the breakfast dishes. After what had happened recently with Clyde, and seeing Jem's distress, she was in no mood to speak further on the matter.

As she washed the dishes at the sink, slowly dropping the crockery into the soapy water, a tear trickled down her cheek and she swallowed to prevent any more from falling. She didn't want to be upset but she was. What a mess she'd made of her life going from one disastrous relationship to another. Her first marriage had been violent and her second, not quite the dream it appeared to be. For what she hadn't told people and had been keeping to herself, was the fact that not only had Oliver been a gambler but he'd been a womaniser too. Initially, she'd thought his late nights and weekends away without warning were only linked to the gambling side of things which he'd made out was a way of making money. He'd convinced her he was doing so well that he was planning on having another wing built on the manor house and a new summer house built by the lake. But in essence, it was pure fantasy. His finances were running at a loss. And to add insult to injury, she had smelled perfume on his shirts and seen the smudges of rouge powder on more than one occasion.

Of course, the women might have been hostesses who played up to the men at such clubs but then she'd found it, a red velvet box hidden at the back of his walk-in wardrobe on one of the shelves. Trembling, she'd thought it was a gift for her for the following week would have been their first anniversary. She'd toyed with taking a peek and curiosity had got the better of her. She'd gasped when she'd opened the box to see a gold heart-shaped locket inside and she'd opened it to see an engraved inscription as her blood ran cold. *To Annabelle, from Oliver with love always.*

Her first thought had been, who on earth is Annabelle? A cheap whore? But surely he wouldn't have bought an expensive gift for one of those? The answer arrived, strangely enough, a few days later when she'd asked Oliver where he'd been and he'd mentioned he'd visited a friend who he'd known since childhood called Annabelle. On further investigation, she discovered that Annabelle was one of the young beautiful women on the many portraits around the house and Oliver had claimed she'd been like a cousin to him. Some cousin though!

Then when their anniversary had arrived a couple of days later, he forgot it even though she'd managed to persuade Cook to make a special meal for the two of them in the dining room, getting the woman to agree to that had been no mean feat.

Angrily, she'd accused him of having an affair with Annabelle which he'd denied and he'd even made love to her that very same night, apologising profusely he'd forgotten such an important date. But Cassie knew in her heart then that their marriage was now in name only and in a way she was now in the same position as his wife had been—on the outside looking in and for that she now felt supremely guilty even though the woman had sanctioned their affair.

Oliver never approached her to make love again and so, in her heart, she realised the night of their anniversary and the night she'd discovered who Annabelle was, was the night she had conceived this life growing inside of her. And to that end, she didn't know how she should feel.

Chapter Six

Christmas was fast approaching and Polly and Cassie were busy decorating the tea room. Polly wouldn't even allow Cassie to stand on a chair to place some holly over the eaves and insisted on doing it herself.

'Can't afford to 'ave you come a cropper by falling off that chair if yer faint or stumble or something,' she said firmly.

Of course, Cassie knew she was right, she was a little older carrying this baby and working too, so as a result was far more exhausted than when she'd carried Emily.

From outside the window and across the street, the Salvation Army brass band was playing *God Rest Ye Merry Gentleman* while a woman dressed all in black with a bonnet to match, marched around with a wooden collection box rattling it as she went under the noses of folk who had stopped to listen to the charming Carols played. This branch of The Salvation Army was based in Hocklea and Cassie didn't reckon they'd make much money from the people of Wakeford but as Polly had reminded her, 'The Sally Army make a lot of their brass from those inebriated sorts in the pubs!' She'd declared with a big grin on her face. 'In fact, I won't mind betting a fair bit of copper for their coffers comes from those places!'

Now as Cassie stepped back to admire their decorating skills she was fair pleased with the result: boughs of holly and ivy were strung across the walls, a small Christmas tree in the corner with white candles and delicate baubles drew the eye and warmed the heart, and there was even a sprig or two of mistletoe to be found here and there for willing customers.

Polly had even indulged herself in some festive baking especially for the run-up to the big day itself. Her delicious mince pies dusted with icing sugar were a favourite, along with neat slices of iced Christmas cake and a non-alcoholic hot punch for customers

Things were going amazingly well and for Jem too in his furniture store next door. He was so busy he barely had time to think but he was happy enough. Clyde, too, seemed none the worse for his recent ordeal and Emily was looking forward to starting as a pupil at the church school in the New Year. All in all, life was good now for them all.

The bell over the door jangled and Cassie looked up in amazement to see Mrs Hewitt enter the shop followed by a nervous-looking Mrs Peterson who was shuffling along in the woman's wake. 'Please think what you're doing,

Edna,' she was saying to the woman as Mrs Hewitt strode towards the counter with a determined look on her face. Indeed her lips were pursed and white with fury and her whole demeanour seemed to be one of anger.

The woman's eyes were dark, beady and bright as she addressed Cassie. 'You might have abused me by trying to brush me off the pavement with that broom of yours the other week when I had a right and a perfectly good reason to be outside this tea room of which you'll soon discover. You think yourself clever with that tongue of yours, but you'll not brush me off this time! Oh no, you won't, madam!' She stuck her chin out in defiance as she waved a brown envelope in Cassie's face.

Cassie studied the woman in a bemused fashion, indeed she appeared fit to burst. 'And what is that?' she asked referring to the envelope.

'It's a written notice for you to quit!' The woman spat out the words angrily at her.

'To quit?' Cassie folded her arms and looked at the woman as if she had a screw loose and then she looked at Polly beside her who shrugged her shoulders.

'Beats me!' said Polly.

'To quit what might I ask?' Cassie raised a quizzical brow.

'This shop of course. I understand you are renting both sides of the shop from Madame Claudette for a furniture business and this tea room, are you not?'

'I am indeed,' said Cassie, 'though I don't see what that has to do with you!' She gritted her teeth

Mrs Hewitt shook her head. 'Oh, don't you? It is indeed my business as my husband now owns the property. He has purchased it as he wishes to open a business here himself. That's why I was perusing the premises recently. My husband and myself were shown around here by the owner a couple of days afterwards. We weren't sure he was going to purchase it at first, but after the way you treated me that day and how you have conducted yourself in this village and at the manor house over the years, it has made it a deciding factor in all of this. Mr Hewitt shall be doing his good deed for the folk of Wakeford by taking your livelihood away from you!'

Surely the woman had to be having her on just to wind her up? This couldn't possibly be true, could it?

'Didn't Madame Claudette tell you that she hoped to sell the property?' Mrs Hewitt demanded with a hard stare.

In truth, she had, but the woman had made it sound as if she was in no immediate rush to sell up. Cassie had been hoping she could build the business up with time and put a deposit down on it herself with a view to purchasing it for her and Jem. Jem had some money left to him from his father and there was money tied up in the cottage he now owned as collateral and she owned property herself. Both their businesses were beginning to thrive so all of this was unexpected news to her and had thwarted their plans for the future.

Suddenly, she felt faint. Noticing her distress, Polly steered her towards an unoccupied table and drew out a chair for her to sit down, then she brought a glass of water to her. 'Here, sip this,' she instructed. 'You've had a nasty shock.' Then glancing at Mrs Hewitt in disgust she said, 'That is of course if *she* is telling the truth!'

'I am. I have the official documentation here to prove it!' Mrs Hewitt said indignantly, slapping the letter down on the table in front of Cassie. 'I'll leave it with you to digest, but we want you and Mr Clement to vacate this property with all of your paraphernalia by the first week of January!' The woman's eyes widened with fury which made Cassie realise the woman *was* telling the truth.

Cassie opened her mouth and closed it again as she watched Mrs Hewitt marching out of the shop with Mrs Peterson on her tail. She glanced at Polly. There was a feeling of disbelief as if this was all a bad dream she'd wake up out of at any moment. This couldn't be happening to her.

'Well open it then,' Polly urged.

Cassie hesitated as if she realised by reading that letter it would make the whole debacle real for her and there'd be no going back afterwards.

She shook her head. 'I don't know if I can…'

'Only one way to find out.' Polly approached and stood behind her as Cassie gently prised open the envelope with trembling hands and she spread the letter out on the table. The notice read:

Notice to Quit

To whom it may concern,

I hearby give you notice to quit and yield up to me on or before Friday the 7ᵗʰ day of January 1876, the quiet and peaceable possession of number 3 and 4 Rowan Road in the parish of Wakeford in the county of Marshfield.

In failure of your compliance herewith, legal measures will be adopted to compel the same by application at the District Police Court.

Dated this fourth day of December in the year of our Lord, 1875.

Yours etc,

Landlord Mr William Montague Hewitt

(The tenant in possession of the above)

The agreement was witnessed by a Mr Josuah Arthur Smythe, who Cassie recognised as a clerk at the solicitors' firm Walker Brothers and Sons at Hocklea. She'd had dealings with the firm over her husband's recent death and the collection and payments of his debts. It was Josuah who had been so kind to her to explain everything in detail and bring her a cup of tea when she'd been in such a distressed state to hear of how the manor house would have to be sold along with other things belonging to the estate to pay off the lord's debts. She wondered what Josuah now thought of this notice to quit. But then again, he might not know her actual name as it wasn't stated on the notice to quit, it just said 'To Whom it May Concern.'

She put her head in her hands as she felt like weeping. Polly laid a reassuring hand on her shoulder. 'Maybe you could visit the solicitor's office to find out if this is legal?' she said hopefully. 'It all seems a bit sudden to me. In any case, you'll have a contract with that Madame Claudette, won't you? Go and dig it out to check what the terms of the tenancy agreement are.'

Cassie looked at her blankly. 'I...didn't...have one,' she said through shuddering sobs.

'You mean there was never anything official between you and her in writing when you took on the tea room and Jem the other side?'

'No,' Cassie sniffed. 'It was all done verbally.'

Polly noticed the final customers leaving. She smiled and waved at Mr and Mrs Moody who were becoming good customers. As soon as they'd departed. She locked the door and turned the sign around to 'Closed'. It was a little early to shut up shop but this was important. She dug into her pocket and handed Cassie a clean handkerchief. 'Now stay where you are. Dry your eyes and blow your nose. I'm going to make us a cup of coffee to discuss this. Where's Jem? We need to speak to him too as this will affect him and Clyde, after all.'

Gratefully, Cassie took the handkerchief and dabbing at her eyes said, 'Yes, it will. This is all my fault. He's gone with Clyde to pick up some furniture for the schoolroom at the church. Reverend Ainsworth requested his help and Jem was only too pleased to oblige.'

'It's evil what that old trout has done trying to get you and Jem turfed out of your shops, you both provide a valuable service to the community. In any case, I can't think what her husband can be opening here. He has no particular skills I can think of. He was some sort of wages clerk at Marshfield Coal Pit many years ago until he rose up the ranks to a position of being a manager there and got himself that nice house, but he has no sort of experience of the retail trade like what you and Jem have.'

'I suppose it doesn't very much matter as long as he can buy something to sell and make a profit.'

'I'll go and fetch the coffee,' Polly said smiling reassuringly. 'Now don't you go worrying. That woman is horrible doing this just before Christmas and although on occasion when I've encountered her husband, he seemed affable enough. He appeared to be on good terms with his lordship, who spoke highly of the man. Well respected by the men at the coal pit, he is.'

'I didn't realise Oliver knew the family.'

'Oh, aye. Used to be a regular visit to the house before your time,' Polly said knowledgeably.

Soon they were both seated with a steaming cup of coffee each and a couple of mince pies but Cassie had no appetite to eat so she just sipped away at her coffee, blowing on it from time to time to cool it down.

'So what sort of verbal agreement did you have with Madame C then?' Polly said finally.

Cassie laid down her cup on its saucer. 'Just that Jem and myself would pay the agreed rent monthly on both shops.'

'Nothing else?'

'No, not really other than we weren't to cause any damage and she wanted us to fork out for the upkeep of the buildings.'

Polly arched an eyebrow. 'That for a start sounds a bit unfair to me. Surely as a landlord, she would have been responsible for the upkeep of the buildings herself?'

'You would think that, wouldn't you? But in all honesty, I'd been so keen for us to move in and set up as it were that I thought nothing of it, thinking that as Jem is a carpenter and all round handyman if any paint or woodwork were necessary, he'd be the man for the job.'

'Aye. I get that. But when you say that it was arranged that Jem and yourself pay the agreed rent monthly on both shops, it does sound as if Madame C wasn't planning on selling at that point.'

'I suppose.' Cassie took a sip of coffee which

had now cooled down nicely.

'So then,' said Polly, 'it sounds to me as if Mr and Mrs Hewitt went out of their way to bribe the woman into selling to them. Maybe they offered her some extra money to persuade her to sell up.'

'Possibly. But whatever the case might be it doesn't help me one iota.'

'You never know though. Go and visit the solicitor to find out if this is legal for a start.'

'But it must be Polly, the solicitor is responsible for this letter.'

Polly shook her head and then began to nibble on her fingernails. Cassie hadn't seen her do that in a long while, it was a nervous habit she had when stressed. The last time she'd seen the woman do that was when she'd got the news that her ladyship had passed away a couple of years ago because before she was nursemaid to Emily, she'd been the woman's personal maid and sometimes companion and even Polly, hadn't judged and had seemed to somehow understand the situation going on with Cassie and his lordship. Sometimes Cassie wondered if Lady Bellingham had informed Polly that she had given her approval to it, but Polly had never mentioned anything of the sort to her.

Cassie fought to think to clear her head. There had to be some sort of solution, she'd need to speak to Jem when he returned. He had a way of working things out.

***

Jem and Clyde were sitting on the horse and cart on their return journey from the church hall. Reverend Ainsworth had been delighted with the furniture they'd delivered to him. Several bookcases, a large desk and chair for the teacher and several small desks and chairs for the pupils which they'd purchased from an old school in a neighbouring village that had closed down. All the children there had been transferred to a brand new school with new equipment so he'd bought this lot for a song at auction. Only thing was, Jem felt bad charging the vicar for this stuff and making money on it but the good reverend had insisted, informing him it would be the kind benefactor who was paying for the furniture, not the church itself so that in itself had eased his troubled mind. He had a living to make to keep him and his brother so he could hardly refuse. Yes, it had been a satisfying day's work.

As they pulled up outside the shop he blinked several times. Were his eyes deceiving him? There was a lantern burning in the window of the tea room at this time of evening. Usually, Cassie and Polly would have locked up long before now. Unless maybe they were staying behind to prepare for tomorrow's trade? Cassie had told him yesterday how she'd planned to decorate the tea room for Christmas and he'd even managed to purchase a small Christmas tree from the marketplace for her. It was a Norwegian Spruce too, a fine sort of Christmas tree in his book.

'Take the horse and cart back home, Clyde,' Jem ordered. 'I'll be along later. Make sure you feed t'horse and stable her for the night.'

Clyde nodded. 'W...what's up?' he asked as if sensing something was wrong.

'I'm not altogether sure,' Jem said truthfully, 'but I'm about to find out. Now get off home as the temperature is dropping and that horse needs feeding and stabling for the night.'

'I'll g...go now,' Clyde said and Jem watched him gee the horse up the incline.

Jem's stomach flipped over as he knocked on the tea room door. Polly was immediately on her feet to allow him access. 'Is something wrong, Pol?' he asked removing his flat cap as he stepped over the threshold.

'Aye, you could say that. Mrs Hewitt was around here earlier on and she's given Cassie a notice to quit the shop.'

Jem's gaze travelled to where Cassie was sitting at the table. He could tell from her red-rimmed, puffy eyes, she'd been crying. 'But I don't get it,' he said. 'How can Mrs Hewitt give you a notice to quit, the shop's bugger all to do with her?' His face flamed, he didn't often use curse words and now that had slipped out in anger he felt shame but Cassie didn't appear to notice.

'Because her husband now owns the property.' She passed the letter over to him for his perusal.

He raised his eyebrows as he looked at the notice. 'Looks very official and above board. Though I can't understand why that Madame Claudette one couldn't have forewarned you of her intention to sell the property when you signed an agreement with her.'

'That's just it though, Jem. I didn't sign anything at all. It was a verbal agreement I had with the woman and she didn't appear to be in a rush to sell. I was hoping given time that maybe if both businesses, that is mine and yours, had done well enough we could have secured a down payment on the shop and maybe acquired a bank loan for the rest.'

'That were wishful thinking by the sound of it, Cassie, and might I say a tad naïve on your part.' He cast her a stern glance.

'Now, you're angry with me?'

He didn't want to hurt her but she had been foolish not to have had anything in writing from their landlady. He forced a smile. 'Now let's not go worrying as we're no worse off than either of us were a few weeks back when we weren't in the shop. In fact, we're a darn sight better off as both of us have done well. We'll try to get another property maybe, something like this one.'

'But there are none,' Cassie said blankly.

Polly moved towards them. 'If you don't mind me butting in,' she said, 'but there is an obvious solution.'

'There is?' Cassie blinked profusely as Jem scratched his head.

'Yes, why don't you both go and have a word with William Hewitt to ask what his intention is in buying this place and if he's willing to rent it out to you as in the agreement you had with Madame C. Afterall, it would be easy money in his pocket.'

A big grin appeared on Jem's face. 'Polly, I could kiss you!' he said. 'That's a fantastic idea!'

'We don't know if the Hewitt's will go for it though?' Cassie furrowed her brow.

'There's only one way to find out,' Jem said. 'Tomorrow we'll call around to see them both.'

Cassie shook her head. Mrs Hewitt hated her and she'd love to see her on her doorstep with cap in hand, pleading to be allowed to keep the shop on and she didn't want to give the woman the satisfaction of her being beholden towards her. Though as she gently patted her ever-increasing tummy, she realised that pride came with a pinch and she must put any harsh feelings she had towards the woman well and truly behind her.

***

From the top of the horse and cart where she was seated, Cassie looked down on the village of Wakeford. From up here, she could see for miles towards Drisdale in one direction, Marshfield in another (which gave her a lump in her throat) and the bustling town of Hocklea in another. The Hewitt family home was on the border between Wakeford and another small village over the other side of the mountain called Castleford, as Wakeford was slightly nearer and easier by foot, the Hewitt family mostly conducted their business in Wakeford. They were better off than most folk in the area and often had no need to be out walking as they owned their own coach and horses which put them in the better off bracket. There were only several other people in the vicinity who owned their own coach and horses too and those were the Petersons who lived close by, Doctor Mason who was an elderly medic for the wealthy folk in the area, the village butcher, Mr Rumbelow, and the village baker, Mr Greening. They were the only folk of affluence and standing, and all lived on the mountain in the same area or "the nobs' area" as Clyde often referred to it.

As Jem pulled up the cart outside the large imposing house that was ensconced into the side of the mountain, Cassie's stomach flipped over with fear and she now regretted having any previous dealings with Mrs Hewitt whatsoever. The woman had the opportunity to now make or break her. Jem, himself though, didn't feel that way. His plan was if they couldn't appeal to Edna or William's better natures then he was not about to beg, he would dust himself down and start all over again and find a new property to rent, for Cassie, that felt more difficult. She'd already lost her husband and her home and now she felt she was about to lose her business. The unexpected pregnancy brought up all manner of feelings for her. It was as if the rug was about to be pulled from beneath her feet and she didn't much care for that sensation, after all, it was scary.

She glanced up at the grey house which had six large framed windows, a big wooden door at its centre and a meticulously tiled roof. She gulped. The dwelling looked foreboding and fierce like Mrs Hewitt herself. No cosiness or welcome here.

Jem heaved himself down from the cart and walked around to her side. He reached out his arms to her to aid her down. Looking up at her, he shot her a disarming smile as if to say, 'Don't worry yourself so, Cassie. All will be well.' She hadn't as yet informed him of her pregnancy so she was grateful for the fact he was the gentlemanly type who would help her down anyhow whether she were pregnant or not. Allowing him to help, he took her hands and guided her on to terra firma. Feeling the gravel beneath the soles of her boots, she winced. It was as if the small pieces of crushed stone were impressing themselves into her boots to remind her this wasn't going to be an easy task. Jem, as he strode beside her, didn't appear to have the same problem, but then again he was wearing boots with hobnail soles—which were embedded with short nails with a thick head used to increase the durability of boot soles, suitable for a hardworking sort like him.

As they stood outside the front door, Cassie

noticed an elaborate sign painted in gold-leaf paint which read, "Hewitt Hall". She surveyed the scene around them, there was no sign of the couple's coach, she half hoped they were out for the day and that they'd need to return at some other point as she felt she couldn't possibly face the woman's wrath today. But then again, what would that achieve? It would only be delaying the inevitable. She noted the sharply sculptured shrubbery, it was almost as though a weed wouldn't dare show its ugly head in this garden. She'd never seen such a neat garden in all her born days.

Jem rapped on the door knocker and the pair stood back, Cassie nervously licked her dry lips. *Please be out*, she whispered inwardly to herself. Finally, the door swung open and a young maid stood there. 'The tradesman's entrance is around the back of the property,' she said curtly, glancing at Jem's horse and cart.

'We're not here to do business like that,' Jem explained, 'I mean we are here to do business but we're not selling anything.'

The maid quirked a puzzled brow and folded her arms as if she meant business. 'I don't understand,' she said impatiently tapping her foot. Cassie guessed the young woman was a maid of all work and had jobs she needed to attend to. She smiled at the girl. 'It's about the property Mr Hewitt has purchased. We currently trade from it, I have the tea room and the other side, Mr

Clement sells furniture.'

The maid returned the smile. 'Oh, I know who you both are now. Please forgive me. I've been dying to try the tea room I was going to wait until my next afternoon off. But you say Mr Hewitt has now purchased the property?'

'Yes,' said Jem. 'We're here to ask if we may rent it from him instead.'

The maid glanced behind her into the house. 'Mr Hewitt is out at the moment conducting some business in Hocklea and Mrs Hewitt is entertaining some of her friends from the Women's Guild for afternoon tea in her conservatory. Shall I fetch her for you?'

'Oh, no, no, no!' said Cassie too firmly. 'Do you know when Mr Hewitt will return?'

The maid shook her head. 'I'm sorry, I don't. May I pass a message on for you?'

Cassie thought for a moment. 'Please could you ask him if it's at all possible to call to see me? I'm Cassandra Bellingham and I'll be working at the tea room all week. At a time to suit his convenience, of course.' She smiled.

'Very well,' the girl nodded. 'I will be sure to pass the message on.'

'One more thing,' added Cassie, 'if you could ensure that only he receives the message as we do not wish to disturb or worry Mrs Hewitt...' She wondered if she had gone a step too far by saying that but in for a penny in for a pound.

A small smile played upon the girl's lips as

if she understood her mistress all too well and knew what a tyrant she was. 'You have my word,' she said and then she shut the door firmly behind herself before they'd even had a chance to thank her.

'I don't know if you did the right thing there,' Jem said glumly. 'That one might go straight to Mrs Hewitt and report back every word we've said.'

'I don't believe she will,' said Cassie with confidence. 'I could see it in the girl's eyes. She's on our side and has incurred the wrath of that old biddy on more than one occasion!'

'I only hope you're right,' Jem muttered under his breath as he kicked a small stone out of his path and dug his hands deep into his trouser pockets.

***

But Jem needn't have worried as the following day William Hewitt showed up at the tea room, alone. When the doorbell jangled and Cassie glanced up from the counter she was almost surprised to see that the man had dared to come without his wife.

He was smartly dressed in his grey frockcoat, pristine white shirt and silver-grey cravat. On entering the premises, he removed his black bowler hat and tucked it beneath his arm. Cassie put him at middle age. He was a man who although he carried a little too much weight, carried it well. His salt and peppered, thick bushy sideburns and handlebar moustache made up for the lack of hair on his head. His twinkling indigo eyes made his appearance more than attractive, in sharp contrast to his wife's dour demeanour.

As he approached the counter, he raised his brows. 'Excuse me, Madame, would you be Cassandra Bellingham? I was given a message to call in to see her?'

'Yes, that's me, Mr Hewitt I assume?'

'You assume correctly,' he smiled.

The tea room was quiet that afternoon so Cassie led him to a corner table in case any customers called so they might speak in confidence. Jem, unfortunately, was at the marketplace where he still traded on his stall twice a week.

Polly appeared at their table and Cassie gave her an order to bring a pot of tea over to them.

'That's most kind of you,' said William Hewitt. 'I have had a busy morning, so some refreshment would be most welcome. Now, what did you wish to see me about?'

'It's about this place,' Cassie said with some trepidation. 'You see, I was served a notice to quit a couple of nights ago...'

'And you don't agree with it?'

'It's not that, Mr Hewitt, it's just that I made an agreement with Madame Claudette that I would be renting this place for the minimum of six months and as business is beginning to build up and I'm establishing a regular clientele, it is heart-wrenching for me to give it all up right now.'

William's face clouded over. Oh dear, what was he thinking? She swallowed hard.

'I purchased this property in good faith on the proviso that I would take vacant possession. Madame Claudette, or Mrs Robertson as I know of her, has assured me there would be no problem with it. She said it was rented out on a short term lease of weeks rather than months. Do you have the contract for me to peruse?'

She shook her head. 'Unfortunately, no. It was a verbal agreement.'

'Then I'm afraid that you wouldn't have a leg to stand on in court.'

As she sat there feeling flummoxed, several customers made their way in through the door and headed towards the window tables which were popular. It was all a bad dream to Cassie and normally she'd have been on her feet to meet and greet them, but somehow she blocked out their chatter as she fought to think. She was oblivious to the fact that William Hewitt was looking at the customers with avid interest.

Polly brought the tea tray to the table and went off to serve the customers who spoke of sandwiches, iced slices, mince pies, pots of tea and coffee as other people drifted inside.

It's of no use, thought Cassie, he's not interested.

But then William said something that made her prick up her ears and take stock. He cleared his throat. 'I know that's not what you wanted to hear but I can see you have established some trade here. I wonder if we might come to some sort of agreement?'

'Agreement?' She looked at him quizzically with her chin rested on her hands on the table.

'Yes, if you'd please pour the tea as I'm parched and I'll tell you what I propose we do.'

***

'He what?' said Polly as she listened with interest to what Cassie had to say when William Hewitt had departed from the premises.

'He said although legally I didn't have a leg to stand on as there was no written agreement between myself and Madame Claudette who he knows as Mrs Robertson...'

'I flamin' well knew it,' said Polly throwing her tea towel down on the counter. The bloomin' old fraud!' She glanced at Cassie then urged, 'But do go on.'

'Anyhow, he's come up with a solution. He said he only needs the one side of the shop as he wishes to set up a new business there, a hardware store by all accounts, but he'd be prepared to keep this on as a tea room for the same rent.'

'Hey there, what's the bloomin' catch though?'

'There isn't one really except he would like a small percentage of the profit, only five per cent though.'

'Hmmm,' Polly sniffed. 'I don't know whether that's a good idea. Not only that but where will this proposal leave Jem and his business?'

'Mr Hewitt suggested Jem use the upper floor to sell his furniture. There's a staircase people can use and he said he'd put a notice in the hardware store below to send trade upstairs as often when people are decorating they are seeking new furniture.'

'I suppose so,' said Polly reluctantly. 'And I suppose Jem would have to cough up 5 per cent of his business as well as the rent an' all?'

'Precisely.'

Polly sniffed even louder and crossed one hand over the other as if considering it all. Finally, she said, 'I suppose you 'ave little choice for time being.'

'I suppose we don't,' said Cassie with a resigned sigh, though secretly she was pleased as they'd been granted a reprieve and just before Christmas and all. She couldn't wait to tell Jem the good news and didn't think he'd mind too much moving his business upstairs, though hefting furniture up and down the stairs would, of course, involve hard work and he wasn't afraid of that; nor was Clyde for that matter. Both men had enough muscle power to shift the furniture when needed. What she was really concerned about though was Mrs Hewitt. Did the woman know of what her husband had proposed? In any case, whether she did or not the deal would be sealed in the New Year as the man had left the tea room with a promise for his solicitor to draw up the paperwork. When the time arose, it would be a simple case of her and Jem going to the offices and signing their names on the tenancy agreement.

Chapter Seven

Jem was as happy as Cassie was about the new proposed tenancy agreement with Mr Hewitt but he was very sceptical about the man's wife. They were seated in Clem's cottage at the table while Clyde was out the back of the property seeing to the horse.

'No, I agree,' Jem said stroking his stubbled chin. He looked tired today, the dark rings beneath his eyes seemed testament to that. 'I can't see Mrs Hewitt agreeing to her husband's proposal...that is...not unless...'

'Not unless what, Jem?' Cassie shifted further forwards in her chair.

'Not unless the pair have something up their sleeves.'

'But Mr Hewitt seemed most sincere to me.' She frowned.

'Aye, maybe the man was. I've not had any dealing with him to tell the truth, but that wife of his has the most malicious tongue of anyone in this village. I can't see her being happy with it.'

'Not even the extra five per cent a month coming from each of us?' Cassie quirked a brow.

'When you put it like that...she is the sort

what likes the finer sort of things in life so maybe that will soften the blow, like.'

Cassie chuckled and then she became startled. 'Oh!' she said suddenly.

'What's the matter?' Jem touched her hand across the table which brought tears to her eyes. Now was the time to tell him. 'I haven't told you this but now I need to, Jem.'

'Is anything wrong?' Cassie could see the genuine concern the man had for her in his eyes.

She shook her head and swallowed hard. 'No, not wrong exactly it's more that something unexpected has happened and I only found out about it a couple of weeks ago.'

'Oh?' In that moment the way he was looking at her made her feel a great swell of deep feeling for him.

'It's just that I'm pregnant?' She looked deep into his troubled eyes to see if she could gauge his reaction.

'P...pregnant?' She nodded. 'And how do you feel about that?'

She shrugged. 'The honest truth is I don't really know how to feel, I've not had the time with working at the tea room and his lordship's death dwelling on my mind this past couple of months.'

He smiled at her. 'Well, you've got us at any rate, me and Clyde and your own family. Things will have a way of working themselves out and at least the baby isn't being born out of wedlock.'

That was true. A thought suddenly occurred to her as she said with some alarm, 'But what if people do think this is someone else's baby I'm carrying? Some folk around here think badly of me anyhow, they may assume I've been playing fast and loose with my morals.' She bit her bottom lip.

'If you ask me, if they think that way of you anyhow, naming no names, then what does it matter? You're a marked woman Cassie Bellingham and make no mistake!' She noticed the glint in his eyes and she laughed realising he was only teasing her.

***

Cassie and Jem heard no more about the tenancy agreement until William Hewitt marched into the tea room a few days later with a request they should both attend a solicitor's office in Hocklea as the tenancy agreement was now drawn up. Both were only too happy to comply and made arrangements to attend a different solicitor's firm to the one William Hewitt used as he'd explained there would be a 'conflict of interest' for them to use the same firm. So the prepared papers were sent to the offices of Messers Blake, Martin and Dimbleby, a solicitor's firm that Jem's own father had previously used when he made his will leaving the cottage to his sons.

As Jem was about to sign, he glanced across at Cassie with trepidation in his eyes.

She noticed his hand tremble as he held the

fountain pen over the document. 'What's the matter, Jem? Have you had second thoughts?'

He shook his head and laid the pen down on the large oak desk. 'It's not that. I'm just not very good at reading and writing, I had little schooling, you see. I'm afraid I'll mess it up and make a mistake.'

The beak-nosed solicitor, Mr Martin, smiled. 'Are you able to write your full name at least, sir?'

Jem nodded and smiled. 'Yes, though it's been a while since I've done so in an official manner. I've had no need to, you see.'

Mr Martin shuffled some papers on the desk and then drew one out. 'Then if I suggest you practise a little first on this blank sheet of paper, Mr Clement?'

The solicitor placed the parchment on the desk in front of Jem. Jem lifted the fountain pen and wrote his name several times: Jeremy Winston Clement. Unfortunately, he made a couple of spelling mistakes and so, Cassie wrote his name for him and encouraged him to copy that onto the form. She found it hard to believe that Jem did so well in life and business without being able to read and write properly. Maybe Clyde had the same problem too, she would have to speak to them about it.

When the document was signed by both parties and witnessed by both Mr Martin and his clerk, Mr Jeffery, the solicitor shook their hands. 'You're far better off getting something legal drawn up like this in writing than having a verbal agreement which of course, you found detrimental to your cost.' He sniffed loudly, causing Jem to sneak a glance at Cassie who held herself up straight with her chin jutting out.

'Yes, you are correct of course, Mr Martin,' she said, 'though life is most certainly a series of lessons and my partner and I, have both learned a valuable lesson indeed. Nothing or no one will ever pull the wool over our eyes again.' She shot the solicitor a hard stare which caused his face to redden.

Mr Martin ran his index finger under the rim of his shirt collar. Suddenly, he didn't seem quite so formidable. If she were to deal with such people in the future she was going to put on her 'lady of the manor' act to put them in their place. She could, on occasion, be formidable herself, she decided.

As they made their way down the wooden staircase of Messers Blake, Martin and Dimbleby, Jem began to chuckle, so much that it echoed all around. Cassie feeling puzzled, said nothing until they were on the pavement outside. 'What on earth were you laughing at just then?'

He smiled so broadly she could see his even white teeth set against the florid tone of his skin. His green eyes glinting with merriment. 'It was just the way you put that stuffed shirt in there rightly in his place! I can see there will be no messing with you, madame!'

She smiled shyly at him for the first time she'd known him. For some reason, he had broken down a boundary with his understanding of her and she wasn't used to that. It was almost as though the ice around her heart was melting. 'Well,' she said brusquely, 'I was messed around by that Madame Claudette and won't be messed around by anyone else in future.'

'I believe you,' said Jem taking her by the arm to escort her back to the inn where he'd stabled his horse while they were in Hocklea.

Hocklea was a vibrant town compared with the village of Wakeford. Here you could purchase almost anything from the busy daily market-place or any of its wide expanse of little shops dotted on the high street or in the arcades. It was here that all manner of business was conducted not just by retail trading but in several solicitors offices, one of which they'd just visited. It was a thriving place where the hubbub from folk was loud and varied. There was no peaceful solitude here.

A storefront caught Cassie's eye. The sign over the door read: M. K. Jackson & Co (Opticians to the principal Ophthalmic Hospital St. Joseph's in Hocklea). In the window were several notices. One read: "Improved ladies and gents eyeglasses – speciality frames and lenses to oculist's prescriptions. Please enter to book an appointment." The other notices had drawings of several people wearing a variety of spectacles. Cassie chuckled when she read the description beneath one of the images which read: "Suitable for Reading, Distance, Shooting, Billiards and Fishing".

'Why are you laughing?' Jem asked curiously.

'Because I was thinking about my aunt and maybe encouraging her to make an appointment somewhere like this. I couldn't imagine her shooting a gun or playing billiards, mind you!'

Jem drew nearer to the window. 'That might not be a bad idea for her to have her eyes tested after what you've told me about her eyesight.'

Cassie looked at him. 'I know, it's a good idea but the hardest part will be persuading her there's something wrong with her eyes in the first place. She simply won't admit they're as bad as they are. I think she tries to cover it up sometimes. The other day I caught her reading a book upside down!'

Jem nodded as if he understood all too well. 'It's probably a question of pride,' he said. 'There's none of us getting any younger...'

'You're probably right,' she admitted with a resigned shrug of her shoulders.

Jem guided her along the high street where she marvelled at several of the shops which were decorated ready for the festive season. There was an enormous turkey in the poulterer's window and the sweetest doll that would suit Emily in the toy shop. But all of that could wait for time being, she'd return again someday soon.

'Fancy something to eat?' Jem asked as he

helped her across the busy main thoroughfare of the town as they dodged horses and carts, shiny coaches, the odd costermonger trolley and even one of those horse-drawn omnibuses, packed with people, on its way to Demford which was the next town over about seven miles yonder.

She was ravenous now as on rising she had felt nauseous again but had managed to keep a few spoonful's of porridge down. She found the sickness worse if she ate nothing at all and so, contrived to keep something in her stomach whenever she could, particularly in the morning.

'Yes, that would be lovely, Jem.' She smiled at him and he led her across the cobbled courtyard to check on the horse.

The straw-covered cobbles were a little hazardous as splodges of manure were splattered here and there and so she realised she had to be careful not to lose her footing. A stable boy appeared as if on cue and came over to them. The lad could have been no more than twelve-years-old but had a world-weary countenance about him as he looked at Jem. 'You ready for the 'oss, sir?' he asked. The lad's face had a smattering of freckles and his flat cap was perched precariously on his head. Over his striped shirt which was rolled up at the sleeves was a long brown leather apron and his ragged trousers looked like a threadbare corduroy to Cassie. The tongues were hanging out of his hobnail boots as if the laces had broken and he prised both hands into the front pocket of his apron while he waited for an answer.

'No, not yet, lad,' Jem replied. 'If you can keep hold of her for say another hour I'll give you another sixpence for yer time!'

The lad grinned widely displaying a set of uneven teeth as Jem dropped the first sixpence into his grubby palm. 'As you wish, guv. And thank you kindly.' He tipped his cap to Jem. 'I'll give her some more water and something to eat then, shall I?'

'Yes, you do that, lad, and I'll see you alright!' Jem grinned. 'We're just going inside to have something to eat ourselves. What do you recommend?'

'The steak and ale pie is good, gets some titbits of that from Cook now and again I do.' He rubbed his tummy in a circular fashion.

'Then that is what we shall plump for,' said Jem leading Cassie away.

'Very well then, sir! Hope you and yer wife enjoy yer meals!' The lad called after them which made Jem chuckle.

Cassie looked up at her now very dapper looking companion. He was smartly turned out this afternoon in his Sunday best which was a dark woollen jacket, thin striped trousers, white shirt, black cravat and bowler hat. She had to admit she had feelings for him that were surfacing that she'd never experienced before and now they were both out of their work environment, there seemed to be a gaiety about his persona, almost as though just for this afternoon they could block out the rest of the world and make merry with one another.

The inside of the inn was swathed with garlands of holly and ivy and on each windowsill, a red candle burned brightly. At the far end, near the bar, was a fir tree decorated with candles and baubles. A barmaid stepped forward to greet them. 'Are you looking for a table, sir? Madam?' She asked with a round tin tray tucked beneath her arm for glass collection.

Cassie's eyes scanned the room, it did look rather full at the moment. As if sensing her thoughts, the barmaid elaborated, 'We just had a coach party from Scarsfield turn up on their way to London, that's why we're so full...but yer in luck as if you follow me out to the back room, we have a couple of spare tables.'

'Thank you, that'll do nicely,' said Jem looking rather pleased with himself.

The barmaid led them through the alcove and into a small select room that had a smaller Christmas tree in the corner and looked out onto the busy street outside. There was a roaring fire in the grate and on the mantle was a decorative centrepiece of red candles surrounded by holly. It did look cosy.

They were the only patrons present and had the room to themselves. Jem drew out a chair to allow her to sit down.

'And what can I get you to drink while you decide what yer'd like to eat?' Asked the barmaid.

Jem looked at Cassie. 'Have you any lemonade?' she asked.

The barmaid nodded. 'Though we have a rum punch if yer'd like it to warm you up?'

In truth, Cassie would have loved to have had one but she wondered if it might be bad for the baby.

'Or we have one with no alcohol in it, it's got fruit juices, lemonade and spices in it? It will be good an' hot and all.'

Cassie's eyes lit up. 'Yes, please, and a glass of water too.'

'And you, sir?' The barmaid drew near and Cassie noticed the way the young woman was looking at Jem that she was impressed by him.

'I'd like the rum punch, please.'

'Very well, sir.' The barmaid fluttered her eyelashes and smiled at him.

When the girl had departed, Cassie looked across the table at him. 'I think you have an admirer there, Jem.'

'Go on with you!' he chuckled.

'No, seriously. She has her eye on you, I can tell.'

'But she's not my sort at all!'

And what would your sort be then?'

'Oh, I like a more sophisticated lady. A lady who maybe has seen a bit of life. A lady who can think for herself and who has a brain.' His gaze met her own and she felt a flutter in the recesses of her stomach. That wasn't the baby moving either it was the way he was looking at her for the first time—it felt so intimate.

'And would this lady have a name?'

He nodded. 'She does indeed. She's sitting right opposite me.'

Cassie licked her lips. 'But why would you have your sights set on someone like me? Twice widowed and someone who has a young child and another on the way?'

'Because, Cassie,' he reached out and took her hand across the table, 'you're kind and uncomplicated and you just get on with things. Besides, Clyde adores you.'

'And that's important to you?'

'Very.' He drew in a long breath and let it out again. 'Cassie, there's a reason I brought you here today...I'm not rich, but neither am I poor, but I do have a lot of love to give you.' Was this what she thought it was going to be? 'Your father's not alive for me to ask him for your hand in marriage, so I'm asking you right now.'

Then he was on his knees to her. Her hand flew to her mouth. She hadn't been expecting this at all. It was the last thing she imagined.

'B...but Jem are you proposing to me because of what I said the other day about the fact that people might not think this is Lord Bellingham's baby I'm carrying?'

He shook his head. 'Not at all. I've never been

more serious. I think I loved you from that first moment when you came to my furniture stall. You looked so beautiful all dressed in black with your alabaster skin and your mysterious sad blue eyes. I fell for you there and then.'

'And do I look at all sad these days to you?'

'Not as you did back then, but you'd only just buried your husband. Now you seem hopeful for the future but at times I detect there is still a sense of melancholia behind your words.'

She nodded. It was true, every word he said. 'You are correct of course and know me so well by now.'

'You still haven't answered my question and it's very uncomfortable kneeling here,' he chuckled.

'Arise, Sir Galahad!' she announced.

Instead of now towering over her he chose to return to his seat. 'I get the impression this wasn't the right place to propose to you.' His eyes were questioning hers.

'No, it's not that...' She looked away for a moment. 'The venue is fine, I like it here. It is not the place but the time you have chosen for it's far too soon for me to be thinking of remarriage.'

He swallowed hard. 'I will ask you again at some point,' he said firmly, his eyes darkening with intent and then softening as they began to water slightly. Now it was his turn to have sad eyes as he reached out and patted her hand across the table and with a tremor to his voice he added, 'I'll keep asking until you're ready to accept.'

***

The meal went by in a blur as Cassie tried to think of something else other than the unexpected marriage proposal. Somehow, she managed to fork pieces of the steak and ale pie into her mouth, after all, her growing baby needed sustenance and she couldn't leave him or her without nourishment however perplexed she now was. It wasn't as if she wasn't attracted to Jem, quite the opposite. It was just that she couldn't see pleasure mixing with business. She preferred to lead with her head, not her heart. Always had and as far as she was concerned, always would. It was the best way because if she kept being guided by her heart then she would not have set up a new life for herself and Emily after all that had gone wrong with two failed marriages. Yes, maybe that's what it was, she feared failing a third time.

Up until now, she had been looking down into her plate of food but as she raised her eyes upwards she caught Jem's questioning gaze. 'Tell me what you were thinking of, please,' he implored.

She laid her fork on the side of her plate and took a few sips from the glass of water she had ordered with her meal. 'Do you really want me to be honest with you?'

He nodded. 'Yes, I do. Is there any other way?'

She patted her lips with her cotton napkin and laid it down by the side of her plate before looking at him once again. 'I was thinking of what a mess I've made of my previous marriages. My first husband was a brute who treated me badly and...this is a dreadful thing to say, but I thanked my lucky stars when he dropped down dead!' She said vehemently. If Jem was shocked then he wasn't showing it. 'Then my second husband turned out to be an inveterate gambler and also a womaniser like the first. He scattered money around like rice tossed at the bride and groom at a wedding!'

'I see,' said Jem.

'No, you don't see at all!' Cassie's eyes flashed with indignance. 'Can't you tell what a poor judge of character I am? I thought both men were admirable yet once I married both of them they became obnoxious oafs!' There, she'd said it and she shocked even herself as she had never said that about his lordship before, never even thought those particular words. Yet, something from her subconscious mind had arisen here.

'So,' said Jem, 'you think that if you marry me I'll change from being an easy-going affable chap into some kind of monster or at least an obnoxious oaf?'

She shrugged. 'There's no way of telling, is there? And look at what's at stake here as well as my heart it's my livelihood which doesn't just include me and you but also my daughter and my aunt and even Polly. I could wreck it all again as I did with his lordship and we'd end up penniless as being my husband you would be entitled to everything. Women don't have a say, do they? It's a man's world for sure.'

As if not knowing what to say regarding her outburst, he just nodded at her and carried on eating his meal. The rest of the meal went by in silence and it felt awkward, what should have been a lovely moment as two business partners secured their tenancy with one another, and should have been somewhat of a celebration for them both, had somehow slipped into something sordid.

Cassie was relieved when Jem dropped her back off at the cottage. By now it was dark and he carefully helped her down from the cart. 'Watch you don't slip on them cobbles,' he advised. 'Although it's been a fine day, it's mighty frosty tonight.'

She nodded gratefully at him. Ordinarily, she might have invited him in for a warm and a cup of tea before he set off back home but she knew he was anxious to return as he'd left Clyde alone all day. Since he'd almost taken a beating recently, Jem had been even more watchful of his younger brother. It was almost sometimes as though he were holding his breath around Clyde, just waiting for something to happen to him. It wasn't healthy of course, him feeling that way and being on pins for the lad's safety but what else could he do?

As Cassie opened the cottage door, she heard Polly call out. 'Thank goodness you're back home, your aunt has taken a tumble!'

Chapter Eight

With a racing heart, Cassie rushed towards Aunt Bertha who was sitting in the armchair as Polly held a glass of water to her trembling lips. 'I just this minute managed to get her to her feet.'

'How did it happen?' Cassie frowned.

'Not sure exactly but I found her on the flagstone floor near the hearth. Maybe she tripped over the rag rug.'

Cassie watched as her aunt took several sips of water. Then Polly blotted the woman's mouth dry with a tea towel and placed the glass on the table.

'It weren't the rug really,' her aunt explained. 'It's my eyesight, it's not getting any better.'

'Then if that's the case,' said Cassie firmly, 'we must get you to see some kind of specialist.' She figured she had enough money put by, she'd been saving hard since they'd first opened the tea room and although the money was meant for a rainy day, maybe now that day had finally arrived. 'When we were in Hocklea earlier I noticed that there was an optician's practice that examines the eyes.'

'Aye, maybe I ought to have sorted myself out

with glasses before now but I didn't like to admit it even to myself that my eyes are failing me.'

'At least now you have, Auntie. I'll sort all this out for you and pay for your eye examination and the glasses too,' said Cassie kindly. She could no longer bear to think about the woman having any further accidents.

Aunt Bertha nodded gratefully. Thankfully, now, at last, the woman was about to accept help. Her previous prideful manner had come at considerable cost.

When Polly had settled Bertha in her bed, with Emily already asleep in the bedroom next door, she made a cup of cocoa for herself and Cassie and they settled themselves down by the fireside.

'So, how did Hocklea go today? Sorry, I ain't had a chance to ask afore now but I was so concerned about your aunt when she fell.'

'Thats' all right,' said Cassie. She took a sip of her cocoa and gazed into the flames of the fire. 'Put it this way, it was interesting, to say the least.'

Polly raised a thoughtful brow. 'Interesting how?'

'The tenancy agreement has been sorted with no bother, but it was Jem and how he was behaving towards me afterwards. He took me to an inn for a meal.'

'Don't see nothing wrong with that at all!' Polly shook her head.

'No, and there wasn't and it was nice there.

Really Christmassy but it was his intention that concerned me most.'

'Intention?' Polly wrinkled her brow and gasped.

'Yes...' For a moment Cassie wasn't sure if she ought to tell the woman what happened but she needed to confide in someone and Polly was trustworthy. 'He ended up going down on one knee...'

'He didn't! You mean he proposed marriage to you?' Polly covered her mouth with her hand in surprise.

'He did indeed. I mean it took me right aback as I wasn't expecting it. I've had enough things on my mind regarding the business and the thought I might lose it along with everything that's happened since the lord's death. I couldn't fathom what he was saying to me, it felt like a dream.'

Polly dropped her hand to her side. 'I bet it did an' all!' There was a note of indignation to her voice. 'I didn't know Jem had it in him, to be honest. He just seems a quiet sort to me but they reckon it's them quiet ones you 'ave to watch! So how did you answer?'

'I turned him down of course but he says he's not going to stop asking me.'

Polly tutted then she sucked in a breath between her teeth. 'If you ask me a man of his age is desperate to find himself a good wife, especially one like you. You'd be a meal ticket for him.'

'Oh no!' Cassie shook her head vehemently. 'Jem's not like that at all. I believe he was sincere. He does have his own business.'

'Which you helped set him up in. Before you came along he was just selling bits and pieces on the odd market day. Now he's involved in house clearances and started selling antique pieces.'

It was true. Jem had become involved with a couple of dealers and had recently started making good money. 'But if he's on the make as you suggest why would he need my money when he's already making enough of his own?'

Polly folded her arms and shook her head. 'Dunno. Maybe he's getting greedy.'

'I hardly think so, Pol. Look, since I've known Jem he's been very dependable and trustworthy.'

'If that is indeed the case, then perhaps he's asked you to marry him as he feels he can offer you something, a future with him maybe? But be prepared as you'd have to take on that Clyde one too and he's not without his problems. Like an overgrown child, he is. Look at how he went missing with your Emily that night? We were all out looking for them. He caused us a great deal of upset! I mean I'm very fond of the lad but that was most unsettling.'

Cassie shook her head and sighed. 'That was hardly Clyde's fault though. In fact, he helped Emily as who knows what those boys may have done to her and Sammy otherwise.'

'Aye, maybe,' said Pol with a shrewd look in her

eyes. 'Just take care though as if you ever change your mind and marry Jem you'll be taking that great big lummox on an' all. Yer've got enough on yer plate with your daughter, prospective new baby and Aunt Bertha as well as me of course!' She pointed a thumb at herself and chuckled.

***

The following day all Cassie saw of Jem was him passing back and forth up the stairway. He and Clyde were hefting furniture up the stairs to his new shop accommodation. The sound of their hobnail boots on the bare wooden stairs was quite loud on occasion. Cassie guessed the loud clomping sounds were more likely to have arisen from Clyde though than Jem as Clyde was very heavy-footed. At one point it had sounded like thunder when a chest of drawers tumbled down the stairs.

'Heaven help us!' Polly had shouted throwing the apron from her pinafore over her face. 'There's a wonder the customers haven't walked out of here today!'

Cassie had found herself agreeing with the woman. It certainly wasn't good for business and of course, would and could happen again whenever someone walked up the stairs to view any furniture or any was transported up and down it.

'You're going to have to have a word with Jem about this!' Polly moaned later that day. 'It's not on when we have customers in the tea room, they come 'ere for a bit o' peace and quiet not to listen to Thump! Thump! Thumpety thump!'

Cassie sighed heavily. This was all she needed. She wiped her damp hands in a tea towel and made for the door where she found Jem stood in the hallway in the process of instructing Clyde to take the front end of a desk and he'd take the back.

He looked at her with guarded eyes. 'I'm sorry if I've been shouting too much!' he said.

Cassie let out a long breath of resignation. 'It's not that so much, Jem, it's the clomping up and down the stairs all the time—it sounds like thunder in the tea room and it's disturbing the customers.'

'Sorry about that. I promise it won't go on for much longer as we've shifted the best part of it. Mr Hewitt wants the downstairs shop cleared out by tomorrow morning.'

'Oh?' she arched an eyebrow, this was news to her.

'Yes, he called to see me at the cottage early this morning. Apparently, his son is going to be taking over the shop. We had a good old chat and he seemed to take a lot of interest in Clyde, chatting to him and asking him questions about what he was getting up to. He was right nice to the both of us. Anyhow, his son will be here soon.'

'His son?' she wrinkled her nose. 'I didn't know he had one.'

'Yes.' Jem sniffed. 'His son went to Oxford by

all accounts but left for some reason before his time was up. After that, and you can imagine the disgrace, especially for someone like Mrs Hewitt, he was sent away to work in his uncle's law firm in London. Now he's back home and wants to start his own business his father reckoned.'

Cassie folded her arms. 'Wonder what it will be?'

'Don't much care,' said Jem. 'As long as it's not furniture.'

'I very much doubt that. Couldn't imagine someone of his standing selling old chairs and sideboards.'

'Aye, maybe not,' Jem chuckled.

'I can't hold this for much longer!' yelled Clyde.

Jem looked up to see his brother holding up one end of the elaborate oak desk while attempting to drag it up the stairs.

'Don't do that, Clitheroe!' said Jem angrily. 'Wait till I help you, you'll scuff the legs otherwise.' Then looking at Cassie he said, 'Maybe I'll ask Mr Hewitt about carpeting the stairs to keep the noise down. How's that?'

Cassie smiled and nodded gratefully. It would definitely be an improvement.

***

The following morning Emily was up bright and early and playing with Sammy in front of the fireplace as Polly made breakfast. Aunt Bertha had taken to her bed since her fall and Cassie was extremely worried about her, she had been complaining of headaches this past few months and she hoped there wasn't anything seriously wrong with the woman.

'The sooner we can get her to see that optical specialist in Hocklea all the better,' she said as she carried some bowls for their porridge into the living room and set them down on the table.

Polly, who arrived behind her carrying the saucepan of porridge, laid it down in the centre of the table. 'Aye, you're right an' all. That fall shook her up, think it's robbed her of all her confidence as now she fears she'll 'ave another fall. Have you got enough money to pay for her appointment?'

Cassie nodded as she began ladling out wooden spoonful's of oatmeal into the awaiting bowls. 'Yes, that's not the problem. It's getting her out of her pit and onto some form of transport to get her there. I mean Jem is willing to take her on his cart but it's bitterly cold at the moment. I could pay someone to take her in a cab I suppose...' she chewed on her bottom lip. It was all a dilemma for her as the longer the situation persisted then the longer it would take to resolve.

'Never mind,' said Polly sympathetically. 'Sit down and 'ave yer breakfast, else you'll be the one fainting off for the want of good food inside you. Yer still working long hours at the tea room and in your condition too. When are you going to take on a young girl to take over from you?'

Cassie seated herself as told and she looked

at Polly. 'I thought after Christmas when Emily begins at the new school.'

On hearing her name mentioned, Emily stood, leaving Sammy curled up in his bed, contented by the fireplace. 'How many more days till I begin school, Mama?' she asked, her big brown eyes shining brightly. She had her father's eyes that was for sure, but thankfully, she had her mother's nature. She was a kind child and one who was wise beyond her years.

'Not much longer now, dear,' Cassie smiled. 'About three weeks' time. You will start after Christmas. We've got that to get out of the way first.'

Polly seated herself opposite Cassie. 'Yer make it sound a bit of a chore, Cassie? You always used to love the festive season.'

'I still do, it's just that with all this tenancy business…' she lowered her voice a notch, 'and you know what happening,' she tapped her tummy, 'and the business with Jem the other day, my mind is all over the place.'

Polly glanced at Emily who was now seated beside her mother. 'You're going to have to say something soon.'

'I thought to leave that until after Christmas too.'

Emily seemed oblivious to what the grown-ups were talking about. All she was interested in was eating her breakfast as quickly as possible so she could return to her beloved Sammy.

***

Emily now had to go to the tea room with her mother and Polly as Cassie felt it unsafe to leave the little girl under Aunt Bessie's care at the cottage. It was so unlike her aunt to absolve herself of all responsibility when it came to her great-niece. But Emily was no bother. Sammy slept in his bed at the back of the tea room well away from the customers and on occasion, Emily took him outside to the yard for some exercise. There was a long lane at the back of the shops where she could take him on a lead when necessary. There was rarely anyone else around there apart from the odd shop worker sometimes out in their own yard, either having a quick break in the fresh air or stacking old wooden pallets or something of that nature.

It was almost midday when Polly noticed a carriage drawing up outside the front of the shop. 'Hey, there's some posh nob just got out of his carriage! And he's headed in this direction!' she exclaimed excitedly looking at Cassie.

'How exciting,' said Cassie. 'It's not often we get that sort in here. Maybe we'll start attracting a new type of customer.'

The gentleman in question wore a long dark cape and a black silk top hat on his head. In his hand, he held a gold-tipped cane. Cassie had to admit he was extraordinarily handsome. What would he drink? she wondered. A pot of tea? Coffee? Cordial? But as she pondered the question the man bypassed their side of the shop and inserted a key in the other. Cassie stood there opened-mouthed.

'Hey, that's got to be the Hewitt son!' Polly yelled. 'He must be the one taking over Jem's shop!'

'It certainly seems like it!' Cassie shook her head in disbelief. This was all happening too fast for her.

'Do you think we ought to go and introduce ourselves and maybe offer him a cup of tea?' Polly wanted to know.

'No,' Cassie said firmly. 'I'd rather not. Let him come to us.' She knew she shouldn't but for some reason, she felt annoyed by the man. After all, if it wasn't for the Hewitt family Jem would still be in that shop right now. But on the other hand, she reminded herself, if it wasn't the Hewitt family who had bought the property then it might be another family. She tried to concentrate by serving customers and then began to feel a shard of guilt for not welcoming the man.

Untying her apron strings, she removed it and hung it on a hook behind the counter. She patted down her hair. 'I'm just popping next door to have a word with the new owner,' she said curtly to Polly.

'Hey, I thought you said you wouldn't...' Polly's voice trailed off in disbelief as she watched Cassie make her way to the shop next door.

***

Cassie swallowed hard and then tapped her knuckles on the shop door. 'Enter!' boomed a voice that caused her to startle.

An authoritarian type of man who knows what he wants, she thought and she hoped his presence in the shop next door would not cause future trouble for her.

She gingerly pushed open the door to see the man had now removed his hat and cape which were placed on the counter before him. The sleeves of his pristine white shirt were rolled up to the elbow. The chain of a gold watch looped over the pocket of his black and grey pinstriped waistcoat and she thought she detected the faint aroma of pomade as if he had recently slicked down his dark locks. This was obviously a man who took care of his appearance.

His eyes showed interest as she approached him. 'Cassandra Bellingham,' she introduced.

'Harry Hewitt,' the man responded. 'I'm William Hewitt's son and new owner of this establishment.' He smiled.

Puzzled momentarily, she frowned. She hadn't even been aware that William and Edna Hewitt had a son until recently when Jem had mentioned him, for some reason she'd assumed the couple were childless. She swallowed hard. 'I see.'

'You're the proprietress of the tea room I've been informed.' He asked looking her in the eyes, making her feel a little unnerved.

'Yes. I was wondering what shop you will be

opening up here but I was given the impression it was going to be a hardware store of sorts?'

'It's going to be a book shop now instead,' he smiled. 'I've always been an avid reader and love all the great works. My father thought it best that I take over the shop instead of him.'

She arched an eyebrow of surprise. It wasn't what she had expected but then she thought maybe that would do her business some good as often when people browsed books they might wish to read them there and then with a cup of tea or coffee. 'That's interesting,' she said. 'I think that sort of shop may do well here.'

'Yes,' he elaborated. 'My mother has had an excellent idea too...'

'Your mother?'

'Yes, she thinks I should also provide tea and coffee to customers that sort of thing. Maybe the odd slice of cake...'

Cassie's hackles rose. So that was the woman's game to provide some competition to her business. Not content with trying to get shot of her and Jem and that had fallen flat, she had now changed her tactics to compete with her tea room. Granted, there wouldn't be a lot of space there when the books were installed on the shelves as that would be the primary trade but people might enjoy a cuppa when they were browsing the shelves. They might even fancy a seat to read their recent purchase or purchases.

'What's the matter?' Harry stared intently into

her eyes as if astonished by her reaction. 'You look a little unsettled?'

'Unsettled? Me?' she spat the words out. 'First of all, I get the news that myself and Jem are to be evicted, then your father agrees we can stay put as long as Jem moves his business upstairs here, which of course makes it more difficult for him as he has to heft heavy furniture up and down the stairs and then, you open up a rival tea room opposite mine!' She folded her arms and stuck her chin out in defiance.

'I'd hardly call it a tea room, madame!' Harry's face flushed from the neck up as if affronted at such a suggestion from her.

'Then just what would you call it?'

'In all honesty, there's not enough room to install lots of tables and chairs. I just thought maybe I'd place one or two small tables and chairs near the bay window where people can sit and enjoy their purchases. I certainly do not want them spilling tea or coffee over the pages of any books before purchase and I won't be selling any jam buns either as those would surely stick the pages together!'

Cassie caught the gleam in his eyes and she chuckled and so did he. 'I get your point,' she smiled.

He nodded affably at her. 'I'm pleased you do. In fact…' he glanced around, 'we could do one another a favour instead. If you point customers in my direction, I'll do the same for you. Honestly, this will not be a tea room. I'll probably only offer sustenance on my side of the premises if it warrants it. Understood?'

She nodded. He held out his hand and she shook it. 'That's a deal!' she said smiling.

***

Cassie had decided that anything Edna Hewitt decided to do to cause problems for her she would try to turn to her own advantage. She imagined the woman spitting feathers when she discovered her plan to thwart Cassie's tea room would have backfired on her. Within the week Harry Hewitt had set up his new book store with Jem's paid assistance as he and Clyde managed to acquire some walnut bookcases, tables and chairs and the counter previously made was left behind at a small cost to Harry. Cassie had to admit the book shop looked very smart with its coloured bookbindings of various shades and textures, some were vellum or leather-bound, others of a woven cloth material. Some of the books even had embossed gold lettering on them and fancy illustrations on their covers and inside, others were arranged in sets like 'The Complete Works of Charles Dickens or William Shakespeare'. She thought whoever purchased those would need to have plenty of coppers in the coffers. It was popular to give books with decorative bindings as gifts to friends and family, and so, customers' requirements for novelty in these bindings often resulted in unusual combinations of materials and the techniques employed.

The book shop had a special feel to it. A couple of Queen Anne velvet-covered chairs were placed at an angle, facing one another, near the counter for customers to take the weight off their feet. These usually turned out to be well-dressed ladies or the elderly. She was impressed how Harry took care of his customers and their particular needs and how he'd go out of his way to acquire a certain title for someone. He selected his books from specialist shops in London and second-hand ones from marketplaces and small select shops. Nothing was too much trouble for the man.

It was one afternoon a few days after opening that Cassie noticed Harry's mother enter the book shop. No doubt she'd come to see how her son was doing. 'Go over there,' Cassie urged when she'd explained to Polly what had occurred.

'But why would you want me to do that?' Polly asked with an amused look on her face.

'Because she's not so sure of you. Take your pinny off and browse the shelves, see if you can make out what she's saying to him.'

Polly nodded, and removing her pinafore, hung it on a peg behind the counter and then patted her hair down before entering the shop next door. It was a quarter of an hour or so before she returned. Longer than Cassie was expecting. The tea room was filling up with eager customers and she was now struggling to cope so she was grateful when the shop bell jangled as Polly entered looking a little flustered as she approached the counter.

'Cor! This place has filled up since I left. Sorry about that. She rushed to don her pinafore and tying the strings went to serve some customers. 'I'll tell you what I discovered when it quietens down here,' she said over her shoulder to Cassie.

Cassie nodded, now feeling quite concerned.

***

The last of the stragglers had departed so Polly put the "Closed" sign up in the window, locked the door and sat at a table while Cassie placed two cups of steaming coffee down on the table before them.

'So, what did you discover?' she asked breathlessly as she slowly eased herself down onto the wooden chair. It was getting harder to move around now even though her pregnancy wasn't showing as yet, her stomach just felt swollen and heavy and her ankles were often thicker by the end of the day, she badly needed to take the weight off them.

'Well...' said Polly in a conspiratorial tone, 'I didn't get too close and there were quite a few customers in the store so I wasn't really noticed but Harry and his mother were deep in conversation. Ma Hewitt was wagging a finger in his face.'

Cassie chewed on her bottom lip. 'I expect he's told her of our arrangement about recommending one another's businesses and she's cross that he's helping me out.'

'Oh, I don't think so,' said Polly firmly. 'She was talking about some young lady called, Annabelle. Apparently, our new friend Harry is taking too long in proposing to her and his mother is not happy about it at all.'

'Annabelle, you say?' Cassie frowned.

'Yes, why do you ask? Do you think you might know her?'

'This may be a coincidence but there was an Annabelle who Oliver claimed was his cousin. She comes from wealthy stock and there's a portrait of her at Marshfield Manor. He seemed obsessed with her. By all accounts, she's the sort to turn up to lots of social gatherings at the best of places. She's a proper social butterfly from what I've been told. Indeed, I believe she's descended from aristocratic stock.'

'Yes, that would make sense as your husband was one of those sorts himself and if he was a cousin of hers...Hey,' she narrowed her gaze, 'you thought there was something going on between them?'

'I'm not sure.' She swallowed hard and carrying on in a wistful manner said, 'All I know is that he became cold towards me around the time I found out about her existence. If it's the same woman she's very beautiful. I wonder though why Harry's not rushing into marrying her. She's the heiress to a fortune I understand.

I asked around the staff at Marshfield Manor, and although they barely spoke to me, this was one topic of discussion the housekeeper couldn't resist opening up about.' Something suddenly occurred to her, maybe that's why her husband had been so interested in Annabelle as he had debts that needed paying. Maybe he never really loved Annabelle at all as she'd imagined. And maybe his concern about money was the reason he'd gone cold on her, his wife. Now though, she'd never know for sure whether he'd gone to his grave loving or hating her.

Chapter Nine

The following day, Cassie sent Polly and her aunt in a hansom cab to Hocklea so that Aunt Bertha might have her eyes tested there. Truth be told for Cassie, it wasn't the best time to be alone at the tea room as business had picked up on the approach to Christmas and she was rushed off her feet. But she figured she couldn't leave Aunt Bertha to make the journey alone and she did need to have her eyes tested before she suffered the prospect of yet another fall.

Emily did her best to help out in the tea room collecting the used crockery and cutlery from the tables but Cassie wouldn't allow her to serve up any hot beverages in case she accidentally scalded herself or someone else for that matter. By midday, Cassie'd had quite enough and decided to close the tea room until Polly returned later that day. She put the sign up in the window for customers to see they were closed and she and Emily cleared away the final plates. She then sat down for a few minutes to rest her weary legs when there was a tapping on the door. Feeling irritated, she was about to shout out, 'We're closed!' when she noticed Harry at the door. She stood and then slowly made her way over to the door, unlocking it for him to allow him to enter the tea room.

'Closed for afternoon tea?' He quirked a curious eyebrow and chuckled. 'Fancy a tea room closing for tea!'

She forced a smile at his ill-considered quip. She was in no mood for jokes. 'No, nothing as leisurely as that I'm afraid. It's imperative I allow Polly some time off for a few hours so she can escort my aunt to Hocklea on some medical business there.'

'Oh? So now you can't cope on your own? Though I see you have a little helper with you?' he smiled at Emily who beamed back at him. 'So, this young lady is your daughter?'

'Yes, and a very good help she's been and all. But no, it's all too much for me at the moment. Suddenly her eyes filled with tears and she slumped down in a chair beside one of the tables, put her head in her hands and wept. Being mindful it was too awful to contemplate weeping in front of a stranger, she tried to hold back but it was as if there was a torrent of emotion inside which had come to the fore.

'My dear,' Harry said softly, then drawing out a chair and taking the seat opposite hers he passed a large silk handkerchief across the table to her which she gratefully accepted. Then looking at Emily he stood and said, 'Could you please fetch your Mama a glass of cold water?'

Emily nodded, wide-eyed and puzzled at her mother's sudden emotional distress, and complying with Harry's request, she headed off towards the counter.

When the child had gone, Harry reseated himself as Cassie dabbed at her watery eyes. 'I don't know what's going on for you but I'm here to help,' he said taking her hand across the table. To her surprise, she felt an instantaneous connection with him as if he was making her feel safe and as though she had somehow known him all of her life. 'What's the matter, Cassandra?' he asked gently.

After Emily had given her the glass of water and gone off to play with Sammy in the backyard, she found herself pouring out the story of what had recently occurred for her regarding the death of her husband and how she now found herself pregnant.

She blinked away the tears, wondering now what he must think of her but he was smiling and looking entirely sympathetic towards her plight. 'I knew Oliver quite well as we sometimes frequented the same social events and gentlemen's clubs,' he said. 'He was quite a character. I had heard though he'd squandered his fortune and of course, if he hadn't you'd be sitting on a pretty penny right now.'

She nodded. Then her eyes met his. 'Do you know of someone named Annabelle?' she asked, then regretted asking him as it was really none of her business.

He took a sharp breath before nodding, but now his smile had all but disappeared. 'I do. I have been courting her for some time and I know she has marriage in mind but...' he bit his lip.

'But?'

'But in all honesty, I don't think I'm the marrying kind. I wouldn't make a good husband for anyone never mind someone like her.'

'Like her?' Cassie tilted her head to one side.

'She enjoys the finer things in life. I could give her all of that but the one thing I guard fiercely is my own heart.'

She was surprised to hear him speak with such candour as he had known her all of five minutes but it was refreshing to hear. It meant to her that he was an honest trustworthy sort something that had been lacking in both of her husbands.

'Do you know if...' she hesitated, wondering whether she ought to ask but then pressed ahead anyhow, 'if Annabelle and Oliver knew one another very well and if they were cousins at all?'

He rubbed his chin as if in contemplation. 'Why are you asking me this?' His eyes darkened.

Oh dear, had she said the wrong thing? 'I...I... don't know.'

'It's all right. I'm not annoyed, just curious. I think they were related but somehow by marriage and not blood and referred to one another as cousins. And yes, they did know one another very well indeed.'

She thought she'd ask no more in case it upset him but she had the answer she needed for now. She wasn't going mad, the pair had been close. Maybe even lovers but she could never ask him that as although he claimed he wasn't ready for marriage, maybe in time he would change his mind and wed Annabelle.

How could a man this charming have a mother like Edna Hewitt? It was beyond her way of thinking.

Eventually, Harry looked deep into her eyes. 'Are you feeling better now?'

'Yes, I am as a matter of fact. Thank you.' She made to offer him his handkerchief back but he waved it away.

'You can keep it,' he said casually. 'I have so many—there's an entire drawerful of them back at Hewitt Hall, Mother has somewhat of a thing about clean handkerchiefs, she says they are the markings of a gentleman!' He chuckled. 'Now why don't you return home for a while and have a lie down until Polly returns?'

She nodded gratefully. 'Thank you. I think I will. You've been so kind to me.'

'Think nothing of it,' he said standing. 'Any time.' He smiled and left the tea room as quickly as he'd arrived. He cut a dapper-looking figure as he departed and she felt something for him in that moment that maybe she shouldn't.

***

From the pavement outside the tea room,

Jem stared in disbelief. He'd seen Harry spending time talking to Cassie inside. He was a right charmer that was for sure. He'd watched as the man had been looking into her eyes and at one point had even touched her hand across the table. It had been a very intimate scene and one he'd felt jealous of. What was making him so mad was the fact he himself had proposed to her and she didn't want to know, yet she appeared to be confiding in a stranger. He'd even noticed the man pass his handkerchief across the table to her.

All very cosy an' all. He shook his head and scowled.

Before he knew it the man would have his feet under the table there. He obviously had designs on Cassandra as she was a very attractive young woman with good prospects. Her tea room business was doing nicely. That Harry Hewitt was a cad, a bounder if ever he met one. He knew the sort. Quick to turn on the charm with all his banter, moving in for the kill and then he'd be off like there was no tomorrow, leaving Cassie both high and dry. Oh, he'd be looking out for that one that was for sure.

He noticed the man leaving the tea room with a little skip to his step as if delighted with his progress. Jem deliberated whether he ought to go inside and clear the air with Cassie as ever since his proposal things had felt awkward between them, it was almost as though a barrier was in place.

It was then it struck him that maybe he ought not to stick around any longer. He would be proposing forever and a day and she'd still turn him down as she preferred the likes of Harry Hewitt to him. How could he possibly compete? The man had the looks and confident assurance of a toff, whilst he, Jem Clement, was just a humble man selling second-hand furniture and doing odd job carpentry work for folk. He didn't have the eloquence nor the brass to compete with Harry, maybe not the nouse either. Cassie, although coming from humble origins, had got used to the finer things in life, being able to wear ball gowns and the like, she was used to fine dining too and he could never compete with that and felt foolish for ever expecting her to. What an imbecile he'd been to propose, she'd never give someone like him a second look in that sort of manner.

***

Cassie and Emily waited impatiently for Aunt Bertha and Polly's return from Hocklea. Every so often, Emily took a peek by the window but she was to be sadly disappointed, whenever the bell over the door jangled or a cab or carriage drew up outside, she'd either dash off towards the door or press her nose against the window in expectation but it was never them.

Oddly enough, after Harry had spoken to her, Cassie felt strangely revived again, and so, after taking an hour's lie down back at the cottage, she and Emily had returned to the tea room. There was no rush that afternoon though, it was as if the good folk of Wakeford realised that Cassie needed a break and hence, there was only the odd customer or two spread out over the afternoon.

Darkness had now descended and Cassie was becoming quite concerned. What if something had happened to them both? Had Aunt Bertha tripped and fallen again? Had something happened to their cab? Why was it all taking so long? She chastised herself for not taking her aunt to Hocklea instead and leaving Polly in charge of the tea room. However, finally, there was the sound of wheels and horse's hooves as a cab drew up outside.

'They're here!' shouted Emily with great excitement.

The driver was helping both women down from his cab and escorted them as far as the tea room steps. Then he doffed his bowler hat at them both as Cassie made her way to the door as she insisted on paying the cab fare.

Aunt Bertha waved an insistent hand at her. 'Don't fret, Cassandra!' she said in a pronounced manner. 'I'm quite capable of paying the cab fare for myself and my escort! Allow me that much at least!'

Cassie knew better than to argue with the woman and she secretly smiled. Her bombastic tone meant that she was now feeling her feet again which could only mean one thing: her appointment with the oculist had gone well.

Cassie watched her aunt delve into her reticule to pay the driver and she noticed Polly peering over the woman's shoulder, no doubt to ensure the driver gave the correct change in return. There were no flies on Polly—that was for sure.

'Come in out of the cold then, Auntie,' said Cassie in a warm, welcoming fashion. 'You've hardly set foot in this tea room since it opened.'

'I don't mind if I do,' said the woman, linking arms with her niece and now beaming. 'And I'd like to try one of your special afternoon teas if I may?'

'You certainly may,' smiled Cassie. 'This afternoon it's a pot of tea or coffee with cheese and chive sandwiches and a mince pie.'

'That sounds grand!' enthused Aunt Bertha.

Aunt Bertha always wore a lavender scent that permeated the air whenever she was around, for some reason, Cassie found that a comfort to her, it was familiar and friendly and reminded her of childhood days when her parents were still alive. The woman had stopped wearing the scent after the fall she'd had but now she had applied it again and that cheered Cassie to know her aunt was now more her old self once again.

When she was settled at a table, Auntie explained all that had gone on at the appointment. 'The oculist was a lovely gentleman. He used something called an ophthalmoscope to examine my eyes...'

'What on earth is that?' Cassie raised her brows.

'It's a special device for examining the interior of the human eye by means of a beam of light which illuminates otherwise invisible tissues. Apparently, they can tell a lot about the eye from using one. It examines the back of the eye too, something called the retina I think he mentioned and the optic disc.'

'My word, Auntie. You are sounding really knowledgeable there!' chuckled Cassie.

'I don't know the full term for what's wrong with my eyes as there was a long Latin sounding name for it which I can't recall, but in layman's terms: I am short-sighted. He explained that my cornea is curved too steeply. That's why my vision has been blurred of late. He said I've had excessive eye strain from working as a seamstress and that's why I was getting headaches all the time. There is some good news though...'

'Oh, Auntie, what is that?' Cassie asked excitedly.

'The eye doctor explained it can be treated with special spectacles. He said not to expect miracles as of course, my eyes are ageing, but he's going to prescribe special spectacles for me to wear. They'll be ready next week.'

'That is good news, Auntie.' Cassie beamed.

'The only bit of bad news is he doesn't think I ought to consider carrying on with the sewing.

It's not good for my eyes.'

'You'll be able to do other things you enjoy, gal!' Polly reassured, laying a comforting hand on the woman's shoulder. 'You can avoid close work but at least you'll be able to enjoy the view around here and you won't be tripping over things no more!'

Auntie smiled, but Cassie could tell by the wistful look in the woman's eyes that losing one of her lifelong passions wasn't going to be easy for her to bear.

***

Cassie yawned and drew back the bedroom curtains. She'd always been an early riser but now, especially since being in confinement, she'd found it difficult to drag herself out of bed in the mornings. In the distance, she heard the low murmur of voices down below. Polly was preparing breakfast for everyone and would soon knock on the door with a cup of tea for her. It was something she had insisted upon doing this past few days and Cassie was so grateful for it too. She stared through the window with her elbows on the wooden sill marvelling in wonder at the distant snow-capped mountains. She hoped for time being the snow would remain there and not fall on the pavements and streets of Wakeford as it had done a couple of weeks ago. It certainly felt chilly in the mornings. She stretched her arm out to take a woollen blanket from the bed to wrap around her shivering frame when she noticed something: red spots on the bedsheet. Oh no! This couldn't be happening, could it? She lifted her flannel nightgown to check her underwear, and that too was blood spotted. Not a lot but enough to have seeped through to the bed's undersheet. Rushing to the landing she called Polly's name and tried to keep any fear from her voice not to upset Emily.

Fortunately, Polly heard her the first time and standing at the foot of the stairs shouted up, 'Your cup of tea won't be long, it's just brewing.'

Cassie lowered her voice. 'Please Polly, bring my tea as normal, there's something I need to tell you but I do not wish to alarm my aunt nor Emily.'

Polly nodded with a grave look of concern on her face. 'I'll pour your tea immediately. They won't miss me for a couple of minutes as they're both tucking into their breakfast. Go and lie on the bed until I return.'

Feeling as if all the blood had drained from her body as if it were limp and her legs as boneless as her daughter's rag doll, Cassie made her way over to the bed and drew the covers up to her chin. Within minutes, Polly was placing a cup of tea down on the bedside cabinet beside her. 'I'm guessing it's something to do with the baby?' she said softly.

Cassie nodded. Then she pulled back the counterpane to show Polly the blood-stained sheet.

'Now try not to worry too much,' Polly said. 'I

know of a woman that happened to and she worried about it but she gave birth to an eight-pound bouncing baby boy.'

Cassie forced a smile. 'It's just that I worry due to my age. I'm not as young as when I gave birth to Emily.'

'That's perfectly understandable,' said Polly in a reassuring manner. 'But first things first. You need to rest. Sip your tea. Then I'll bring you a bowl of warm water so you can have a little wash, I'll change the bed and give you some fresh undergarments. Then if this carries on, I'll fetch a doctor to you.'

Cassie nodded gratefully. 'Perhaps you'd better close the tea room today, at least for the morning.'

'Aye, I'll do that. I'll put a notice in the window to say it will be open later but I won't specify a particular time.'

Cassie sat herself up to sip the welcome cup of tea and closed her eyes. 'Thank you.' She was so grateful to have someone as level headed as Polly around, the woman was a Godsend.

'Maybe you've been doing too much lately?' Polly questioned. 'You work long hours at the tea room and you're on your feet most of the day.'

Cassie nodded. 'You're probably right. I had intended taking on a young girl to work there after the Christmas period but maybe now would be the right time.'

Polly smiled and tucked the counterpane in.

'Now you rest and I'll just tell Emily and your Aunt you're a bit tired that's all and having a little lie-in today.'

She left the room leaving Cassie to her thoughts.

She must have drifted off to sleep as when she awoke the room seemed a lot brighter. There was no sound of any voices down below either. Where was everyone? She made her way to the window and noticed it had been snowing after all as the back garden was carpeted in a white blanket. In the distance, she could see Emily building a snowman as Polly looked on. Joyfully, the little girl scooped up handfuls of snow to add to the voluminous creature and stood back to admire her own efforts. Then Polly, as if sensing someone was watching them, caught her eye and nodded. She said something to Emily as she left her there to attend to Cassie.

Moments later, Polly appeared in the bedroom. 'You'd better get back into bed. I did look in on you an hour or so ago but you were sleeping so peacefully, I didn't like to disturb you. Any more signs of bleeding?'

'I...I don't know. I haven't dared look.'

Polly whipped back the counterpane and blankets. 'That looks all right to me, better check your drawers.'

Cassie nodded and did as told, then tidied herself up. 'No sign of anything here.'

'I still think you'd better return to bed, just in

case.'

Cassie did as told but now she was feeling rested she felt keen to return to the tea room as they'd be losing money but she realised Polly would object to that so instead she said, 'I'm feeling fine but will do as you suggest but I think you need to open up the tea room. If you just carry on with the story of me having a lie-in and that Emily and Aunt Bertha are to check in on me from time to time, that way I can send for you if something does happen.'

'Right you are then,' said Polly. 'It's just gone eleven o'clock so we've only missed a couple of hours of business. I'll place a message in the window to say we're looking for an assistant, shall I?'

'Yes, best do that.' Cassie smiled. She disliked the idea of giving up her job but if it meant keeping the pregnancy safe and secure, then she realised she must.

'I'll just fetch you a jug of water and a sandwich so you have something to eat and drink when I'm away. I might lock up for a short while if it gets quiet to check on you, mind!' Polly said firmly.

'I'd appreciate that.'

'I think it might be an idea though to get checked over by the doctor even if the bleeding has stopped.'

Cassie nodded. She knew the woman spoke sense. How much her life had changed just overnight. She'd gone from an active person to practically an invalid and she didn't much like the feeling at all.

Before Polly left, she brought the food and drink and some books she thought Cassie might like to read. Cassie chose one she liked the look of but found herself reading the same page over and over as she couldn't concentrate so she was quite relieved when Emily knocked on the door and entered.

The little girl had Sammy in her arms and looked quite concerned. 'Are you unwell, Mama?' she asked, her big brown eyes shiny and questioning.

'I'm all right, Emily. I just need to rest that's all. Why don't you and Sammy cuddle up on the bed beside me and I'll tell you a story. Is Aunt Bertha all right downstairs?'

Emily nodded eagerly. 'Yes, she's having a nap by the fireside. Can you tell me the story about the naughty little elf again?'

Cassie chuckled. It wasn't a story from a book as such but one that Cassie herself had created to amuse her daughter. For some reason, Emily loved it and pleaded for her mother to tell her the story over and over again. Each time, Cassie added something new to it.

She patted the bed beside her for Emily and the little dog to sit next to her. Soon Cassie was animated once again as she told Emily various stories and the child was captivated by tales of elves and goblins, fairies and pixies and wild woods and secret doors in large towering oak trees. The next couple of hours passed by quickly and Polly returned for a few minutes with some cakes from the tea room for everyone.

When Emily had left the room to take Sammy outside, Polly looked at Cassie and smiled. 'How are you feeling now?'

'A little better, thanks. I'm not as tired as I was but I do fear something bad will happen if I'm not careful.'

Polly's eyes reflected her grave concern. 'When I close the shop I'm going to fetch the doctor to you. I've made some enquiries from various customers and the one they all seem to favour is Doctor Bryant who charges reasonable rates for his services, they all appear

to put their trust into the man. I placed that notice in the window and already there have been some enquiries. One young girl who told me she's sixteen years old, dropped by. She said her name is Rose Barton. She's never worked in a tea room before but is used to helping her mother at home. The girl seems keen as mustard. I've told her to call again this afternoon after I'd spoken to you. What do you think?'

Cassie smiled. 'I trust your opinion, you're a good judge of folk. There are only ten days to Christmas so tell her we'll take her on until then and see how it goes. If she's a good worker, we'll take her on after Christmas too.'

'Sounds good to me,' said Polly with a satisfied

smile as she sat on Cassie's bed. 'No more bleeding then?'

'No, not for time being. Maybe if I rest all will be well.'

'I'm sure it will,' said Polly, taking Cassie's hand. 'You really need to look after yourself, you know.'

When the woman had gone, Polly's words echoed in her mind. What she said was true though as she had been driving herself so hard of late. Who was she trying to impress? It was hardly a crime to rest and take some time from the tea room. Maybe it was the feeling that she was the one keeping them all together and with a roof over their heads and she silently cursed Oliver Bellingham for putting them all in this mess. And then she broke down and wept because she still loved him so and this was his child she was carrying.

***

Polly turned up later with Doctor Bryant when the tea room had been closed for the day. Doctor Bryant was a tall upstanding man with well-trimmed salt and pepper sideburns. He wore a pipe stove shiny hat and a black necktie. He reminded Cassie more of an undertaker than a doctor but he seemed to have a vast medical knowledge. Stroking his pencil slim moustache he said, 'So then, my dear...I understand that you've been bleeding a little today?'

'Yes, Doctor,' Cassie said. She was sitting upright, propped up in bed by plenty of pillows. She was glad she'd taken the time to freshen up her appearance by washing her face and hands and brushing her hair. 'But it's only happened the once today and must have occurred overnight.'

He nodded. 'I see.' His face was giving nothing away. 'And have you had any bleeding prior to this or during any other pregnancy?'

She shook her head. 'No, not at all. Never, Doctor.'

He nodded and smiled. 'That in itself is a good sign. If you could lift your nightgown above your abdomen so I might palpate your stomach.'

She nodded as he removed his hat and placed it on a chair beside the bed along with his bag which he opened to locate his stethoscope. 'Don't worry,' he smiled, 'my hands aren't that cold—I've been wearing leather gloves, I swear by them in this weather.'

He sat on the bed as he gently palpated her stomach and listened with his stethoscope. He frowned for a moment and listened again. *Oh, surely not! He can't find a heartbeat,* Cassie thought. She held her breath and waited for a moment to hear the bad news but then the doctor smiled.

'There's a heartbeat all right,' he said, 'but there's not just one, there's two! That's why I took so long I wanted to be absolutely sure. I thought it was strange. Have you felt much movement lately?'

Cassie gulped, she had been unprepared for this and struggled to focus on what the doctor had just asked her. Jolting back to reality as she fought to take in what he'd said, 'No, not an awful lot of movement, Doctor.'

He stood with the stethoscope still around his neck. 'That's because they're taking up more space than one baby as there are two. Now, I suspect the bleeding is something to do with that. I can't be one hundred per cent sure but I think it best if you go on bed rest for a fortnight, just in case.'

She nodded at him and opened her mouth to say something but then closed it again.

'Vaginal pregnancy bleeding or spotting is more common during a twin pregnancy, my dear. And believe me, it's not always a cause for concern. You see your body is adjusting to a multiple pregnancy. Some women are known to bleed at the scheduled time of their next period and may not even realise they are expecting in the first place.'

That was reassuring to know but didn't help her one iota. How on earth was she to cope with one extra child, never mind two?

Polly caught her eye. Was that sympathy for her she saw there?

The doctor packed his equipment away and replaced his hat. Polly addressed him. 'Doctor, I think Mrs Bellingham has had something of a shock. It will take time for her to digest this information.'

His eyes crinkled at the edges as he said, 'Of course it will. You weren't prepared for this news at all but I am sure all will turn out well in the end if you look after yourself. Now don't worry about my bill for now. I'll have someone hand-deliver it in a few days when you've had more time to come to terms with this.'

'Thank you, Doctor.' Polly saw him downstairs and out through the door where she thanked him again and watched him depart. No doubt he had other patients to visit on his round.

She bounded back up the stairs and sat on Cassie's bed where she found her gnawing at her fist with tears in her eyes. She removed her hand from her mouth when she saw the woman. 'Oh, Polly, what am I to do?' she cried. Polly held her close allowing her to cry. 'Now don't go worrying, we're all here to help you through this,' she said kindly.

Chapter Ten

Cassie spent the next few days on bed rest while the new girl, Rose, worked at the tea room and Polly stepped into Cassie's shoes. The woman knew the job well enough though Cassie worried it might be too much for her as she also had to bake for the business, but Polly seemed to manage things efficiently as she informed Cassie that Rose was an asset as she was a hardworking young lady. That, in itself, was a load off Cassie's mind

The other thing that troubled her was the fact that Jem had not been in touch even though Polly had informed him of what had occurred regarding the pregnancy.

'Keeps to himself these days,' Polly said, 'hardly makes any conversation anymore though Clyde is still friendly enough—that lad hasn't changed.'

'Oh?' Cassie raised a brow.

'Do you know who had the cheek to call into the tea room to apply for the waitress job?'

Cassie furrowed her brow, she was reclining on the bed, her hair long and loose and spread over the pillow, tiredness consumed her. 'No?'

'That May Malone one, the young woman who lay on the floor and claimed that Clyde had jumped on top of her!'

Cassie sat up in the bed. 'I hope you sent that little madam packing!'

'I did and all, I sent her out with a flea in her ear. She's a rum sort and make no mistake. I don't like what she and that Artie did to Clyde. He's such a gentle giant. He seems to have taken something of a shine to Rose. I often find them chatting in the passageway between both shops whenever business is quiet. To be honest, I think she likes him too.'

'How's Jem?' she looked at Polly. Every day she enquired about him and every day she got the same response that he seemed to be doing all right but was still keeping himself to himself but today, Polly's eyes were all over the place as if she couldn't meet her gaze.

'Polly, what's up?'

'I found out from Clyde today that they're leaving Wakeford. How long was that tenancy agreement you both signed for?'

'Three months to begin with.'

'Clyde informed me that as soon as that time is up, they're both off to begin elsewhere. Jem's going to put the cottage up for sale.'

Cassie frowned. 'This must be my fault,' she said shaking her head.

Polly approached and then seated herself on the bed beside her. 'Why on earth would you say that, Cass?'

'Because of that day I turned down his proposal of marriage!'

Polly widened her eyes. 'No, surely not. He'd never leave because of that.'

'But it was so sudden and I wasn't expecting it at all so that was the real reason I turned him down.'

'That's understandable. You've had so much going on in your life of late. Forgive me for saying so but his lordship has hardly gone cold in his coffin, has he? So it was unfair of Jem to propose to you out of the blue like that.'

Cassie startled. 'That is the very thing though, Pol. Even though his lordship did what he did and deceived me, I still love him. My heart is still with him and it has no room for anyone else as yet...'

Polly patted her hand gently. 'Pretty soon that heart of yours is going to have to make room for two new loves in your life. I know it's different with children, it's an all-consuming love that you won't get for any man. For a child, a mother will be fiercely protective like a lioness, woe betide if anyone: man or woman tries to come between her and her offspring, she'll snap your head off. It's always been my feeling that just as a lioness is the provider who goes out hunting to support her cubs while the lion often sleeps waiting for her to return, it is she who is the strong one. Picture yourself like that lioness for time being. You don't need no lion, darlin'. You're all those children will ever need.'

Cassie nodded and smiled, realising that Polly was absolutely right. Yes, she'd miss Jem if he left Wakeford but the truth was that proposal had already come between them. She'd survive and make no mistake, she'd live to fight another day just like that lioness.

***

It had snowed so much overnight and the wind had blown a gale, causing high snowdrifts to rise up against the front door and windows of the little cottage. Even if they could get out to open up the tea room, it was unlikely many customers would even make it to the end of their own streets never mind there.

Cassie was now sitting downstairs in the comfy armchair nearest the fire, there had been no sign of any further bleeding but she was still taking it easy. Polly wouldn't allow her to lift anything.

'We're lucky I suppose,' said Polly with a long sigh. 'We have a plentiful supply of food in for the next few days and enough coal and stick for the fire.' Fortunately, they were able to make it out through the back door to get to the privy as the snow hadn't drifted there, though Polly had to break the sheet of ice that had hardened over the pan and their feet were like lumps of ice on their return to the cottage, taking several minutes to thaw out.

'Yes, there's plenty what are a lot worse off than us!' Polly went on as she stretched out a pair of Aunt Bertha's bloomers over the wooden clothes horse near the fire. The laundry let off steam as it dried but there was no other way to dry their clothing until the weather settled back down and even then, there were days when it was so cold that when the washing was brought in from the clothesline they were like boards of frost.

Auntie, herself, was in the scullery seated at the small table there with Emily regaling tales from days long gone. She was telling the little girl how back then Christmas could come and go as people were so poor they were lucky if they got to eat any day never mind the day itself. But she said she'd been one of the lucky ones as her father had been a fruiterer by trade so there was always an assortment of nuts, oranges and even boxes of dates and figs for the festive season. When she said her father had been a fruiterer, she explained to Emily that her father had indeed been a costermonger in Hocklea with his own donkey and cart. That story had the little girl enthralled as Auntie spoke about as a child seeing Christmas festivities in the big houses she visited with her father. On occasion, they'd even been invited into the servants' quarters for a cup of tea and something to eat on a particularly cold day. The Christmas tree in one house had been "up to the ceiling" of the ballroom as Auntie put it as Emily sat there, mouth wide open with surprise. The Christmas tree at Marshfield Manor had been a fairly modest one considering that was a big house but looking back on it, maybe that was at the Lord's bidding as he was penny-pinching due to his accumulative debts.

Cassie, who had been eavesdropping, knew there was truth in the woman's stories but sometimes her tales were so elaborate that she wondered if Aunt Bertha wasn't adding yards on as a form of entertainment. But Emily was bewitched as she sat with both elbows on the table gazing up into her great aunt's round and wrinkled face. It was so good to see how well the pair got on. Sammy had just molished his breakfast and was fast asleep in the corner in his bed, snoozing away.

Who'd have thought this time last year that they'd all be living in a new home and Cassie would now own a tea room?

***

Clyde was annoyed. He kicked the table leg with his hobnail leather boot. He didn't usually get this angry but why did Jem suddenly want to up sticks and leave the only home either of them had ever known? It was beyond him. No matter how he tried to talk to his brother he never got a straight answer as to what was going on. All Jem would say was that there was nothing worth sticking around for and they'd be better off moving on to another village somewhere else like Foxbridge or Evesley which were about thirty miles or so away in either direction. It was evident when Jem spoke about getting "a fresh start" or "beginning again" that he wasn't thinking straight and nor was he taking Clyde's feelings into consideration. Clyde didn't want to move not now that he was having no more trouble from Artie and his gang. Since that time the lad avoided him for fear of those men with pitchforks who had chased him and he must have warned off his gang too. Now the members either avoided him altogether or the odd one or two actually said "Good day" to him. And it wasn't as a mark of disrespect either as in as if they were making fun of him, they seemed genuine greetings to him. And now that he'd encountered the new waitress, Rose Barton, at the tea room, he actually looked forward to going into Jem's shop as he had to pass the tea room window and could see her there. She was so pretty with her yellow ringleted hair and she often looked at him and waved. She even kept a sticky bun for him once.

If they moved away he'd not get to see Rose anymore. Wakeford was his home so he didn't much fancy going to a new village and having to get to know folk all over again. In any case, it would be bad for him as people who didn't know him would make fun of his stutter and treat him as though he were a simpleton when he was not. So, no, he definitely did not want to move and go through all that again, the people of Wakeford had finally accepted him for who he was after all these years.

The sound of cartwheels brought him up sharp as he realised Jem had returned. He was in no mood for his brother's company so he left via the back door. He was already dressed warmly in two layers of clothing, his thickest woollen jacket, a cap, muffler and gloves. He marched over to the barn to fetch a shovel.

Noticing him, Jem shouted: 'Hey, where are you off to? The weather's too bad for you to go out, only just made it home with the cart, the horse is exhausted.'

'Don't need no horse and cart!' Clyde shouted back. 'I'm off to Cassie's c...cottage to see if they need d...digging out. Was the tea room open?'

'No, of course not!' Jem shouted back. 'That can wait. There's nothing we can do.'

But Clyde defied his brother and made his way from their property with a shovel in his hand.

'Don't be a fool!' Jem shouted after him. 'It might snow again later and you'll be found dead on the mountain pass.'

Stubbornly, Jem made his way through the gate. The old path could no longer be seen but he knew it well enough and if he went now, he'd make it back before it got dark. The last thing he heard was his brother's muffled voice shouting after him, 'Come back here, you fool!' That was enough to spur him on as all his life people had been calling him a fool and now to hear Jem use those very same words cut him to the quick.

He was halfway there when he realised he ought to have listened to his brother's words. But there was no point in him turning around as it was about the same distance to get back home, so instead, he plodded on, trudging through the thick snow. It was coming down thick and fast and blowing into his eyes, every so often he'd stop and blink it away or wipe it with the back of his gloved hand. There was an angry howl to the wind that he hadn't heard in a long while. Usually, in the distance, he'd be able to see the Hewitt family home and several others dotted on the mountainside but in the swirl of heavy snowfall, he couldn't even see those—they were obscured from view. Locating those houses would have been a way to keep his bearings as a frame of reference but now he realised, he didn't know where the hell he was and he was beginning to feel light-headed too.

***

Jem couldn't leave his brother go off like that. Pulling on an extra coat over the one he wore, he went in search of him calling out his name. What on earth had possessed the man to go off like that? It wasn't like him at all but if he didn't get to him then he had serious concerns for his welfare on the mountain like that. He toyed with the idea of taking the horse once again but the poor animal had already struggled to get back to their cottage across the rocky mountain pass in such hazardous conditions.

'Clyde!' he cried out. 'Clyde!' He had now been searching for about half an hour and had left minutes after his brother in his footsteps. He reckoned he couldn't have gone all that far ahead of him but as the snow was falling so thick and fast it would have already covered any of Clyde's tracks.

He thought he heard a cry and struggled to work out in which direction it might have come from. The snow was blinding him, apart from the dazzling whiteness of it all it was blowing into his eyes, every so often he wiped it from both his eyes and mouth. His lungs felt sore and as if he was now struggling to catch a breath. He felt nauseous too. 'Clyde!' he forced out a shout and then he heard a distinct reply. Relief flooded through him.

'Jem!'

'Where are you, lad?'

'Over here!'

This time, Jem managed to locate in which direction the voice was emanating from and headed towards it to find Clyde huddled up against a tree as if the trunk was the only thing holding him up.

'Thank goodness!' he wept. 'Why did you go off like that?'

'B...because I was angry. I don't want to m... move from Wakeford!' He began to sob like a baby as Jem knelt in the snow to hold his brother in his arms. He couldn't break his heart like this. If he'd felt strong enough to go off in a huff in blizzard-like conditions then he figured it must mean a lot to him.

'Don't fear,' he said, 'we won't have to move. We're going to stay put.' He held his brother close to him as he felt tears trickle down his cheeks not knowing whether they were Clyde's or his own. He realised if they stayed out too long they may be unlikely to rise to their feet once more and be at the mercy of the elements. Removing his glove, he fished in his trouser pocket for a barley sugar sweet. 'Here, suck this to revive you, Clyde,' he ordered. 'It may help keep you going. He took one himself and then helped his brother to his feet and put the glove back on his own hand. It was perishing cold but somehow the brothers helped one another slowly back to their cottage as they clung on to each other for support.

When they got back home, Clyde realised he'd left the shovel near the tree but Jem told him not to fret about it as they had a spare in the barn and in any case, they could return for it once the snow melted. Clyde worried in case someone else would get there before them but Jem reassured him that no one else would be foolish enough to go out in these conditions. Clyde smiled at his brother as they both sat warming up in front of the fire with fresh clothes on and wrapped in blankets. This time he didn't mind being referred to as a fool as coming from his brother, he realised it was meant with affection.

Later that evening, Clyde looked at Jem. 'Did you mean what you said about us not having to leave this cottage any longer or were you j...j... just saying that to get me to return home?'

Jem nodded. 'I'm a man of my word, aren't I?'

Clyde supposed he was. 'Yes.'

'And I've rarely let you down?' He raised a brow of expectation.

'No, never p...purposely, our Jem.'

'There you go then, lad.'

'B...but why did you want to leave here in the first place? I d...don't understand.'

'To be truthful, Clyde, I don't either. It was just a mad thought to escape all me troubles but one thing is for sure, I now know deep down that my heart is still here in Wakeford.'

Clyde looked at his brother and smiled but he failed to notice the look of anguish in Jem's eyes as he turned away.

**

'Who on earth is that?' Polly asked looking at Cassie. It was a couple of days since they'd heard anything from the outside world as the weather conditions were so dire.

'Sounds like someone's tapping on the back door,' said Aunt Bertha who since her recent sight problems seemed to have acquired an acute sense of hearing.

'There's only one way to find out.' Cassie made

to heave herself out of the armchair but Polly stopped her by laying a hand on her shoulder.

'You stay where you are, I'll attend to this.' Polly rolled up the sleeves of her Cambrian blouse as if she meant business which made Cassie smile. Within moments, she could hear voices in the scullery. A man? Jem? It didn't sound like his voice though.

Polly appeared in the doorway looking all flustered. 'There's a gentleman what's here to see you, Cassie,' she said, her face red and the curls on her forehead appeared to be sticking to it even though it wasn't all that hot in the cottage. What had made the woman look so disconcerted all of a sudden? In Cassie's mind, it had to be that the woman was either somehow in awe of the caller or maybe feared him? Why didn't she just explain who the caller was?

'Well, who is it, Pol?'

'It's Mr Harry Hewitt,' she said, patting her hair down.

Cassie smiled broadly. 'Please show him in and put the kettle on to boil on the hob, I'm sure he'd be grateful for some refreshment.'

Polly nodded and smiled and for a brief moment, Cassie felt as though the woman was about to curtsy as she would have done at Marshfield Manor. She hadn't realised it before but Polly was in absolute awe of the man.

More voices and then Harry Hewitt lowered his head to enter the low ceilinged room, removing his top hat. His cheeks looked slightly pink from the cold outside but his eyes held a mischievous sparkle to them. 'Good day to you all,' he said.

'Good day, Harry,' Cassie welcomed. 'Please remove your coat and sit near the fire.'

He nodded, and Polly who had been standing there open-mouthed throughout, took the man's astrakhan coat with its fur collar, his top hat and leather gloves and placed them neatly on a spare chair, but the scarf remained around his neck. Aunt Bertha went to shift herself from the other armchair for him to sit, but Harry shook his head. 'Please do not move on my account,' he said. 'I'm quite happy to take a chair.'

Before anyone had a chance to protest at their prestigious visitor having to rough it, he drew out a hardback chair from the table and seated himself.

'What brings you here today in these terrible conditions?' Cassie asked.

'You, of course.' He looked at her with some intent.

Cassie noticed Polly still stood in the doorway as if a spell had been cast over the woman. 'Tea, Polly?' she reminded. Polly's glazed eyes finally came back into focus and she nodded and smiled and then left the room to prepare for the task-in-hand.

'Me?' Cassie looked into his eyes.

'Yes. It was the first time the ostler's managed

to get the coach and horses out this past couple of days so I made it to the shop and noticed that yours was closed, not that you'd have much custom with the severe weather conditions, of course. I'd been speaking with Polly previously about you and she'd explained you'd been put on bed rest.'

'Oh did she!' Cassie chuckled not at all annoyed that Polly had mentioned this, she was more amused than anything.

'Yes, it's true, I'm afraid. Polly brought the doctor to me who thought it best if I rest up for a while.'

'So, that's why the new girl has started at the shop?' She nodded as he swept his hand through his dark floppy fringe.

'I was just wondering if there is anything I might do to help?' He flashed her a grin.

'In what sort of way do you mean?'

'I can send some lads down to dig out a path from your front door for a start and maybe clear near the shop too. That way it can be opened up again, the weather seems to be subsiding a little.'

She nodded gratefully. 'That would be most kind of you and now, may I offer you a cup of tea for your trouble?'

He nodded. 'That would be very welcome indeed, thank you. I have been up very early this morning cataloguing some trunks of books that turned up a few days ago from London. I hadn't had a chance to sort them out as yet, so that's where I've been this morning at the shop sorting those out. And as the snow hadn't been cleared away, I had to trudge through it and soaked my trousers up to the knee!' He chuckled.

'You must be famished though?'

He smiled. 'I suppose so.'

'I'll ask Polly to fry a couple of rashers of bacon, eggs and bread for you to go with that tea. How does that sound?'

'Marvellous!' he enthused.

'One good turn deserves another,' she said, supposing it wasn't the sort of cuisine he was used to at Hewitt Hall. His mother had delusions of grandeur though that much was evident as although they lived in a mighty fine house which was larger than most, it could hardly be described as a palatial dwelling. They had wealth that much was for sure but she'd hardly have described Edna as a well-bred sort. She had married a man who through his own efforts had worked his way up the ladder, though had originated from humble stock. Maybe they had more in common than she realised, particularly when it came to Harry.

Harry stopped for an hour or so as everyone watched him eagerly tucking into his cooked breakfast. Polly stood with one hand on the door jamb observing with delight how he relished the food she'd prepared.

Then when everyone else had departed the room and he and Cassie were alone, he looked at her in earnest to enquire about the pregnancy. 'Oh, I had a surprise I can tell you!' Cassie announced. 'There are going to be two babies and not just one!'

Harry lifted a curious eyebrow. 'Twins? My word but you'll have your hands full.'

'I know,' she said, letting out a long sigh. 'It's not what I'd planned and to be truthful after my husband's death, I had no idea I was expecting, you see...'

'See what?'

'I don't want to cause trouble but I was convinced that he and Annabelle had something going on between them.'

'I see,' was all he replied, then he said no more on the subject which she thought curious considering his mother was expecting to marry him off to the young woman. Within minutes he was making his excuses to leave, all of a sudden he looked wary and she guessed that maybe she had touched a nerve and that she shouldn't have brought her suspicion up to him.

Before leaving he said softly, 'I meant what I said, if there is anything I can do to help you, you only have to say the word. I will send around some of the hired help at Hewitt Hall to clear a path for you from your cottage to the tea room by this afternoon.'

She smiled and marvelled at how thoughtful he was. Afterall, she'd seen neither hide nor hair of Jem of late and that really rankled with her as

in a way they were supposed to be business partners but now it appeared if what she'd heard was
true, he was deserting a sinking ship.

Chapter Eleven

After a couple of days, the weather had cleared up enough for Jem and Clyde to get the cart out to travel to Cassie's cottage. They'd taken the shovel from the barn and retrieved the abandoned one near the tree so they could help clear a path for her. When they arrived outside her home, Jem frowned.

'What's wrong?' Clyde looked at his brother.

'Someone's already one step ahead of us. Look at this! The path between the cottage and the shop has been cleared!'

Clyde grinned. 'T…that's g…good isn't it? S…saves us the work!'

'I suppose so.' Jem shook his head in disbelief, but he was irritated that someone had beaten them to it. He was the one who wanted to take care of Cassie even though she'd annoyed him lately. He realised how childish he'd been though, he'd had an awakening of sorts. He'd dropped the idea of marrying him on her toes and taken her by surprise when he should have bided his time. No doubt as she was recently widowed and pregnant to boot, she felt it inappropriate to wed right now.

'What do we do then?' Clyde sniffed.

'Use yer handkerchief!' Jem chastised. 'We got to open up the shop anyhow, so we'll get to it. Someone's done us a favour I suppose as the path to the building is clear.

Clyde blew his nose and returned his handkerchief to his jacket pocket. When they'd dismounted from the cart, Clyde immediately made his way to the tea room and pressed his face against the glass.

'What on earth?' Jem watched his brother waving to someone through the window and he grinned. Of course, he might have guessed: Clyde was sweet on that new waitress Rose Barton. A very pleasant young lady she was an' all. He glanced in the window himself to see if Cassie was in there but all he saw was Rose waving back enthusiastically at his brother and Polly attending to something or other behind the counter. His heart sank. Cassie couldn't be feeling up to the mark again then.

As he went to enter the main door between the two downstairs shops, Harry emerged and smiled at him. 'Good morning, Jem. It's nice to be getting back down to business.' He raised a brow of expectation as if a reply ought to be forthcoming but Jem just nodded at him and brushing past, made his way towards the staircase.

'I suppose you noticed the snow has all been cleared away from the shop?'

Jem had just put his foot on the first step. He

turned to face Harry. How could he fail to notice that the shop front had been cleared of snow? The man was incredible. 'Yes, I did. I suppose that had something to do with you?'

Harry drew closer and lowered his voice. 'Yes, I called to see Cassandra at the cottage yesterday morning. She's had a rough deal lately that's for sure. I got some boys to clear the front of their cottage and make a path all the way here to the shop for fear if she does decide to come into work she may fall.'

'Very commendable of you.'

'Especially now as she will have double the trouble in the future.'

'Double the trouble?' Jem furrowed his brow.

'Yes, old boy. Haven't you heard? She's not just expecting one baby but two. The doctor has confirmed the presence of twins.'

Jem felt as though the air had been sucked out of his lungs. Twins? He opened his mouth to say something and closed it again.

'Ah, obviously she hasn't mentioned it to you but she won't have had the opportunity to after being told to rest up by the doc.'

No, she hadn't mentioned it but Polly might have. He felt so foolish. A complete stranger like Harry Hewitt knew more about what was going on with Cassie than he did and the man had already stepped in and been responsible for a job he'd like to have undertaken himself.

'Thank you for informing me of the situation.'

Jem forced a smile. Obviously, Hewitt meant more to her than he did.

When Harry had stepped back into his book shop, Jem retraced his steps to where Clyde was still smiling like a fool through the window at Rose. 'C'mon!' Jem said gruffly. 'Get up them stairs, there's work to be done. Don't ever let a silly female hold you up for work what needs doing!'

Clyde's happy expression changed to one of puzzlement. Why had Jem's mood darkened this morning when he'd been perfectly happy when they'd left home? It was almost as though he'd been looking forward to the day ahead and now it seemed as if something had upset him.

'W...what have I d...done?' Clyde wanted to know.

Jem's jaw tightened and through clenched teeth, he said, 'There are some people in this world, Clyde, that you can waste too much time on because when a better option comes along they drop you like a hot potato!' And with that thought, Clyde followed his brother up the stairs.

***

Polly opened up the tearoom for the day. People were up and around and going about their business once again. 'Come on, Rose!' she chastised. 'No time for dawdling about with that dimwit out there!' she chuckled and then thought better of her words. After all, Clyde wasn't harming anyone by waving to Rose through the window but he had been distracting her for the past ten minutes when the girl needed to work.

Rose blushed. 'Sorry, Miss Hedge.' She lowered her head.

'It's me who ought to be sorry,' Polly said. 'I shouldn't have referred to Clyde as a dimwit, he's nothing of the kind. He's a very intelligent person really, he just comes across as childlike but he has more brains and more manners than many I know.'

Rose smiled. 'It's 'orright, Miss Hedge. I'll tell him he's not to distract me when I'm working.'

'Good gal,' said Polly. 'I tell you what, tell him to call a bit later when it's quiet and I'll keep a couple of mince pies for him and I'll brew up a cuppa.'

'He'll like that, Miss Hedge. Thank you.'

The rest of the day went by in a bit of a blur for Polly. Rose was a good worker and kept up with demand, not just serving customers, but she was quick to clear the tables and change the table cloths when needs be. Some customers were a bit clumsy, spilling their teacups over or leaving smudges of jam and cream on the pristine white linen. The girl was a Godsend. It was while things had quietened down and Rose was seated at a table with Clyde as he took advantage of Polly's earlier offer of refreshment, that Polly's eyes were drawn to the coach that had just drawn up outside. The driver opened the door to help down the young lady who was emerging from the cab. The lady was astonishingly beautiful, dark chestnut hair hung in waves on her shoulders. She wore a dark blue velvet cape with a matching bonnet and a fur-trimmed muff hung around her neck, ready to plunge her hands into in the freezing cold weather. She glanced across at the tea room and Polly noticed what a vivid shade of violet her eyes were, her stare was penetrative and caused Polly to look away. Where had she seen that young lady before?

Then it came to her—Marshfield Manor. Her face was on one of the portraits that hung there. She'd once caught his lordship gazing at it and his face had reddened at the time as if he'd been caught doing something he shouldn't have.

Of course, it was Annabelle, the young woman that Cassie had mentioned to her. But where was she going? The tea room or to the book shop next door or even Jem's furniture emporium above? She didn't have long to find out as the woman tipped the driver and made her way to the book shop. Hadn't Cassie told her that Harry was courting her and his mother had big plans for him to marry her?

She disappeared inside the shop, emerging just five minutes later. That was odd. She'd already paid the coach driver, why hadn't she asked him to wait if she was going to be that quick? Then she noticed Harry coming out after her. They shared a heated exchange and then she angrily walked away for him with her chin in the air. As if not realising what to do next as she had no form of transport, she made her way into the tea room.

Polly gulped.

The young lady had the confident exterior of one who was in command, yet had the countenance of someone whose emotions had been severely shaken. Polly watched as she headed towards the counter.

'Psst! Rose!' Polly hissed at the girl who had her hands plunged into a sink full of dirty dishes.

Rose blew a breath upwards causing a thick strand of hair to move away from her forehead. She quickly wiped her hands on a clean tea towel. 'Yes, Miss Hedge?' Her eyes were wide and enquiring.

'Put your pinafore on, gal. Then go and escort the lady to a table.'

'Yes, Miss Hedge.' Rose complied and went to attend to the lady who smiled at them both through glazed eyes.

After Rose had seated her at a window table, which Polly thought was no coincidence as the young lady might then be in a good position to see who entered and exited the shop next door, she returned to the counter with the young woman's order.

'What's it to be then, gal?'

Rose studied her small notepad. 'The lady would like a pot of coffee for one, Columbian if we have it and a fruit scone with jam and cream, please?'

Polly nodded. 'Well she'll have to make do with our usual roast blend coffee this ain't no flippin' posh London coffee shop. Go and ask if that's all right. I think it's a Brazilian blend that Mrs Bellingham buys in.'

Rose stood there vacantly.

'Get to it then, girl!' Polly chastised and she raised her eyes heavenwards wondering what on earth was wrong with Rose this morning, she seemed miles away. No doubt that Clyde one had something to do with that the way he'd been hanging around lately.

Rose returned to the counter and said, 'Yes, the lady says Belgian coffee will be fine, thank you.'

Polly smiled as she nodded her head. How could Rose confuse Belgium with Brazil she'd never know. Rose's mind was in the clouds this morning, in any case, Miss Annabelle would probably be none the wiser. 'Young love,' she tutted as she turned away to attend to the task in hand, all the while wondering what had gone on between Annabelle and Harry next door. Whatever it was, it had brought tears to that young woman's eyes.

Annabelle stayed at the tea room for about twenty minutes, she hardly touched her fruit scone. Polly had watched as she'd just nibbled delicately on it, her eyes fixed on the outside world. She did though drink all of her coffee.

''Ere,' said Polly as Rose returned to the counter with a tray of dirty dishes from nearby tables. 'Did that lady by the window ask to be seated there or did you direct her there?'

Rose's eyes grew wide as if she had done something wrong. She swallowed hard. 'Oh, no, I didn't lead her there, I promise. I know everyone likes that table but she 'specially asked to be seated there. Is it reserved for someone else then?'

Realising that Rose had got the wrong end of the stick, Polly smiled. 'Don't be so silly, gal. I wasn't having a go at you. I just noticed since she's been in here it's as if she's watching for someone or something.'

Rose nodded with a look of relief on her face. 'I do see what you mean.'

'Go over to her table,' whispered Polly, 'ask her if there's anything else you may get for her.'

Rose laid down the tray, pleased to relieve herself of her heavy burden and made her way to the woman's table. Polly watched the woman shake her head and glance in her direction. Polly made her way to the table, 'Is there something I can help you with, miss?' she asked.

Annabelle looked up at her, her eyes shiny and bright from unshed tears. 'I only wish there was,' she said sadly. 'I'll pay my bill, if I may?'

'I'll send the girl over with it,' Polly said, almost feeling as though she ought to curtsy.

'Oh, one other thing? Is there anywhere around here where I might hail a hansom?'

'Yes, there is, Miss er?'

'Davenport.'

Polly made a mental note of the name to double-check with Cassie later if it really was Annabelle from the portrait, though she guessed it had to be if she were visiting Harry Hewitt next door. 'There's a point down the hill on the left where the cabs wait to pick up passengers, sometimes you might be lucky and can hail a passing one on this street though. In fact, would you like me to send the girl down to fetch one here for you, miss?'

Annabelle nodded. 'That would be extremely kind of you.'

Polly sent Rose to fetch the hansom to the tea room. She was lucky the driver allowed her a free ride back to the shop as many wouldn't allow it, but old Bill Compton had known her family before she was a babe-in-arms so he was more than happy to oblige.

Breathlessly, and red-cheeked, Rose entered the shop as the bell jangled. 'Your cab's here, miss,' she said approaching the table as if pleased with herself.

Annabelle dropped some coinage into the palm of her hand. 'For your trouble, thank you,' she said smiling sweetly. Rose looked at her full of awe. 'What a lovely lady,' she said looking at Polly as they watched her being aided into the cab by Bill.

'Yes, she is,' said Polly thoughtfully. 'She really

is.' She looked down at the saucer on the table and noted the woman had also left a large tip as well as paying the bill. She couldn't quite envisage that lady she met there as the wanton hussy Cassie seemed to imagine she was.

***

Back at Hawthorn Cottage, Cassie and Polly were seated at the scullery table while Polly peeled some potatoes and carrots for their evening meal. She'd just prepared a steak pie and had planned on popping it in the oven later when the vegetables were put on the hob to boil.

'Davenport did you say?' Cassie arched an interested eyebrow.

'Yes,' said Polly. 'I'm almost positive she's the same Annabelle what was on that portrait back at the big house.'

Cassie let out a long breath. 'Then there's no doubt about it, she is the one and the same if she's involved with Harry. You said she seemed upset?'

Polly nodded vigorously. 'Yes, it looked as if either she was on the verge of tears or had already been crying before visiting the tea room. A sort of altercation took place previous to that right outside the shop.'

'What sort of altercation?'

'Harry Hewitt ran after her and she looked angry to me. She turned to face him and they had words and then she stepped inside our shop as if to get away from him as she probably realised he wouldn't like to make a scene in there in front of staff and customers. Wouldn't want everyone knowing his business kind of thing.'

'That might have been nothing though, a lovers' tiff, maybe.'

Polly stopped peeling and placed a large potato and the knife on the table and then rubbed her chin. 'Possibly. But what makes me think there might have been more to it is the way that coach drew up outside the book shop. She wasn't inside there more than five minutes before she came storming out of there and he, I mean Mr Hewitt, came after her. I think he'd told her something she didn't want to hear.'

'Now what makes you say that, Pol?' Polly had a habit sometimes of over-egging the pudding with her descriptions so Cassie wanted to know why she should think that was the case.

'It's because her coach had already been dismissed after she arrived as if she'd planned on stopping awhile. As it turns out, after some refreshment at our shop, a hansom had to be summoned for her.' She folded her arms. 'Now you tell me why that would be?' She closed one eye as the other widened.

'Hmmm, I suppose you have a point there, Pol. If a quick visit to see Harry was her intention, she'd have asked her coach driver to hang around and wait for her. Must have been something big for her to storm off on the verge of tears like that. Maybe a certain name had been mentioned.'

Cassie thought back to the time she'd asked Harry about Annabelle and who she was to Oliver. Maybe she'd planted a seed of doubt without meaning to.

'Surely though, you don't still think his lordship had been up to any shenanigans with Miss Annabelle?'

Cassie shrugged her shoulders. 'To be truthful, I don't know what to think.'

''Ere, why don't you ask Mr Hewitt yourself? You're on good terms with him.'

Cassie smiled. To Polly Hedge, life was simplistic. She could no more ask Harry what he'd argued with Annabelle about than she could ask his mother what colour her drawers were. 'I don't think that I would, should or could do that, it would be intrusive and impolite, Polly. I've only been acquainted with the man for a short while.'

'If it were me I would do a little digging around as it might have something to do with his lordship!'

Hearing Polly say that made a shiver course Cassie's spine. It wasn't something she felt like facing up to at the moment. Harry hadn't as yet given her any indication that might be the case so why go digging up the past? A lump had grown in her throat and she swallowed it before saying, 'I think I'll go and have a lie down before supper.'

'Aye, you go and rest. I'll call you when it's ready.' Polly retrieved the knife and carried on peeling the potato.

Chapter Twelve

William Hewitt was in the midst of inspecting the underground stables at Marshfield Coal Mine. As pit manager, he needed to keep things in order and oversee the men and young lads who toiled there. The stables consisted of a long and wide gallery that was divided off into around thirty stalls for the horses and pit ponies. The stables were fairly comfortable and well-kept to facilitate a large number of horses. He inhaled the smell of the Dutch peat which was healthier, cleaner and easier to handle than the sawdust had been previously, and less flammable, he hoped. The horses and ponies seemed accustomed to the darkness to which they were condemned but William, on this occasion, wasn't. It was something he never really got used to. He realised that once in a while he had to meet with the men actually underground like this afternoon, but more often than not, life was spent above ground at the office.

He prided himself though on making thorough checks of the stables to ensure the horses had adequate bedding and food. The poor animals became tired and weary worn after spending years underground, so on his say so, he decided when they should be put out to pasture. There were several farmers in the area who were more than happy to take on the horses for light duties, but in the main, their final years were good ones. It was a generous payback for their service to the pit and the local community and was a kind of respect for the beasts of burden, William often thought.

Most of their lives had been spent underground and they were only brought to the surface for special reasons such as a pit strike. Most of the horses were exceedingly bright and intelligent as they went about their work wearing eye-guards and harnesses most of the day. In some cases, they hardly needed any supervision. The only time they ever annoyed the men was if they had their tucker nicked from their jacket pocket or hiding place by a horse, that was why most of the men carried their bread and cheese in a metal snap tin. It was far safer from both the horses and pit rats that way, and the rats underground grew as large as cats at times.

Today, William was investigating a strange odour that some of the men had noticed underground and he pondered on whether to bring them to the surface as a safety measure or not. Underground gas was a deadly menace to contend with—it was mostly a mixture of methane and other gases that could convert to carbon dioxide. There had already been a bad explosion at the pit about ten years previously, so he was mindful of that. In fact, a strange aroma had arisen about two weeks previous to this but it was not thought to be hazardous by the pit owner, but today, William was guarded. He didn't want to offend his own boss but his instincts told him something wasn't right. His men thought him a firm but fair manager who intervened at times between themselves and the pit owner.

Every mine needed two shafts and a circulation of air. The air was channelled into the innermost recesses of the mine and was then divided and distributed into the different districts of the mine, and so conducted as to sweep away any noxious gases which may be produced either from the coal or the exhausted workings but sometimes things went badly wrong.

As William strode deliberately across the stable area towards one of the seams, the foreman, Tom Langstone, came to meet him. Tom's face was smeared with coal dust so that only the whites of his eyes were visible and his tongue and teeth as he spoke. 'Something bad down here, Mr Hewitt. Canary's dropped off its perch about a quarter of a mile along the seam.' He held up the cage for inspection.

William held up his Davy lamp and studied the birdcage. True enough, the canary was gone for good and he'd seen this happen before at this pit when twenty men and young lads had died ten years since and also at another pit before that where the death toll was far more severe. Now what to do without terrifying everyone underground? There'd be a stampede to get out if he wasn't careful. He'd seen that happen before now where it wasn't an explosion that caused deaths, it was the fear and stampede for every man and boy to spare his own skin.

'Thanks, Tom. I think we need to get everyone to the surface. I better extinguish this, I suppose even though it's a safety lamp occasionally the sparks can set off an explosion.' Where they were stood there was a small ray of light but once in the seam if all extinguished their lanterns then it would be pitch black. 'We'll have to be careful the horses and ponies don't block any entrances, preventing escape, so I think we need to get those out first. I'll get on to the stable lads to get what's here out and if you can get the ones already working on that seam out, Tom, then we'll get the young lads and then the men out. Make sure they extinguish their lamps in case of any firedamp.'

'Right, Mr Hewitt,' Tom said with a nod, realising how serious the situation was.

The evacuation worked like a dream as the men and boys moved swiftly but without panic and William was pleased with how things had gone, but just when he thought everyone was out, Tom informed him that young Benny Brewster wasn't accounted for.

William looked at him. 'You get back outside, Tom. Keep the men calm and ensure they move well away from the pit. I'll go back in to search for the lad...'

Tom had intended searching for the lad himself as he knew that coal seam like the back of his hand, but he knew better than to argue with his boss, so he just nodded and went to round the men up above and remove them far enough away from the danger of an explosion.

With only an hour to go until the end of the shift, a massive explosion ripped through the pit workings. The earth above where Tom and the men stood shook and dense columns of smoke and debris flew through the air. It appeared to Tom as if there were black snowflakes falling from the sky. He stood in disbelief, shaking his head, realising at that moment that his boss and young Benny were dead. Tom put his head in his hands and wept, the lad was only a baby and he'd known him all of his young life. He'd just turned twelve years old when he'd been sent to work underground with his dad to help the family finances. A boy doing a man's job. It didn't seem right somehow. And he cursed the pit owner, Josiah Samuel Wilkinson, and raised a furious fist in mid-air. The man had been told of the colliers' suspicions of the presence of gas underground a couple of days ago but he'd done sod all about it, claiming it was something else causing the smell as no canary had dropped off its perch at that time, which was true, but that must have been the start of it. It was too much of a coincidence.

That night in the pub, Tom explained how the pit had gone up like a volcano and it had shaken the houses for miles around, in a scene like Armageddon, as women ran with babes in arms and toddlers dragged on their mothers' skirts as the womenfolk went to check on their men. Thankfully, on this occasion, most were spared, apart from the two left underground.

Sometime later, Tom and a few others had managed to drag out the charred remains of William Hewitt and Benny Brewster. A scene he never wanted to picture ever again in his life but he realised it would be one he'd relive many times over in his worst possible nightmares. The men in the pub had patted him on the back and bought him copious pints of ale, treating him like a hero. But he didn't feel like one. Instead, he went home feeling shame that not one of the higher-ups, apart from William Hewitt, had heeded the warnings.

Part Two

Chapter Thirteen

Harry stared out of the coach window in a state of disbelief. His father was gone and there was nothing he could do about it, no money nor medical help in all the world could bring back the man he'd so admired and respected. He glanced at his mother who was seated opposite him, she was dressed head-to-foot in black with a veil covering her face. She'd said practically nothing these past few days nor eaten, she was numb with the shock of it all that much was evident. He wondered if she'd break down later during the service, this just couldn't go on.

When the pit foreman, Tom Langstone, had called to the house with the news of his father's death, Edna Hewitt had collapsed and had been taken to her bed by the servants and Doctor Mason immediately summoned. Harry, himself, had been in the book shop at the time serving a customer when he'd heard the distant rumble which at first he'd mistaken for thunder until a sickening feeling in his stomach had warned him about the pit. He'd hoped he was mistaken but after taking a hansom to the area, he realised as soon as he saw crowds of people headed with extreme purpose in the pit's direction that this was no thunder. In the distance he watched in horror as clouds of grey smoke billowed from the pit, surrounding the area like a shroud of death.

By the time he arrived, the men were outside, some sitting on the grass with their heads in their hands in utter despair. He'd heard someone saying something about "Two still trapped inside" and he'd known in his heart one was his father, which was later confirmed by a doctor at the scene who advised him to leave immediately. He shouldn't be around to watch as it would "not be a pretty sight" when they recovered the bodies. "Go home and be with your mother right now," the doctor had advised and he'd done just that, his heart breaking knowing there was nothing he could do at the site.

Jolting back to reality, he drew in a composing breath. Today of all days, he needed to keep calm. The coach was part of the funeral cortege behind the horse-drawn funeral carriage. He tried to catch his mother's eye to reassure her all would be well but she stared blankly ahead as if wearing blinkers like the horses, so instead, he left his seat and sat beside her taking her gloved hand in his. She seemed so vulnerable, aloof and alone in her little world. He felt a bump as the coach started to pull away down the drive of Hewitt Hall and as he gazed out of the window, he noticed the trees his father had planted many years ago, the small lily pond he'd had installed, the shrubbery and rockery to the left. Everything re-minded him of his father, choking back a tear he stared ahead.

As the coach made its way along the streets to reach the village church, Harry noticed that people were lining the streets, the men removing their hats and the women lowering their heads as the hearse passed them. Such was the testa-ment of the man, he'd been well-loved that much was for sure. A kind-hearted man who did all he could for the people of the village. He needn't have been so generous with Cassie and Jem with regards to the tenancy of both shops. When he'd taken over he could have hiked up the rent as many would have done but he realised both busi-nesses needed to get off the ground and he'd wanted to give them a fair chance. Drawing a silk handkerchief from the inside pocket of his black astrakhan coat, Harry blotted the tears away, he needed to be strong today for Mama.

The other coaches behind theirs contained his uncle and his wife and cousins as well as an aged aunt from London. In some of the other coaches, sat his father's lawyer and associates, Doctor Mason their family doctor, and one or two other notable men from the village of Wakeford. Evi-dent whose coach was missing though was Jos-iah Samuel Wilkinson who had gone to ground since the explosion. Rumour had it among the men that he'd fled somewhere abroad but Harry wasn't so sure. He had the money to pay a good legal team and he also owned another pit about twenty miles away. Harry felt bitter that the man hadn't shown his face and wondered if he might do at the funeral itself. Maybe his coach would turn up at the final hour in time to pay his respects? But somehow he doubted it.

The service went by in a blur and the Reverend Ainsworth's words went around in a swirl in his head. "Respected gentleman", "Benevolent Sort", "Heroic Deeds", "Tried in vain to save a young life." Harry wondered for a moment what sort of a burial poor old Benny Brewster would be getting. His family were as poor as church mice. They were a family of eight and two of the elder sons had already followed their father underground before Benny. If they hadn't been so desperately poor then maybe his death would never have occurred. He made a mental note to check on the family and offer to pay for the burial, it's what his father would have wanted. He ought to have made approaches earlier towards them he supposed but he'd been so full of shock and grief himself that they had dulled his senses.

The vicar was bringing the service to an end and when the final hymn had been sung which was "The Old Rugged Cross", a hymn his father had loved, Reverend Ainsworth said he had an announcement to make. Harry looked up with some surprise. What could this possibly be?

'While William Hewitt was alive he didn't want this made known, only upon his death...'

There were murmurs of surprise amongst the congregation, even his mother's blank expression changed to one of puzzlement. She looked up at Harry who shrugged his shoulders and whispered, 'I have no idea what this is about, Mama.'

'He was known as a generous and benevolent gentleman...' the reverend continued, 'but what most of you won't realise is that William Hewitt is the mystery benefactor who has funded a new school here to begin next month...'

There were gasps of astonishment from the congregation.

'Indeed, not only had he made arrangements to fund this new school for the foreseeable future as he realised the importance of education and all children having a fair start in life, but he has also donated a large sum for the upkeep of this church and its new roof. Provision has also been made for the widows and orphans of this parish.'

Suddenly a scream of rage emanated from deep inside Edna Hewitt. She could hear herself screaming but she thought it was coming from someone else.

'Mother, control yourself!' Harry said, gently shaking her. He felt like slapping her face but to do that today of all days would just be too much.

'Please take me outside for some fresh air...' She fought to get the words out. 'I'm having trouble breathing...'

Gasping, he led her away from the pew with all

eyes upon them. What would people think? This was all too much for Harry.

Once outside the building, he looked at her, she had drawn her veil over her head away from her face and was blotting her eyes with a lace handkerchief. 'Don't you know what this means?' she yelled at Harry.

He shook his head, in truth he didn't.

'We're penniless, he's left us nothing.'

Surely that couldn't be right? Even though Father had funded the church and was leaving money for the widows and orphans of the parish, they still had the house and shop. He shook his head. 'That can't possibly be right. I'll find one of Father's lawyers from Walker Brothers and Sons, they're in the church. I'll approach Nathaniel, he'll be the best to deal with.'

She nodded and sniffed. 'Better not make a spectacle of us, wait until they emerge for the burial. Do not tell anyone else of this and if anyone asks you why I screamed, just tell them it's grief and not anger.'

For someone who had seemed numbed by it earlier, Edna Hewitt had made a remarkable recovery from it. Hearing all that from the vicar had been like a bucket of ice-cold water poured over her.

***

When the burial had taken place, Harry went in search of Nathaniel Walker, one of the sons of Walker Brothers and Sons. He figured he would be the best one to ask regarding his father's affairs. His father Alfred Walker, head of the firm of solicitors, was not a well man these days and in any case, he did not wish to disturb him as the man had been a friend of his father's for years. Nathaniel's brother, Sebastian, was approachable but Harry felt him being the youngest, he wasn't as experienced as his elder brother who had now been with the firm for ten years.

Harry drew Nathaniel to one side, 'Nat, can this really be true that my father has donated all this money to the church for the new school, roof and its general upkeep as well as dishing out dough to the widows and orphans of the area?'

Nathaniel bit his lower lip and nodded, his grey eyes slightly guarded. 'I'm afraid it is true.'

Harry drew in a breath and let it out again. 'So you knew about this?'

'Yes, we did, but it's not as underhand as you might think—there was nothing clandestine about it whatsoever. In fact, the meetings we had to represent your father were all above board.'

'And you didn't think to tell either myself or my mother about those meetings?'

Nathaniel rubbed his chin and lowered his voice a notch. 'It's a tricky situation, granted. Your father came to see us around six months ago to arrange it all. As we are bound by confidentiality as a firm, we couldn't go contacting your mother or yourself behind his back, after all, it was *his* money. As you know, some of it was a legacy from his uncle from when he kept the lead mines—he was left a substantial sum then and of course, his earnings as pit manager.' He paused for a moment and smiled, 'But do not fret, dear chap. You are to inherit the book shop and tea room and the property above those—that I can tell you.'

Harry nodded, feeling slightly better, but he hadn't realised his father had inherited a large sum of money from his uncle's will, he'd thought it a nominal sum only. He met Nathaniel's persistent gaze. 'And Mother?'

'Don't fear...she won't be turned out of Hewitt Hall right now today, that I can promise you—there's no immediate rush for her to vacate the property.'

Harry's lips tightened and he clenched his teeth. 'I had hoped she wouldn't be turned out at all!'

Nathaniel's forehead creased into a frown. 'I'm afraid it's your father's wishes that the big house is to be given to a third party.'

'But that's preposterous!' Harry spat angrily. 'Where is my mother to live now and just who on earth is the third party?'

Nathaniel released a breath. 'Provision has been made for her to move into a two-bed cottage at Drisdale.'

Harry's head was swimming, he could hardly believe his ears. 'But why would my father do this to her? He must have been out of his mind.' His eyes searched the graveyard where people were in the midst of leaving, one or two chatting leisurely to the Reverend Ainsworth and shaking him by the hand. Somehow, as he scanned the area as if for something that would make sense, he felt as though he were in a dream and a very bad one at that. How would he explain this to Mother?

'I know it's a shock for you, Harry,' Nat said laying a hand on his shoulder, 'I couldn't tell you this before but at least you are now a man of property which will be transferred to your name. Your mother will also have a roof over her head as he's also made provision that she might have a modest, regular allowance for food, clothing, et cetera'

A modest allowance? For the woman who had been used to servants catering to her every whim?

***

On the coach ride back home, Harry explained all that Nathaniel had said to him while Edna Hewitt put her head in her hands, shaking it as she did so. It was some moments later before she looked up at her son and threw her veil from her face backwards over her head.

'A two-bedroom cottage!' Her bottom lip was trembling now. 'Me in a poky little cottage! This has to be a joke of your father's! He wouldn't do this to me, would he?'

Harry took her hand. 'I'm afraid he has. It was

all arranged six months ago legally without our knowledge. According to Nathaniel, he will make monetary provision for you so you will have enough food to eat and clothing to wear.'

'But what if that runs out?' His mother's eyes widened with alarm. 'He's throwing our money away from his grave that's what he's doing! He'd rather give to the wretched before he'd give it to me! Or you for that matter!'

Harry felt awkward for a moment. 'There's something I haven't mentioned…he's leaving the book shop, tea room and the premises above to me. Those will all be in my name.'

'Oh, he's seen you all right then!' She spat out the words.

'Maybe he has and I'll always be grateful for that but we could try contesting the will, maybe he wasn't in his right mind or something at the time.'

She shook her head. 'There was nothing wrong with his mind, he was of sound mind. He must have planned this to get back at me.'

Harry frowned. 'Whatever do you mean, Mother?'

She waved a hand at him. 'Never you mind. How am I supposed to host a funeral tea back at our house knowing what I now know.'

'I can always cancel it and say you've taken ill?'

She shook her head vehemently. 'Please do not do that. His family have come a long way and his poor aunt is so elderly to have made the journey. Could you say I'm ill but perhaps take them somewhere else?'

Harry fought to think for a moment, he could hardly take them to The Ploughman's Arms, his relatives wouldn't appreciate that though maybe the solicitors and acquaintances would. The only place he could think of was the tea room. It would be open and they tended to be quiet at this time of day. 'No need to fret, Mother,' he said, 'I think I have the perfect solution.'

***

'A party of twelve you say?' Polly wrinkled her nose as she stared in disbelief at Harry who had just entered the tea room. She glanced over his shoulder at the carriages lined up outside. She had of course realised that today was the day of his father's funeral and would have expected him to take the funeral mourners elsewhere either somewhere more upmarket or back at Hewitt Hall itself.

'Please, Miss Hedge. You would be doing me a great favour, I can't explain right now but I'm in somewhat of a sticky situation.'

Her face relaxed and she let out a breath. 'Yes, of course, that's fine.' She turned to Rose. 'Set out some extra seating then turn the sign to closed,' she ordered.

Rose nodded and smiled, she would never question her boss about such an issue even if she thought it strange.

Harry thanked Polly and then made his way

out to the awaiting carriages. By the time he'd returned with the funeral guests, all the tables were set out and the last customers had departed the tea room. Polly approached him. 'We don't have so much to offer today but would a selection of sandwiches and slices of fruit cake be acceptable to you and your guests? Along with as much tea and coffee as you'd like?'

Harry flashed her a smile. It was the first time he'd wanted to smile all day. The first time he'd felt someone was on his side. 'Thank you, Miss Hedge. That would be most acceptable indeed.'

He returned to the funeral guests and explained the situation, apologising profusely for his mother's absence and explaining that she wasn't in the frame of mind to socialise with anyone right now as it had all been a tremendous shock for her. Without going into detail, what he said was perfectly true. His father's associates and acquaintances didn't seem bothered at all and expected some would end up later at The Ploughman's Arms opposite. He felt like joining them himself and then thought it might be an idea to take the men there afterwards and buy them all a drink as a gesture of goodwill. These were men who had helped his father greatly over the years. It's what William Hewitt would have wanted.

The family members though, weren't that easy to appease as they'd travelled some distance and Harry realised after some time in their company that they'd taken it for granted they'd be spending the night at Hewitt Hall. What could he say to them? They were tired and needed somewhere to rest but his mother wouldn't thank him for bringing them back home with him even though they had the space to put them up.

There was a respectable guest house though at the end of the main street, he could enquire there he supposed but realised it would then only be courteous to foot the bill on their behalf too. Money that he didn't much feel like parting with right now as soon they might be in dire straits. The book shop wasn't making much profit as yet as he'd only just opened it and had to purchase stock and have the place fitted out, though the tenancy payments from both Cassandra and Jem would come in handy.

Once everyone was settled and plates of miniature ham and pickle sandwiches placed before them with a cake stand of buttered slices of fruit cake and a few mince pies that were leftover from that morning, all nicely arranged by Polly, he made an excuse to leave them there as he made off for the guest house.

Mrs Butterworth, who was stood at the small wooden counter in the hallway of the guesthouse, seemed an amiable, attractive sort with dark lustrous hair. She'd been running her establishment for several years; it was the nearest thing Wakeford had to a hotel, apart from the Ploughman's Arms which also offered accommodation but was known as a racy sort of place. It was rumoured that many nefarious sorts stayed there from time to time including the likes of May Malone who offered her services to visiting businessmen who passed on through the village.

Mrs Butterworth ran an index finger down the large dark blue booking register and then glanced up at Harry, who remembering his manners, removed his top hat and placed it on the counter. 'Yes, we can accommodate them all. I have three bedrooms free. One is a single room that would be suitable for your elderly aunt so she might have some privacy, then there are two doubles, so if the married couple takes one and their twin boys the other, that should work fine...'

Harry was just about to ask about the cost for one night when Mrs Butterworth asked, 'And will they be requiring supper tonight and breakfast in the morning before they leave?' Oh dear, Harry hadn't considered that and now it would be an additional cost. He could hardly expect them to go out looking for somewhere to eat or to pay for it themselves as they were supposed to be his guests, after all, so he nodded. 'Yes, please.'

She gazed up at the ceiling as she made some mental calculations, 'Let me see then, the cost of the rooms with evening meal and bed and breakfast thrown in will be three shillings.'

Harry beamed at the woman, that sounded very reasonable indeed but then she added,

'Each.'

His face fell so that would cost him fifteen shillings.

'Noticing his expression she said, 'I suppose I could deduct 1 shilling as your aunt's room will be small.'

He nodded. 'How about if they don't have the evening meal and just the breakfast?'

The woman sighed. 'Then that will bring the cost down to eleven shillings and sixpence.' She shook her head. He wondered what she was thinking as he looked quite affluent, she must assume he was a right penny pincher but the woman would hardly have known that his father was about to sideline his mother out of his will.

He swallowed a lump in his throat. 'I'm sorry about this,' he said feeling forlorn.

Her blue-grey eyes met his with some sympathy. 'Are things hard for you right now, Mr Hewitt, with your father dying an' all? He was a good sort and make no mistake.'

Harry's eyes widened, he had no idea that Mrs Butterworth had even known his father or in what capacity. He narrowed his eyes with suspicion. 'You knew him?'

'Oh, yes. I'd known him for years. He was such a kind man.' Her face flushed. 'A regular caller here, he was.'

It was at that point, a revelation hit Harry straight in the face. The woman had been abandoned by her husband many years ago. His father's many excursions from the house late in the evening when he claimed to have been called to the pit on business might have been to here. Why hadn't he realised it before? But still, he couldn't hold the woman accountable for all of it, if indeed an affair of sorts had taken place.

She reached out a hand across the counter and touched his. 'I'll tell you what I'll do as your father was so good to me, I'll charge you just ten bob for the lot and I'll throw those evening meals in for free. How does that sound?'

He nodded and smiled. 'That sounds very good to me, Mrs Butterworth. Thank you, you are most kind,' He said with some relief. He could just about afford that.

Harry could tell what his father had seen in the woman, she was still attractive for her age, and a warm kindly sort who was the opposite in looks and personality to his mother. No doubt, his father had come here for some comfort in Mrs Butterworth's arms when the reception back had Hewitt Hall had been frosty. Still, he was so grateful to her for cutting the price for him.

He extracted his leather wallet from his inside coat pocket and paid her the ten shillings. She took the money and began scribbling something in her register. She gazed up at him. 'What name shall I book the five guests under, Mr Hewitt?'

'Please book them in under the Hewitt name as they are relations of my father's from London.'

Mrs Butterworth arched an interested eyebrow at him. 'Oh, I see.' It did appear that she was interested in anything to do with his father. Her eyes began to water and then she said in barely a whisper, 'I was so sad to hear of his sudden passing you know...'

He smiled at her. 'I imagine you were,' he said in a kindly fashion. Maybe Mrs Butterworth had given his father far more love than his mother ever had and for that, he would be forever grateful.

He shot her an admiring glance. 'Is it all right if I send the guests over when they're finished at the tea room so they might rest as they've come a long way?'

She smiled at him. 'Yes, by all means. I'll also put the kettle on to boil for them when they arrive. Just mention to them that evening meal is served in the dining room at half-past six and breakfast is at half-past seven in the morning. Though I'm a little more flexible with breakfast time if they need to leave early or should like a lie in for an hour or so.'

He nodded, then replacing his top hat, looked deep into her eyes. 'I am so grateful you know, in more ways than you could possibly imagine.'

Mrs Butterworth blushed like a young woman. 'And do call in any time to see me,' she said. 'The kettle is always on the boil.'

As he departed down the steps he grinned to himself feeling sure the woman had given him an open invitation to socialise with her anytime, and he guessed that he did look like a younger version of his father. Many a man might take her up on that when they fancied a bit of comfort and maybe he might well have but he had enough on his plate with the way Annabelle was behaving of late.

Chapter Fourteen

Cassie was Christmas shopping in Hocklea with Aunt Bertha, the woman needed to pick up her new spectacles from the oculist, so Cassie thought it a good time to venture back outside after receiving the all-clear from Doctor Bryant. She'd not forgotten the sweet doll in the toy shop window when she'd visited there with Jem. It was porcelain with big blue eyes and glossy auburn curls. Its dress was made of pink satin and edged with fine white lace. It was quite expensive but after all, they'd been through lately, she reckoned it would be a lovely Christmas gift for her daughter.

There was an air of festivity around Hocklea that day as people went about with packages under their arms, baskets laden with citrus fruit, nuts and delicacies for the big day itself. Rows of white-feathered geese hung from the eaves outside the poulterer's shop and Cassie thought they'd purchase one of those just before leaving for home.

Aunt Bertha was excited about picking up her new spectacles but Cassie was mindful that the woman needed to take care before they got them in case she slipped on the cobbles which were frosted with a thin layer of ice, so she took the woman's arm to guide her into the shop.

Aunt Bertha's appointment was with Mr Matthias Jackson himself who was the chief oculist at the shop.

'Please don't be nervous,' Cassie whispered as a young lady receptionist led her away to a little room to see Mr Jackson. Cassie kept her fingers crossed that all would go well. Auntie had been through the hardest part of having her eyes tested so now it was just a question of if the spectacles would work.

Aunt Bertha was gone the best part of twenty minutes while Cassie waited but it gave her time to rest her legs as she was quite worn out. The twins inside her seemed to be kicking mercilessly this afternoon.

Finally, Auntie emerged from the oculist's office with a beaming smile on her face, she walked towards Cassie with the aid of her willow stick.

'Your new spectacles look very smart!' Cassie enthused.

'Aren't they marvellous? I can see once again, I am so grateful to you and the eye doctor, Cassie.'

'Take a seat here,' said Cassie, pulling herself onto her feet. 'I'll just settle the bill a moment.' She conversed with the receptionist and was handed a beautifully handwritten bill which read:

One pair of ladies' spectacles: Made of a thin metal with a W bridge, oval frames and long straight side arms with flattened teardrop temples. TWO SHILLINGS AND SIXPENCE

One mother of pearl spectacle case. FOUR SHILL-INGS.

Cassie gulped. This was far more expensive than she'd first realised though her aunt badly needed those spectacles. No doubt her aunt had been persuaded into ordering the mother of pearl spectacle case. 'Excuse me, miss,' she addressed the receptionist.

The girl turned from where she'd been writing in a ledger. 'Yes?'

Cassie lowered her voice so her aunt wouldn't overhear. 'I can afford the spectacles for my aunt but I can't afford the cost of the mother of pearl case for them. I'm afraid my aunt is slightly deaf at times and maybe she didn't quite understand the cost involved.'

'That's quite all right,' the girl said smiling. 'We do have several other style cases, there's a silver-plated design for three shillings?'

Cassie let out a long breath, she was just going to have to be frank with the girl. 'What is the cheapest case for sale?'

The girl arched her eyebrows as if with surprise. 'I suppose the plain leather pouch though it won't afford much protection towards the glasses.' Her eyes lit up as she held up her index finger as if an idea had suddenly occurred to her. 'However, I've just thought of something. We had a pair of glasses returned this morning as the person who purchased them has suddenly passed away. Not a nice thought I know but I could sell you that one. It has a little wear and tear as it has been used but it would afford more protection than the soft leather pouch.'

'That would be marvellous,' said Cassie surprised by the young woman's ingenuity. 'At what cost?'

'Would sixpence be in keeping with your finances?'

'It would indeed!'

The girl made her way from behind the counter and returned with the hard metal case and handed it to Cassie. It looked like silver-plate to her and had a couple of scratches on it but the main thing was the case was affordable within her budget and would protect her aunt's precious new spectacles. She paid up what she owed and they left the shop and returned to the toy shop to pick up the doll for Emily which was nicely gift wrapped in a box with a red bow attached. Finally, they called to the poulterer's shop to pick up the goose before heading back home.

***

Later that evening when Emily was tucked safely in her bed and Aunt Bertha was fast asleep by the fireside, Polly and Cassie sat chatting away in the scullery.

'So, you mean to tell me that the funeral tea

was held at our tea room?'

Polly nodded vigorously. 'Yes, it was.'

'How strange. I would have attended the funeral myself as a mark of respect towards the man but it was the first day I'd felt well enough in ages and I wanted to accompany Aunt Bertha to fetch those spectacles before Christmas.'

Polly smiled sympathetically. 'I don't think anyone would have expected you to be there, not in your condition and especially after what's occurred. In any case, it's mainly men what turn up for funerals except of course, if it's women from a family and even then, many choose not to attend.'

'I suppose so. Was Jem there?'

'No. Why? Did you expect him to attend?'

'I just thought as he'd had recent dealings with the man like myself he might have represented both of us. I'm a bit disappointed in that, to be honest.'

'To be truthful, he told me after the accident that he wouldn't attend as he doesn't much care for Harry.'

'Really?' Cassie shot her a sideways glance. 'Why ever not?'

Polly sniffed loudly. 'I should've thought that was most obvious!'

'It's not obvious to me so pray tell?'

'He's jealous of the man as he thinks Harry has designs upon you!'

'Oh, for goodness sake!' Cassie laughed in disbelief. 'Why ever should he think that? Why on earth would a toff like Harry Hewitt be interested in me? A twice-widowed woman who is heavily pregnant with twin babies and who already has a young daughter?'

Polly pursed her lips. 'It's not so daft though, is it?' She angled her head to one side. 'Just as Jem was interested in you. He knew all that stuff about you being widowed and pregnant, 'cept he didn't know it was twins you're expecting and I doubt even that would have deterred him when he made that proposal to you!'

The truth was, Cassie didn't know how to think she just imagined that someone as sophisticated as Harry Hewitt would never be interested in her in that sort of manner. She knew he liked her but she thought that was as a fellow trader with affiliated interests between the tea room and his book store. 'To be honest with you, Polly, the thought of Harry as a romantic interest hadn't crossed my mind until you brought it up just now...'

'Got you thinking though, gal! Ain't I?' Polly chuckled.

***

The last thing Harry felt like doing was cajoling his mother at the moment. She now seemed to be full of such venom and vitriol towards his father that no matter what he said it didn't appear to pour oil on troubled waters.

Finally, he'd had enough, so he cleared his

throat and taking her hand said softly, 'You hinted on the day of Father's funeral that he must have prevented you from inheriting everything as "he wanted to get back at you"? Mother, what did you mean by that?'

'Oh, nothing!' she sniffed, shaking her head.

'Now come on, don't play those games with me. I need to know!' he said firmly, raising his voice so that he startled even himself.

She looked at him through glazed eyes. 'You see I found out...'

'Found out about what?'

'About his dalliance with that common woman.'

He raised his brow. 'From the guest house? Mrs Butterworth?'

His mother's eyes widened. 'You know about it and didn't say anything?'

'No, in truth I didn't,' he said softly. 'Not until the day of the funeral when I worked things out for myself. You see, I had to put our guests up somewhere and by the way the woman spoke of him and the expression on her face...I worked it out for myself.'

She nodded. 'Yes, he was having a passionate affair with *that woman* for years. I tried to turn a blind eye to it at first, I mean you were very young back then and I had a terrible time giving birth to you so I tried to keep him at arms' length afterwards as I didn't want to go through all that again. So times of intimacy were few and far between, and no man can withstand that for long, I suppose. They have certain needs.'

He nodded. 'But that still doesn't explain why he's practically cut you out of the will though, Mother?'

'I don't know how to find the words to say this b...but...'

'But what?'

'I think he never forgave me...' She lowered her head and for a moment he thought she was about to weep but then he realised there was an element of shame in what she had just said.

'Never forgave you for what exactly?' He narrowed his eyes.

She lifted her head and met his gaze, trembling all the while. 'You see when I discovered his affair with *that woman* I became so angry. I'd given my life to him to be his wife, bore him a son and stuck with him through both good times and bad, so I'm afraid I did a terrible thing which I haven't quite forgiven myself for.' She waited a while before composing herself. 'I tried to set fire to the guest house!'

Harry felt a sense of dread course around his body this wasn't the mother he knew. Oh, she had her airs and graces and sometimes nonsensical approaches to life about her, but he'd never known her to do anything that malicious. He was afraid to hear what she had to say next but he found himself saying gently, 'And what happened when you did?'

His mother drew a breath as if to compose herself. 'It happened to be on the night he was staying there. It was my plan to just cause a little mayhem and smoke them out of there. It was the early hours of the morning and I threw a rag dipped in turpentine in through the letterbox. I'd set fire to it and was shocked at how quick the fire was beginning to spread inside. I was looking in through the glass in the door. I immediately regretted my actions and began hammering on the door and yelling but for some reason, no one responded...' she swallowed. 'It was my guess at the time that your father was in bed with the woman and it was my way of finding this out. I'd had visions of him coming to the door and then I could say, 'Ha, I've caught you out at last!'

Harry shook his head. 'But I'm guessing it didn't happen quite like that?'

'No, it didn't. For a start, your father wasn't even there. On this occasion, he was actually at the pit. For some reason though that night Mrs Butterworth didn't rouse when I called out and banged on the door. Realising this could now be something serious, I ran to the inn up the road which still had some late customers there and asked for their help. I didn't tell them the fire was down to me of course. Some of the men battered the front door of the guest house in and another brought a ladder. Mrs Butterworth was rescued and fortunately, she only had one paying guest there, who thankfully, was fine afterwards.

Though the guest house needed some repair and new decoration afterwards.'

Harry sat there in a state of disbelief that the woman he saw before him, the woman he had called "Mother" for all these years had been capable of doing something like that. It was a mixture of disgust mingled with revulsion for her, yet at the same time, he had a level of sympathy for her too.

'And Mrs Butterworth was she fine after the fire?'

Tears welled up in his mother's eyes. 'No, not really. Oh, physically, she was unharmed but it caused her to shut her business for some time. She became very depressed and anxious.'

'Unsurprisingly.' His mother shot him a surreptitious sideways glance which caused him to feel uneasy. 'Why do I feel there's something you're not telling me, Mother?'

Edna Hewitt swallowed a lump in her throat. She took a long sip of water from a glass tumbler on the small table at her side and set it down again. Then she met her son's persistent gaze. 'You're absolutely right, Harry. There is something I haven't told you...' She swallowed hard as if the words were difficult for her to say. 'But what I hadn't realised is at the time Mrs Butterworth was carrying your father's child.'

Harry's mouth popped open with surprise, he tried to say something but the words just wouldn't come for a while, then finally he said, 'So I'm guessing Mrs Butterworth lost the child?'

'No, he's still very much alive but I blame myself for the way he turned out in life.'

He shook his head vigorously. 'What on earth do you mean?'

'Following the fire, she became unwell and gave birth prematurely...'

Harry nodded as if he understood but then his forehead creased into a frown. 'But he's still alive so he must be all right then?'

Edna shook her head. 'He is strangely but I'd say although he looks like a man, he has the mind of a child...'

This wasn't making any sense to him at all. 'I still don't get it.'

'Jeremiah Clement, you know him?'

'Of course I do as Father had been renting out the shop to him.'

'Well, his younger brother isn't really his brother.'

'Go on, Mother...'

'He's your half-brother. Clitheroe Clement, otherwise known as "Clyde"!'

'B...but that can't possibly be true, can it?' Harry could hardly believe that Jem's so-called brother, that large man who seemed like a gentle sort of giant could possibly be his brother too.

'That's not all I'm afraid...'

'You mean there's more to come?'

She nodded slowly. 'Not only that, but I've always had my suspicions that Jem might be your brother too!'

He put his head in his hands, none of this was making any sense to him. So, his father, who he had admired and looked up to all of his life had possibly fathered two other sons who were his half-brothers. He didn't want to believe it. He'd had some friction from Jem and he had no idea why the man acted so strangely towards him, but Clyde was one of the funniest, softest men he knew.' He dropped his hands to his sides and looked at his mother. 'You've given me this information now Mother but what am I to do with it?'

'I really don't know, Harry.' She shook her head. 'It's up to you whether or not you do anything with it but at least now you know the full facts. It's not something I've ever admitted to anyone before. It feels like a weight has been lifted off my shoulders.' She sighed loudly.

And put onto mine, thought Harry to himself.

Chapter Fifteen

Jem was busy loading up the horse and cart outside the shop. He wiped the sweat from his brow with a handkerchief and returned it to his trouser pocket. He had a wardrobe and matching dressing table, and one or two other items, to deliver to a lady living in Drisdale. Life had settled down once again since he'd sorted things out with Clyde and now that his brother realised they were sticking around for good and not starting a new life elsewhere, he'd calmed down. Jem had been sorely disappointed when Cassandra had turned down his marriage proposal but in hindsight, he realised maybe it was all for the best. Although his intentions had been sincere, he now knew he'd been unfair to put unwarranted pressure on her like that. Her focus needed to be on the life or should he say lives, blossoming inside of her.

He had just finished loading up the cart and was securing the pieces of furniture with some rope when Harry approached him. Jem narrowed his gaze. What did he want now? The man had a serious expression on his face as he strode towards him with extreme purpose with every footstep taken.

'Can I speak to you for a moment?' Harry gazed at him with intent.

'If you must!' Jem was no fool, he realised now the man's father had died that anything to do with the tenancy of the shop would be dealt with by him. 'Look, I know I'm a day or two late paying my rent but once I've dropped this furniture off then I shall have the full amount for you. Things have been tight this past few days...'

Harry waved a hand in front of him as if to dismiss the promise of rent. 'I'm in no immediate rush for that.'

'Oh?' Then what did the man want?

'I need to speak with you about a delicate matter if I may, can you spare me some time?'

Jem shook his head. 'Can it wait? I need to deliver these pieces afore it gets dark. Got to get to Drisdale, see.'

'No problem. On your return journey call into the book shop to see me, it shall be quiet by then.'

'Aye, all right then. I'll do that.' There was no use in falling out with the man as he needed to keep the tenancy of that shop and his father had been right good to him and Cassandra in letting them stay on. 'I was so sorry to hear of your father's death...' he added.

Harry nodded. 'Thank you. It came as a shock to us all. I don't think it's hit me properly yet.'

'I'll call at the shop later, then,' Jem said, and

he clambered aboard the horse and cart and gave the leather rein a quick flick to get the horse started.

Delivering the furniture went smoothly even though he didn't have Clyde around to help him today. He was visiting their Aunt Dorothea in Hocklea. The woman had become a little fragile of late, and so, he and Clyde now helped her whenever they could, doing jobs around the house for her and delivering sacks of potatoes and other provisions to her door.

Jem arrived at the shop as the last customers were departing. Harry flashed a small silver flask at him. 'Fancy a tot of whiskey?' He asked, closing the door behind him.

Jem stepped back in surprise. 'I shouldn't really when I'm in charge of the cart.'

'One won't harm you,' Harry grinned.

Jem returned the smile. 'I dare say it won't.'

'Please take a seat,' Harry gestured towards the bay window area with a flourish of his hand, where two leather button back armchairs were situated.

On the small occasional table between them were two cut-glass tumblers which Harry poured the amber fluid into as Jem seated himself. Harry passed him a glass, 'Here's to your very good health!'

Harry raised his glass and Jem followed suit, then Harry seated himself opposite. Jem remained silent as he waited for Harry to speak, he guessed it might be something to do with Cassandra. Maybe he had a plan to propose to her himself but instead, he began, 'There's no easy way to say this to you Jem…but from something my mother told me yesterday, it appears that Clyde is my half-brother.' He waited to gauge Jem's reaction. Jem almost choked on his whiskey as it went down the wrong way, he spluttered momentarily.

'W…what did you say?'

'You heard correctly and there is something else, *you* may also be my half-brother too, though that has yet to be proved…'

Jem stared at him wide-eyed in astonishment. 'This has got to be some kind of joke, hasn't it? Our parents were Alfred and Annie Clement. They had us late in life and our mother died giving birth to our Clyde…' he began to tremble as he realised as he was growing up his parents seemed a lot older than their friends' parents. They'd been kind people but if he thought about it, there was always an element of secrecy. If Aunt Dorothea visited their farm, she'd often usher their father away to speak privately with him. He couldn't remember so much about his mother though, but until now he'd had no reason to question their parentage. 'B…but why is your mother saying this?'

'I'm as shocked as you are, Jem.' He lifted his glass and taking a long satisfying swig laid it down again. Then he looked him directly in the eyes. 'From what my mother has told me, my father had a long-standing affair with Mrs Butterworth from the guest house. There was a fire and it seems she wasn't right afterwards and my father gave the baby away, Clyde I mean. No doubt due to the scandal as he could hardly bring him back home to our house.'

Jem nodded staring blankly at the small table between them. He raised his eyes to meet with Harry's. 'Then if it's true, how do you know I'm your half-brother too?'

Harry shrugged. 'I don't, at least not for certain. My mother added that she had her suspicions about you too, in truth, that's all I have to go on. I just wondered if you knew anything about this at all?'

'No, I bloody well don't!' Jem finished his drink and slammed it down on the table. 'I think I will take another if you don't mind?'

By the time Harry had got around to locating a bottle of whiskey he had in the cupboard so that there was more to go around, both men were feeling tipsy. Jem realised it was foolish to drink when he needed to get back to the farm but somehow his feet wouldn't lead him away, he needed time to digest all this information. Perhaps Clyde was Harry's half-brother, he could see a vague similarity there as both men were tall and well-built, dark-haired too, but he didn't for one moment think that he himself was related to Harry. He had a sandy reddish sort of hair colouring and if out in the sun too long, his skin turned red and burned easily. He had to be so careful. Yet, thinking about it, Clyde had a swarthy sort of complexion just like Harry. In fact, he looked more like Harry than him.

This realisation made him feel bad as if true, then Clyde wasn't his real brother at all. Not a blood relation at any rate.

**

The advent hymn *O Come Emmanuel* was playing as Cassie entered the church with Emily's hand firmly in hers. She had intended attending the church as soon as she was able following her visit to see the Reverend Ainsworth but her recent unexpected period of bed rest had put pay to that, but now she was feeling more herself. As she searched the pews for somewhere to sit, she noticed several eyes cast upon her and she felt her cheeks grow hot. What were these people thinking? Then she caught the eyes of Mr and Mrs Moody from Dykingdale Farm. The first customers they'd received at the tea room and now their most frequent visitors. The pair nodded and smiled warmly at her. As if realising her predicament, Mrs Moody gestured with her hand for Cassie and Emily to join them in their pew. There was plenty of room, so with some relief, they sat beside them. Their pew was three rows from the front which was good as now they'd get to hear the reverend's sermon without lots of bobbing hats and heads in the way. The sermon hadn't begun as yet, the organist appeared to be play-ing some well-known carols beforehand. Cassie smiled and thanked Mr and Mrs Moody for their kindness.

'It's all right,' Mrs Moody reassured. 'People are particular about their pews here, but we'd be more than happy for you and Emily to sit here at any time, or anyone else who you'd like to join us too for that matter.'

'Thank you.' Cassie smiled.

'I was sorry to hear that you've been on bed rest,' Mrs Moody said sympathetically, 'Polly told me.'

'Yes, I'm fine now though. It's nice to get out of the house for a while.'

As the service progressed Cassie felt as though many eyes were piercing a hole in her back, though she had noticed that some villagers at least had begun to warm towards her as they nodded or smiled at her when they caught her eye. Those were mostly folk who were patrons of the tea room and their friends. Word was ob-viously getting around that she wasn't as black as she'd previously been painted. She wondered where Edna Hewitt was as Harry had informed her they had a family pew at the church. There was no sign of Harry either, she thought it strange as he'd told her he was a regular attendee at the church. She let out a breath, maybe he hadn't been telling the truth though? But then again, the poor man's father had recently passed away and maybe coming here was a reminder of the recent funeral.

***

Harry opened one eye and groaned loudly. Where was he? Had someone hit him over the head with a hammer? He wasn't in his own bedroom or even his own house for that matter. As his eyes gradually focused, he noticed Jem fast asleep in the armchair opposite him, his head rolled to one side. Oh heck! It was a Sunday and wasn't he supposed to take his mother to church as usual? He drew in a long composing breath and let it out again. No, he wasn't. His mother had told him she wouldn't set foot in that church again after what the reverend had said at his father's funeral. She had thrown scorn on the idea of what she felt was rightfully hers being spent on the upkeep of the church, the funding for the new school and the widows and orphans of the area. One name, in particular, she'd spat out at him. '*Cassandra Bellingham*! Why should that widowed whore have any of our money! She's indecent and no longer wears her widow's weeds as she should while in mourning!'

He'd tried to reassure her that Cassie was supporting herself now and would be unlikely to lay claim to any charity the Hewitt family had to offer via his father's bequest. But his mother was having none of it and in fact, that's what had caused him to drink that whiskey last night. That and the news that his father had fathered not just one bastard son but possibly another too. Now as he gazed across at the man who might be his half-brother, he smiled. They'd both got off to a bad start but last night it was as if they were putting the world to rights as they drank whiskey together.

Tentatively, he slowly pulled himself onto his feet and went to rouse Harry, but gently shaking his shoulder. Jem woke up with a startle. 'What? Where am I?' Then he realised. 'My goodness, Clyde will wonder where I am. I've been here all night long. Why didn't you wake me before now?' He rubbed the back of his neck.

Harry could see that Jem was no longer angry with him, his touching concern was for Clyde alone. He was a good brother to him. 'I'm sorry, Jem. I wasn't much use as after a while I passed out myself and only now I've woken up. Thank goodness it's Sunday morning and not Monday when I have to open the shop. Now, no need to panic. I'm sure Clyde can fend for himself. Before you leave I'm going to make you a strong cup of black coffee so you are alert enough to drive the horse and cart back home.'

Harry's head whipped around. 'Bella, she's gone!'

'No, she hasn't. Don't you remember we tethered her to a post in the yard outside? She's got a bit of shelter under that canopy out there and we left a bucket of water for her. I've got an apple you can give her before you set off home.

Go and check on her if you like. The apples are in a bowl by the counter.'

Jem nodded and hauled himself onto his feet and staggered off to find the back door. Harry grinned, he had a vague memory of them leading the horse through the shop and outside to the yard, all the while being careful not to disturb any of the book stands or tables. They must have made a good job of it as there wasn't much out of place.

Jem returned a few minutes later, this time not looking as concerned. 'Aye, you're right. She's fine. Don't seem to be that worried or cold. I forgot we draped a tarpaulin over her to keep her warm. Luckily, I haven't got much on today, so I'm going to get her back home and rested in the barn, then I'm going back to bed myself.'

Harry handed him a cup of coffee and they both reseated themselves in the leather armchairs by the windows like a pair of bookends. 'Will you tell Clyde about what I told you?' Harry asked, then he took a sip of coffee and laid his cup down in its saucer.

Jem shrugged. 'I don't know how to, to be honest.'

'I know what you mean as I felt like that about telling you. Maybe we should try to find out a little more about the circumstances first.'

Jem angled his head on one side. 'How'd you mean?'

'We could call to see Mrs Butterworth for some

clarification…'

'I suppose so and I could have a word with my auntie. She's my father's sister. Quite elderly now, maybe she can shine some light on Clyde's parentage as well as my own.'

'That's settled then,' said Harry smiling. 'Come on drink up!'

'Isn't that what you kept saying to me last night?' Jem chuckled.

***

An official-looking letter had arrived at Hewitt Hall addressed to both Edna Hewitt and Harry. The maid bobbed a curtsy as Harry removed it from the silver tray and she went about her business. Without waiting to consult his mother, and with trembling hands, he broke open the seal as he read its contents.

Since the sudden and sad death of one Mr William Montague Hewitt of Hewitt Hall, Wakeford, it was his request upon his death that the property of the same name be put in the hands of a third named party. Provision has been made to provide you with a property named Hartwell Cottage, Hollybush Row, at Drisdale. Thereby, you are given notice to quit Hewitt Hall in the parish of Wakeford in the county of Marshfield on or before the 31st day of January 1876 so that the quiet and peaceable possession of said property can be taken over by the new owner appointed by William Montague Hewitt.

In failure of your compliance herewith, legal

measures will be adopted to compel the same by application at the District Police Court.

Dated this sixth day of June in the year of our Lord, 1875.

Yours etc,

On behalf of Mr William Montague Hewitt (Deceased)

(The legal owner of the above)

Harry took a shuddering breath, the letter was from his father's firm of solicitors which had also provided a covering letter from themselves. Why was his father doing this to them? It seemed pretty cruel to him. It wasn't so much for himself he felt concern but for his mother. After all, he was now a young man and had been left premises where he could conduct his business and also receive monthly rental payments from the tenants. He could make a go of things and was more fortunate than most, but his mother wasn't getting any younger and had been used to a certain lifestyle, to expect her now to up sticks and settle in a little cottage was beyond him.

She'd previously been informed about the cottage of course, but he'd thought from what Nathaniel had told him following the funeral about there being "no immediate rush for his mother to vacate the property", he'd assumed they'd have at least several months and not weeks to get out of here. How was he to tell her this devastating news?

The end of January wasn't that far away. And

who could the mysterious third party be who was to take over Hewitt Hall? A thought occurred to him...was it Mrs Butterworth his father had hoped to bequeath his property to? Surely not. It was most usual for a spouse or firstborn male child to inherit not someone's long-time lover. But you just never knew with his father, he'd had his secrets over the years, that much was evident.

Harry decided to wait until dinner that evening to inform his mother they needed to be out of the property by the end of January. At least they'd have a roof over their heads for time being. The sensible thing to do right now would be to view the cottage at least. In the covering letter, Nathaniel Walker had suggested calling into the offices for the key. So, taking the letter and documentation with him, he folded them neatly and placed them in the inside pocket of his coat so Mother might not find them until he found out more. Then he summoned the family coach to take him to the solicitor's office at Hocklea in total disbelief at how their lives were about to change in one fell swoop.

Chapter Sixteen

From a corner of the living room, Cassie stared into the flames of the fireplace as she nestled up in the armchair beneath a woollen blanket. By next Christmas things would be very different indeed as then she'd have three young children to cope with and not one. She closed her eyes for a moment and sighed. It was a little hour to herself which she was grateful for. Polly had taken both Emily and Aunt Bertha, who was managing well with her new spectacles, to the tea room so she might rest in peace. Only Sammy remained curled up in his basket at the fireside. She'd almost drifted off to sleep when there was a sharp rap on the door, silently cursing the caller, she tossed her blanket to one side and hefted herself out of the chair.

Sammy, who was now alert with his ears pricked up looked at her quizzically. 'A fine house dog you are an' all staying in your basket,' she chuckled.

As she opened the front door, she gasped when she saw Harry standing there with his top hat in his hand and his coach parked outside. 'May I come inside?' he asked his eyes full of concern.

'Yes, of course.' She drew back the door for him to enter. There was something about the hollow, haunted look in his eyes that told her something was amiss. He followed her into the cottage.

'Take a seat,' she offered.

'Thank you.' He placed his hat on top of the table and sat in the armchair facing hers near the hearth and she sat opposite.

'So, what's brought you here today? I'm guessing this isn't a social visit?' She angled her head to one side.

'No, not really.' He shook his head and then steepled his fingers, almost as though in prayer. 'You see the most awful thing has happened and I don't know what to do about it. You're the only person who is outside of the situation that I felt I could speak to.'

She smiled at him. 'Then I'm all ears...'

'I discovered that after my father died he'd cut off my mother from any legacy. Basically, she now has to leave Hewitt Hall and go to live in a little cottage in Drisdale.'

Cassie's eyes widened. 'Good heavens! That seems a bit harsh. But why on earth would he do something like that, he seemed such a benevolent sort to me.'

'Oh, he is, believe me. He's left the shop premises to me and the rest of his money is to go for the upkeep of the church, some distributed amongst the orphans and widows of Wakeford and the most surprising thing of all is that he is the mystery benefactor of the new school at the church!'

Cassandra sucked in a breath and let it out again. 'Oh, my. I mean I knew that there was some sort of mystery person who was paying for the school, after all, Emily will start there as a pupil in January, but I had no idea your father was the person funding it.'

Harry shrugged his shoulders. 'Why would you? In any case, there is more to this story and I hope I can rely on you keeping this to yourself for time being?'

She nodded. 'But of course.'

'It appears that my father fathered an illegitimate son.'

She gasped. 'How dreadful for your mother.'

'Mother knows all about it, in fact, she's the one who informed me of the situation. I won't name him for time being as he needs to be informed himself first. Suffice to say, it has come as an awful shock to me.'

'I bet it has.'

'I called to the solicitor's office this morning and was given the key for the cottage in Drisdale and it's dire. In a state of disrepair, I can't possibly move mother in there but we need to vacate Hewitt Hall by the end of January. I've tried to think of all possibilities. We can't afford to rent a house in the meantime, and obviously, now, I'll be homeless too. The trouble is the money we could have afforded on rent will now be required to do up the cottage.'

'I'm sorry to hear that but couldn't you sell it instead?'

He rubbed his chin as if in contemplation. 'I had half considered that but I'd prefer to pay out to do it up. It needs a new thatched roof, some painting inside and maybe some new window frames as they're rotting away. If I could get it in a good state of repair then maybe I can sell it at a later date at a good price for her. Meanwhile...'

'Meanwhile, you and your mother have no place to stay?'

'Not exactly. I could bed down at the shop for time being. But I wouldn't want Mother to stay there. Do you have any ideas?'

'She'd be welcome to stay here with us.' Cassie said without hesitation.' I know we've had our differences in the past but as long as she doesn't mind.'

He pursed his lips. 'It's going to be difficult getting her out of Hewitt Hall anyhow but even if I do that I suppose this is the last place she'd want to stay. She seems so jealous and spiteful towards you.'

'There is one thing though, Harry...'

'Oh, what's that?'

'We're more alike than she realises and in a similar predicament. We've both been widowed and let down by the men we thought we knew...'

'There is that,' he said softly as he stared into

the flames of the fire.

***

Jem was gazing thoughtfully at Clyde as he watched him loading up the cart. They were picking up some furniture from an office that had recently closed down in Hocklea. There were some nice pieces of furniture there too: three solid oak desks, several leather back chairs and four walnut bookcases. He'd even decided to purchase some artwork there that he quite fancied as he knew of a dealer in Drisdale who would purchase them from him. Lately, he was discovering he had an eye for things and was developing a passion for antiques. Although not a well-schooled man, he was becoming quite knowledgeable. Thinking about that time when he'd signed his name to the tenancy agreement and how evident it was that he could neither read nor write properly that gave him the determination to do something about it. Cassie had offered to help him to read and write but he decided she had enough on her plate but the Reverend Ainsworth had recently advertised classes for people like him that were to be held twice a week beginning in January. So, he decided to attend those.

Clyde frowned. 'What you looking at our, Jem?'

Jem smiled realising it was time he told his brother what he knew about his parentage. 'When we get back to the cottage there's something I need to speak to you about and when I do we need to visit Aunt Dorothea to set the record straight.'

Clyde scratched his head, seeming mystified with what his brother was saying to him. 'D... don't think I understand?'

Jem shook his head. 'Neither do I, lad. Neither do I. Hopefully, all will become clear before too long.'

***

Telling Mother they had to vacate Hewitt Hall by the end of January, hadn't been easy for Harry. He'd paced the floorboards of his father's study with his hands behind his back, practising what he'd say for ages beforehand, until finally, he'd blurted the words out to her. His mother's hands had flown to her face and when she heard about the state of disrepair to the cottage in Drisdale, she'd collapsed in the armchair. He'd had to send for the maid to bring smelling salts. Finally, when she came around she looked at him with questioning eyes.

'But you want me to go and live with that Wakeford Whore while the cottage is being re-paired?' She held her hand to her chest as if she had been wounded.

'Yes, Mother. Cassandra has even offered to have you there for Christmas to be part of her family celebrations. Isn't that lovely of her?' He forced a smile, realising his mother was not an easy woman to placate.

'Never!' she said pointing an index finger angrily at the ceiling. 'Over my dead body!' Then she'd risen to her feet and left the room. Harry knew where she was going—to her bedchamber, she often went there and took to her bed when she couldn't cope with life. It was such a shame, his father was dead and now it felt like his mother was dying inside too. The woman was mortally wounded by the gun held to her head by his deceased father.

There was something else too he hadn't considered up until now—*the servants!* What would they do when he and his mother left Hewitt Hall? Unless of course, the new owner, whoever he or she was, took them on? He decided to say nothing to them for time being until he found out more about the situation.

He sank into his father's favourite armchair and stared at his portrait on the wall above the fireplace. *Oh, Father, how could you betray us so?*

His father seemed to be boring a hole into his soul with his dark piercing eyes. What could he have been thinking when he made that will? There would be an official reading of it on Monday, January the 3rd at the offices of Walker Brothers and Sons. Mother would need to be there for that as would he of course. As he remained deep in thought he heard coach wheels on the gravelled drive outside and the sound of doors being slammed shut. He rose from the armchair and went to the window to look. *Annabelle?* What on earth could she possibly want? He thought they'd said all they had to the other day. She didn't notice him peering out of the window and she had a solemn expression on her face. He had a half a mind to instruct the maid to say he wasn't at home but then he thought that churlish of him. So, instead, he made his way to the hallway to receive her. Whatever news she had for him, he felt it wasn't going to be good.

The maid went to answer the door and Harry stood there as she allowed Annabelle in through the door. Annabelle was dressed all in blue with a fur-trimmed hat, she looked stunningly beautiful with her flushed cheeks and the sparkle in her eyes but she was frowning. The maid took Annabelle's cape and closed the door and went off to attend to her duties.

'Annebelle!' Harry stepped forwards to greet her taking her hands in his. 'What brings you here today?'

'I'm afraid I have some sad shocking news...' she said, her eyes enlarging. 'I've only just heard it from my father and wanted you to be the first to know as it involves the pit.'

'You'd better come through to the study,' he said, taking her by the arm and leading her along the corridor. He opened the study door and gestured for her to take a seat by the fireplace and he followed suit. 'Would you like some coffee'

She shook her head. 'No, thank you.'

'How about a glass of brandy then? That's good for shock.'

She nodded. 'That would be nice. Yes, please.'

He rose from his chair and poured them a small glass each and handed her one which she immediately took a sip from and he laid his down on the small occasional table beside his armchair as he seated himself.

When she had composed herself, he looked at her and asked, 'What is it that you have come to tell me?'

She met his persistent gaze and laid her glass down on the table beside her. 'It's Josiah Wilkinson...' she bit her bottom lip as if she needed to force out what she had to say to him. 'He's d... dead.'

'Dead? But how? I thought he'd gone missing after the accident when he failed to show up for my father's funeral.'

'He shot himself. Blew his brains out by all account...' her white-gloved hands flew to her mouth as she began to sob, her shoulders wracking with grief.

'How awful for the man but to be honest there were a lot of people gunning for him anyhow. He was a marked man.'

She nodded as she composed herself. 'Oh, it's so awful. Daddy has been over to Marshfield Manor to see his wife. Apparently, he did it somewhere in France days after the explosion.'

'I suppose he could no longer live with himself

after his neglect of the safety situation at the pit. My own father and a young lad lost their lives due to his negligence!' he said angrily. 'No matter how awful it is though, I'm not sorry he's dead.'

Annabelle looked at him with glazed eyes. 'How can you possibly say that? He leaves behind a wife and four young children.'

Harry shook his head. 'For them, I am truly sorry but many of the men and boys at the colliery will celebrate when they find out. He was a hard taskmaster who had a cruel streak running right through him like his father did.'

He lifted his brandy glass and drank the remainder of it in one go as it warmed his blood. 'The only thing I'm sorry for is that no one had the satisfaction of reaching the man first and killing him. I will never be able to forgive him for killing my father. He had blood on his hands. And I don't expect young Benny Brewster's family will much mind he's gone either!' He looked at Annabelle's dishevelled state which he realised he was responsible for as he'd projected his venom onto her. Feeling bad now as he'd forgotten for a moment that Josiah Wilkinson was like an uncle to her as he was her father's best friend, he paused a while before choosing his words carefully, 'Though, I do feel sorry for you, my dear, as you held him in high regard.'

She looked at him and nodded. 'I did indeed. He was my Godfather.'

'I didn't realise that,' his tone of voice softened. 'I'm not sorry the man's dead but I am sorry for your pain.'

Harry didn't know whether it was the right moment or not to mention something to her, but he figured as they might not see much more of one another that he'd be doing Cassie a favour if he found out what the state of play between Annabelle and Lord Bellingham had been. 'If I might be so bold as to ask, was there ever anything going on between you and Lord Bellingham?'

Annabelle's eyes flashed with indignation and her bottom lip trembled. 'How dare you ask me this, today of all days!'

He figured he'd hit a nerve but decided to persist. 'I did always suspect there was something.' He hadn't told Cassandra of this as he had no positive proof when she'd asked him.

Annabelle raised her chin in defiance. 'Is that the reason you've been holding off marrying me?'

He nodded slowly. 'I did love you once upon a time but I felt I could never compete with what you had with *him*.'

There was now a distinctive wobble in her voice as she nodded. 'Very well then, I shall tell you the truth. Yes, we did have something but then Cassandra came along and I was pushed out of the picture. He met up with me a few times afterwards but all his passion was directed towards her. I just could not compete. I am sorry if my feelings for Oliver got in the way of what we had for one another. Now it's out in the open, couldn't we start again, Harry?'

She looked at him with such pleading eyes. Her beauty sometimes robbed him of his breath, but it was the deceit and betrayal he found hardest to live with. Slowly, he shook his head. 'I'm sorry Annabelle, I could never trust you again. We both deserve someone who loves us back in equal measures and I no longer love you, I'm afraid.'

'This is the absolute worst day of my life!' she yelled, as her body shuddered and she gulped back the tears that were threatening to form again.

'It may feel that way right now,' he said, standing and proffering his handkerchief, which she took from his outstretched hand, 'but someday soon, you will realise this day was a turning point for you. You are so beautiful, Annabelle. Youth is still on your side and you will have learned a valuable lesson from this.'

'Being what?' she sniffed.

'That you have to handle love carefully. It is so fragile and if you abuse someone's trust it will slip through your fingers...' He walked over to the window and stared out down into the valley below where all manner of things were taking place. Each home having its own trials and tribulations and he sighed deeply. This was a momentous day indeed.

Chapter Seventeen

Jem and Clyde were sat in Aunt Dorothea's small but cosy living room in her cottage at Hocklea.

'Don't look so serious, the pair of you!' Auntie mocked from her armchair opposite. She leant over to stoke up the fire and then settled back into her chair. A shard of guilt coursed through Jem for raking up the past in case it unsettled the elderly woman.

'I'm afraid, Auntie...that it is a very serious situation.' He shot a sideways glance at his brother who looked equally concerned. Since relating the news to Clyde, his brother had been very quiet as if mulling things over this past few days. Clyde could not remember their mother as they'd both been informed she had died giving birth to him. If that was a lie then Jem thought it a cruel one to hold the lad responsible in a way for his mother's death.

'Oh?' Auntie quirked a silver brow in his direction. Then she clucked her teeth, a bad habit she'd acquired over the years. She sniffed loudly. 'Don't you think you ought to tell me about this serious situation, then?'

'It's like this,' said Jem sitting forward in his

seat. 'We've discovered that our parents weren't our parents, well at least they weren't Clyde's. I'm not sure about my actual parentage.'

'But of course they were your parents,' said Auntie giving a nervous laugh.

'No!' Jem held up the vertical palm of his hand. 'Please, we are grown men now and would like to know the truth.'

Auntie sighed. 'What I mean is to all intents and purposes they were your parents, they brought you up, apart from your mother who died when Clyde was born.' She glanced at him and he nodded.

'But that's not true though, is it? Clyde was William Hewitt's love child by Mrs Butterworth?'

'You know about that?'

'Yes, that's what I'm telling you I know and I have had that information from Harry Hewitt himself, who got it directly from his own mother!'

'Oh!' That had taken the wind out of Auntie's sails.

'Please, I implore you, Auntie. What is the real truth?'

Auntie Dorothea drew in a composing breath and let it out again. 'Jem, your parents were your real parents but yes, it's true, Clyde...you had different parents and they were the people Jem mentioned. You see, your father at the time was working for William Hewitt at the pit. He always liked and respected the man. William was in a sticky situation fathering a child out of wedlock and as Mrs Butterworth had some sort of a breakdown at that time, the child could have ended up a ward of the parish and placed in the workhouse...' she drew a breath. 'Out of the kindness of their hearts, your parents decided to take you on Clyde,' she glanced in his direction.

'H...how old w...was I then, Auntie?'

'Oh, only a few days old. A right little bonnie thing you was an' all. Your mother though had a difficult time giving birth to you. It didn't go smoothly at all and you almost died. You were what is known as a "blue baby" and needed to be brought back to life.'

Jem nodded. 'That's all well and good but what really happened to my mother since she didn't give birth to Clyde?'

'Ah, that's a sad tale indeed.' She glanced at Clyde again. 'She loved you like you were her own as did your father, but one day she was taken poorly with a fever. We never found out what it was but it took her away from us all for good. You were around six months old. So she had you as her own for that amount of time, lad. And she loved you so, both of you.'

Clyde nodded. 'What was my mother like, Auntie?'

'Oh, she was a very pretty woman, Clyde. Believe me, she loved you as if you were her own. You too, Jem. Though you were her child by birth. What I'm trying to say to you Clyde is, although they were not your birth parents, the amount of love and care they gave you more than made up for that.'

Seeming satisfied with what Auntie had told them, Clyde settled back in his armchair. Jem, though, was by no means satisfied and when Clyde later rose from his chair to check on the horse, angrily, Jem said, 'Then why were we given a tale that my mother had died in child-birth almost as though it was Clyde's fault?'

Auntie's previous animated expression changed to one of remorse. 'I am sorry about that, your father and I discussed it at the time and as your mother had passed away we decided it was the best tale to tell you boys at the time. To explain things.'

'Aye, a tale it was and all. All this time my poor brother, but he's not really my brother by blood now is he, has been thinking he caused our mother to die. That was heartless, cruel, I'd call it.'

'But, Jem. It weren't like that at all. We didn't think for a minute you'd think such a thing, in fact, I think your father told you your mother died after Clyde was born. He was six months old.'

'Somehow or another over the years, and I am too young to remember what happened, some-one must have said that Clyde caused her death as that's what we've both always thought.'

'I don't know who that person was, but it

wouldn't have been me nor your father. I am sorry you've both formed that impression over the years.' Her green eyes looked full of hurt at the accusation and he realised he'd hit a chord with her.

'And while I'm thinking about it, after our mother died why wasn't Clyde returned to his rightful mother then? She obviously got better over the years. She wouldn't be running a guest house otherwise.'

Auntie bit her bottom lip as tears filled her eyes. 'The truth is, Jem, Clyde's mother doesn't know he's alive and well.'

'What do you mean?' He stared at his aunt, realising he wasn't going to like the answer she was about to give.

'William Hewitt told her Clyde had been given to a couple who went to live overseas.'

'What on earth? How cruel is that? What possessed the man?'

She shook her head. 'I think he thought it for the best as she seemed so distressed when he was born, she was on the verge of lunacy at the time, even tried to kill herself, she did.'

'If that's the case we can do something about it now. I'm going to take Clyde to see his real mother like he should have been taken to her years since! Auntie, I am so angry I don't know if I'll be coming here ever again!' He raised his voice and then stormed out of the cottage, slamming the door behind him.

Clyde turned to look at his brother. 'Has Auntie sent you out to fetch us in for tea?' he asked with a big grin on his face.

'No, Clyde. We're not stopping—we're heading home. There's someone I'd like you to meet!'

***

When Lizzie Butterworth was introduced to her only son and indeed her only child, she'd been delighted. She'd hugged Clyde so tightly and hadn't wanted to let him go. Jem had watched on but now although he was happy for him, felt that maybe a gulf had emerged between them. They were no longer blood. Clyde now had a new parent and an older, eloquent brother. A feeling of sadness rose to the surface. An indescribable pain that gnawed inside of him. It was almost as though the past wasn't real any longer. Yet, deep down he knew he'd done the right thing in getting the truth out of his Auntie. At least she was still blood even if he didn't much feel like associating with her right now.

Clyde had been delighted to meet with his mother and looking at them together, Jem realised they were mother and son as they were so alike as they stood beside one another. They had the same dark hair and swarthy complexion.

Now all Jem had to do was relay all he'd discovered to Harry.

***

It was Christmas eve midday when Harry turned up at Hawthorn Cottage with his mother.

Polly allowed them in through the door and she shot a sideways glance at Cassie.

Cassie drew in a breath and let it out again not knowing what sort of reception she'd now have from the woman. Expecting to see the strong, determined chin stuck in the air and the beady anger behind her eyes as well as hearing the woman's bombastic tone of voice, Cassie was flabbergasted that she detected none of those. Edna Hewitt looked a shadow of her former herself. In her widow's weeds, her skin looked almost alabaster in tone, her grey eyes uncertain and wary, her voice carried a tremor to it as she said cordially, 'Thank you for inviting us to your home, Cassandra.' Cassie almost fainted with shock. It was the first time the woman had ever addressed her by name.

After a pause of not knowing quite what to say, Cassie smiled and said, 'You are most welcome. I was most sorry to hear of your husband's death.'

Edna nodded in her direction. 'It was so unexpected.' The woman swallowed hard.

'Here, come and sit near the fireside with me, you must be perished,' Cassie said kindly. Then turning to Polly she said, 'Would you please fetch us a pot of tea and some fruit bread, lightly buttered, Pol?'

Polly, who had a look of uncertainty in her eyes, nodded. No doubt the woman was concerned as every time she'd encountered Edna

Hewitt so far, there had been trouble, but now Cassie realised the woman was broken. The shock of her husband's death had been bad enough but to lose everything else too, had all been too much for her. It had been different when Cassie had lost her husband and all the wealth as she'd never been wealthy to begin with, it was just like taking a step back onto familiar ground from the days when she'd had to struggle before she'd met his lordship. But Edna Hewitt, on the other hand, was used to a particular lifestyle.

Edna sat in an armchair opposite Cassie, while Harry drew up a dining chair from the table and sat between them as if about to umpire some sort of game, but the truth was, there no longer was a game. Edna was down on her luck and this was no time to treat Cassie badly as she had done in the past as Cassie's benevolence towards her was astounding.

'Have you eaten today?' Cassie searched Edna's eyes.

'No, I couldn't face anything this morning to tell you the truth,' Edna said in a weak, trembling voice as she met her gaze.

'Then you must have a slice of fruit loaf. It's something we serve at the tea room and is very popular with our customers.'

Edna nodded. 'There was a time when you generously offered me the chance to eat and drink something there but I refused, and for that, I apologise, sincerely. It was most ungracious of me, particularly as you were just setting out. You must have felt as I do right now having lost your husband. I'm afraid, my dear, I treated you badly. I am, oh, so very sorry.'

Then Edna began to weep.

***

Harry sat in the offices of Walker Brothers and Sons Solicitors with Nathaniel Walker seated opposite him across his large walnut imposing desk.

'So, you mean to tell me that there's nothing my mother can do to contest my father's will?'

Nathaniel shook his head. 'No, I'm afraid there isn't. Your father to all accounts and purposes was of sound mind when he made that will, it was properly witnessed at these offices by myself and my father.'

Harry frowned. 'But it's so unfair to cut her off like that. Surely there must be some sort of legal loophole?' Harry realised he was clutching at straws by the look in Nathaniel's eyes.

'No, there isn't. Now if you were living in Scotland it would be a different matter but in England and Wales the law allows someone to leave their home, money, belongings, etcetera to whomever they wish!'

'Then the law is a pompous ass!' said Harry fiercely as he gritted his teeth and his hands balled themselves into fists on the armrests of his chair.

Nathaniel let out a long breath as he fiddled around with his fountain pen, then he looked across his desk at Harry. 'The 1837 Wills Act, and the 1857 Court of Probate Act reformed an inheritance process that has been both archaic and chaotic over the years. It doesn't seem fair I grant you, but those were your father's wishes. I heard about a client who left a silver sixpence to his wife of thirty-five years, the rest he left to some lady he'd had a dalliance with when he was young. To add insult to injury, he also left a substantial sum of money to his butler who'd been with him for years. But it was all perfectly legal and above board.'

'I see,' said Harry, raising his eyebrows with incredulity. 'So, it appears there is nothing Mother can do but accept the cottage and basic allowance he left her?' Nathaniel nodded.

Harry frowned. 'She has little choice but that cottage is in a state and will need repairs.'

'We can give her some of her allowance right now, if that's easier for her?'

Harry shook his head. 'No, thank you. It will eat into the money she needs to live on. I'm going to undertake some of the repairs myself.' He hadn't asked Jem as yet but he was hoping he and Clyde would help him as they were both handymen.

'I'm glad you've got plans and they sound sensible.'

'Before I leave, there is something I need to discuss with you?'

Nathaniel laid down the pen and sat forward in his seat. 'Yes?' he linked his fingers on the desk.

'It's about the third party who is to take over Hewitt Hall, who is it?'

Nathaniel's eyes suddenly became guarded. 'I'm afraid I can't reveal that yet until the reading of your father's will. That person has not been informed they are to inherit the property as yet.'

'It's Mrs Butterworth!' Harry blurted out suddenly. 'Just like that client you mentioned who left something to his old love and his butler. She was my father's mistress, it all makes sense!'

Nathaniel shook his head vehemently. 'There's no use playing guessing games.'

'Very well,' said Harry standing, 'out of respect for this firm I shan't press it. I'll wait for the reading of the will. Monday the third of January?'

Nathaniel nodded. 'Yes, that is correct. At half-past ten at these offices.' He smiled nervously. 'Will you take a drink with me before you leave?'

Harry shook his head. 'I think not, I have things to attend to but thank you for your time all the same,' he said curtly. He rose from his chair and stretched his arm across the table to shake Nathaniel's hand. He was so angry he realised he needed to leave now before he punched a hole in the wall. It wasn't Nathaniel's fault of course but he felt betrayed to know someone he had considered a close acquaintance over the years had known something he had not been privy to himself. Harry badly needed some fresh air and couldn't wait to get out into the frosty air onto the pavement outside.

***

Jem and Harry were discussing "the parentage business" as they'd now termed it over a pint of ale at The Ploughman's Arms.

'So, your aunt and father deceived you both over the years?' Harry said sympathetically.

Jem nodded. 'Oh, aye. But let's not forget it was the same for you an' all. Even worse I reckon in a way.'

'Maybe.' Harry stroked his chin. 'I think the three of us have suffered in a way and don't forget, although you and Clyde are not blood-related, you *are* brothers and I'll never try to come between you both. You have a bond going on there.'

'Aye, I suppose so,' said Jem relaxing. He was beginning to think that maybe Harry wasn't such a bad fella after all. 'You should have seen Clyde's face though earlier when he was reunited with his real mother. It was a bloomin' picture and so was Mrs Butterworth's.'

'Hard to imagine that the poor woman had her son living so near and she never knew though. I really don't understand why my father did that.'

'My auntie said Mrs Butterworth lost her mind at the time and tried to take her own life so it's my guess that maybe he thought it was for the best. He probably thought she'd never cope with an infant to care for.'

'Possibly. So how are things now between you and your aunt since she was forced to tell you the truth.'

Jem shook his head sadly. 'Not so good. I got angry when I spoke to her and maybe said some things I shouldn't have but the red mist had descended.'

'I dare say she was only trying to protect you lads at the time.'

Jem nodded. 'I suppose so. I'm thinking of calling to see her tomorrow to apologise. I made it sound as though I'd never speak to her again.'

'That bad, was it?'

Jem nodded. 'I'm afraid so. She's all we have in the world left of our family and we are all she has.'

'Then make sure you do apologise tomorrow,' said Harry sagely. 'Don't leave it too late.'

Jem shook his head. 'I won't, no fear.'

Harry was just about to summon the barman to bring another couple of pints of ale to their table when he noticed Jem staring at a young man who wore a leather waistcoat and striped shirt with the sleeves rolled up. Around his neck, he wore a red-spotted cotton neckerchief, tied in a knot. 'Who's that you're staring out, Jem?'

Jem averted his gaze back to Harry. 'It's Charlie Baxter. He's a rum sort.' He took a swig of his ale and set his tankard down on the table, wiping the beery foam from his lips with the back of his hand. 'I didn't like the way he acted towards Cassie the night our Clyde and her daughter Emily went missing in a snow storm. We both came in here and he was right obnoxious towards her.'

'How?' Harry frowned.

'Saying dreadful things about her and referring to the cottage as a "Love Nest" when she lived there previously and was his lordship's mistress.'

'I see,' Harry nodded.

'Yes, and when we left here, she told me he'd been eyeing her up, treating her like a piece of meat.'

'Maybe the man needs teaching a lesson,' said Harry with a glint in his eye.

'Aye, maybe.' A salacious smile spread over Jem's face.

'I'll lure him outside and you can do the rest. I won't join in as I think it's wrong to outnumber someone, but it will be a fair fight if it's one on one.'

Jem nodded eagerly. 'I'll have the greatest pleasure in wiping the smile from his chops!'

Harry grinned. 'I'll go and speak to him then.' He stood and made his way over to where Charlie was standing at the bar. 'Hello, my man,' Harry greeted. 'You wouldn't happen to know where I can find a good guest house around these parts, would you?'

Charlie's eyes lit up as if he were appraising the situation of a toff addressing him. In Harry's mind, he guessed the young man was keen to make a bob or two from him. 'Well, it just so happens, I know of a place. I'll show you there myself.'

Harry nodded gratefully. 'That's most kind of you. Would you like a drink so I can return the favour?'

Charlie nodded eagerly and instead of ordering another pint of ale he chose a glass of rum. It was obvious he wanted to get as much as he could out of Harry and Harry was more than happy to take the bait.

Several drinks later, Jem watched Charlie stagger his way out of the pub with Harry at his side, then he followed on discretely behind as he waited for Harry to leave the man to the mercy of Jem's fists. Whistling, Harry made his way to the book store, where he could watch in darkness from the window. It wasn't in his nature to make something an unfair fight. The young man had besmirched Cassandra's name and made her feel uncomfortable that night that Emily went missing. Life was difficult enough for her anyhow, so it rankled with him that she should be humiliated in a pub full of men like that. Hopefully, from now on Charlie would learn his lesson and keep his lips buttoned up.

A thought flashed through Harry's mind, why was Jem so wound up that he needed to punch the fellow? He figured he must have a lot of feeling for her to do so, and then it suddenly occurred to him, Jem was in love with her. Why hadn't he noticed this before? No wonder he'd acted so odd with him when they'd first met. He'd been jealous of him and the attention he was giving to Cassie. Harry grinned. The sly old dog! He'd do no worse than to marry someone like her, she was the most delightful young woman he'd ever met in his life. Not as young and immature as Annabelle, more worldly-wise, granted, but she was the kind of woman any man would be proud to have on his arm. He swallowed hard. *Not the marrying kind then, Harry? Then why can't you stop thinking about her yourself?*

Chapter Eighteen

Harry allowed Jem in through the book shop door later. 'You weren't gone long?' Harry furrowed a brow.

'I couldn't do it,' he said sighing. 'Instead, I just gave him a strict talking to. I didn't feel it fair as he'd already had a few drinks before we'd arrived by the look of it. He did apologise though and said he shouldn't have spoken to Cassandra like that as she was, in his words, "a very nice lady."'

'But what would have made him change his mind like that?' Harry said in an incredulous tone.

'Apparently his mother and aunt have been using the tea room lately and they've spoken highly of her!'

'Oh, I see,' said Harry. 'That's a good thing then. Maybe the villagers are starting to accept her at last and no longer viewing her as a scarlet woman!'

'She was never that!' said Jem angrily.

Harry smiled. 'No, of course she wasn't, old boy. I just meant that's how they perceived her.'

Jem visibly relaxed. 'That's all right then.' He returned the smile.

'Look, why don't you sit down? I'm staying here tonight on a mattress I've brought from the house and Mother is staying with Cassandra and her family.'

'Aye, I'll stop for a bit but don't want to leave Clyde too long.' He flopped down in an armchair and Harry took the other.

Harry sat forward in his seat and looked intently at Jem. 'You're in love with Cassandra, aren't you, Jem?'

Jem's eyes widened. 'How'd you work that out?'

'Because it all makes sense to me now, the way you treated me when you first met me.'

Jem nodded slowly. 'Very perceptive of you!'

'Then why don't you ask her to marry you?'

'I already have and she turned me down.'

Jem's reply stunned Harry. 'Really? What reason or reasons did she give?'

'That the timing was wrong. I think it's too soon after his lordship's death. She also mentioned something about two failed marriages and that she'd fail at this one too.'

'Oh, I see,' said Harry thoughtfully as he nodded. 'Maybe your timing was a little off. I would give it another try at another time. She's going to need a father for those babies and you both seem to work well together.'

'We do. I wouldn't have gone into business with her otherwise. But I've been thinking lately, I'm not the man for her really. She needs someone with a little more class, someone a bit like yourself.'

Harry opened his mouth and closed it again. 'But I'm definitely not the marrying kind. I'm a cad, a bounder of sorts!'

'Of course you're not. You're a fine fellow. Now her last two husbands people might use those words to describe them, but you, never.'

'I'm honoured and I appreciate your kind words. I've only just broken off a long relationship with Annabelle though. Out of the frying pan and into the fire...' he said wistfully.

'Cassie, though, is nothing like your Annabelle. She knows her own mind and she'll fight passionately for what she wants in life.'

'Yes, and don't I just know it. The ructions she's had with my mother of late but now the pair are sitting chatting at the cottage as if they are old friends. If she can win mother over she can win anyone over.'

'True,' agree Jem. 'I know this might sound daft coming from someone like me, but I feel as if you are now my brother too, Harry.'

'That's not so daft though as we both have Clyde in common.'

'Aye. So you won't mind if I sometimes refer to you in that manner?'

'No, of course not. I think you and I bonded that night we both passed out here. Speaking of which, I think there's a bottle of whiskey left, let's raise a toast to Christmas, shall we?'

'I'd like that but then I'll get back to Clyde, don't want to leave him alone too long. Hey, I've just thought of something, you're spending the night here all alone?'

'Yes. But I don't mind too much. I'm staying here as the house is being sorted out for the new owner and we have to vacate in a couple of weeks anyhow, that's why Mother is stopping at Cassie's cottage until the home my father left her is ready. I was going to ask if you and Clyde would help me renovate it as it's in a poor state of repair?'

'We'd be honoured to help out, yes, of course we would. What I was going to suggest though if your mother is nicely settled at the cottage, is if you'd like to stop with me and Clyde at ours? You'll have a bed to sleep in and you can get to know your brother a little better.'

'I'd really like that,' said Harry with tears in his eyes.

And so it was arranged that Harry pack up his gear that night and stay at Rose cottage with his 'two' brothers. Before leaving though, he wanted to check in with his mother at Cassie's home. He was delighted to find her in animated conversation with Emily at the table when he called.

'Everything all right here?' he cast her a glance.

'Shouldn't it be?' His mother glowered at him and then he realised she was jesting with him as she had a twinkle in her eyes.

'Auntie Edna is going to make some clothes for

Raggy Anne!' Emily said excitedly, drawing out the doll from behind her back.

'I didn't know you could sew, Mother?' Harry said in astonishment.

'There are a lot of things you don't know about me,' declared his mother. 'I wasn't born with a silver spoon in my mouth, you know! In fact, we lived in a place rather like this when I was a young girl...'

He noticed a wistful look in her eyes. It was obvious to him in that moment that living with his father, who had acquired a lot of wealth over the years, hadn't exactly been good for her. Maybe in some respects, she'd have been happier remaining poor even if she'd had to struggle to make ends meet.

Polly, who had been hovering in the doorway after letting him in, said, 'I'd invite you, Jem and Clyde here for Christmas dinner tomorrow but as you can see it's rather cramped.'

At that point, Cassie entered the room. 'I've just had the most marvellous idea,' she declared. 'We could all eat together and it needn't be cramped at all.'

Aunt Bertha looked up from where she'd been snoozing by the fireside. 'Pardon?'

'Yes, if we all dined at the tea room instead. Polly could even cook the goose in the oven there. And best of all it's only just up the road.'

Polly smiled. 'It's a nice idea but there's no way that goose will stretch between eight of us!'

Harry chuckled. 'I think I have it,' he said excitedly. 'Jem's outside waiting with the horse and cart as I'll be stopping at his place tonight instead of at the shop. Just you wait here...' He dashed out of the door.

'Well we weren't planning on going on anywhere!' said Aunt Bertha and everyone laughed. Then they waited with expectation for Harry to return.

Finally, Harry burst in through the door, his eyes shining bright. 'Jem says he and Clyde would definitely like to join us but can his Aunt Dorothea come along too?'

Cassie nodded eagerly, wishing she'd purchased another goose as well or maybe even that huge turkey she'd noticed in the poulterer's window.

Then Harry added, 'But don't fret, Jem says he's already bought a goose and a chicken as he had been planning to dine with his aunt. They'd recently fallen out and after he drops me off at the cottage, he's off to see her about dining together tomorrow as he intends making it up to her.'

'That's splendid!' said Cassie clasping her hands together. 'Let's pray it doesn't snow tonight so we can all be together tomorrow...'

They all nodded and murmured in agreement.

***

The following morning Polly was up bright and early to cook the poultry. Jem had already been around on his horse and cart to drop off the extra goose and chicken. His aunt had been delighted to be invited along for the festivities and even more delighted that her nephew had found it in his heart to forgive her for what he'd perceived as a deceitful act, though now he said he understood why she and his father had acted as they did. The tea room windows were steamed up as the large plum pudding Polly had left to mature during the past few weeks, bubbled away on the hob.

Three tables were placed end to end so that all might sit around one big table later and Cassie had even found three matching table cloths and candle centrepieces for the festive touch.

By midday, all was nicely underway. Even the Christmas presents had been transported to the tea room and set beneath the tree. Edna Hewitt had gladly looked after Emily while Polly, Cassie and Aunt Bertha had trooped back and forth between the cottage and the tea room, their arms full of everything that was needed.

Finally, by the stroke of one, everyone had arrived and all were ready to dine. What merriment there was as they all chatted with one another around the table and Emily showed off her new doll to anyone who was interested. Both conversation and company were good and Edna, in particular, seemed glad of it.

From time to time, Harry caught Cassandra's eye across the table and she wondered what was going through his mind. She had worried that maybe Jem might get sentimental and after a couple of glasses of rum punch might propose again, but that never happened. In fact, he made a point of saying after the meal that she was as close as a sister to him.

Clyde was in his element having both brothers with him and Auntie invited someone along and as a surprise for him, Rose Barton appeared later at the tea room after they'd all dined. Cassie had taken it upon herself to invite the girl over to be in Clyde's company. Rose had already dined at home and seemed pleased to see Clyde.

Finally, the gas light was dimmed as Polly brought out the pudding on a silver platter after setting fire to the brandy it was soaked in. Everyone gasped as they watched the flames ignite. It really was a spectacular moment.

Then when the light was turned back on, Jem left the room for a moment and returned with a fiddle beneath his arm.

'I never knew you could play?' Cassie arched a brow of surprise.

Jem grinned. 'Aye, I do an' all. Want to hear something?'

She nodded eagerly.

'My brother's a man of m...many talents...' said Clyde.

Then Jem struck up the song, *Here we come a-wassailing* as everyone sang along and stamped their feet.

Then Harry bowed and took Cassandra's hand and looking up, asked, 'May I have this dance with you?'

She nodded shyly and he took her hand and danced so gently with her she felt like she was floating on air. She didn't want to overdo it but thought one dance would not harm as long as it wasn't too strenuous. Then Auntie was up dancing with Emily, and Clyde with Rose, until everyone was on their feet. It was a most joyous moment indeed and anyone passing the tea room outside might think they'd partaken of the drink to excess but the truth was they were all high on life.

When the song had finished Harry escorted Cassie back to her seat while everyone else carried on dancing and he sat beside her. She looked at him with questioning eyes and he smiled. No words were needed at all, it was a comfortable moment that passed between them and without being seen, he took her hand and held it to his lips as he kissed it lightly and then held her hand while everyone else was oblivious to what was going on between the pair as they carried on dancing. When the others returned to the table, the pair drew away from one another. For that part of Christmas day was the most special of all to Cassie and she'd never forget it as long as she lived. As she gazed wistfully towards the window onto the street outside, she noticed it had started snowing. It was the most perfect Christmas day ever.

***

For days afterwards, everyone kept talking about that special Christmas day. In the days between Christmas and the New Year, the tea shop remained open though custom was sparse as most people were spending time with their families. It was the same at the book shop too, so sometimes, Cassie would leave Polly in charge while she took a pot of tea or coffee over to chat with Harry. They had grown very close of late and in Cassie's heart, convinced though that she was some sort of Jonah as far as relationships were concerned, she feared that someday soon the spell would break and she'd bring about some misfortune once again. But for time being, things were going well. Harry never put any pressure on her at all. At the back of her mind was the fact he'd told her on more than one occasion that he wasn't the marrying kind.

New Year's Eve proved quiet compared with Christmas day itself and Cassie was happy to spend it quietly at home as now she found by early evening with the advancing pregnancy that she was thoroughly exhausted. Edna was still residing at the cottage and to be fair to the woman, much to Cassie's surprise, she helped out whenever she could. It was out of the blue that New Year's evening that Edna sat down on Cassie's bed and taking her hand said softly, 'I think my son really likes you, Cassandra...'

Cassie nodded and smiled. 'I like him too.'

'I've seen the way he looks at you. He can't take his eyes off you. He was never like that when he was with Annabelle.

Cassie chewed her bottom lip. 'It wouldn't be fair though, Edna...'

'What wouldn't be?'

'Expecting him to marry me. I'm twice wed and with another man's babies on the way.'

'Ah but,' said Edna, 'they are his Lordship's babies that's a different thing entirely. They were conceived in wedlock and Oliver was a friend of Harry's. Not a close one admittedly, but they knew one another well enough.'

Cassie nodded. 'But even so, he's told me often enough that he's not the marrying kind.'

Edna threw back her head and laughed. 'Don't you believe him! His father spun me that line too but I managed to reel him in.'

Cassie smiled. 'So, there was a time when you and William were happy together?'

'Oh, yes.' Edna's eyes were shiny and bright as she recalled the past. 'We happiest in the early days, but then...' her voice faded to barely a whisper, 'but then life got in the way. I'm afraid I didn't pay him the attention that was needed when Harry was born and he found comfort elsewhere.' There was a catch now to Edna's voice and Cassie's heart went out to her. She stretched out across the eiderdown and took the woman's hand in hers and gave it a gentle squeeze of reassurance. It was a moment of complete under-standing between both women and the know-ledge that although 1875 was almost over, both had a lot to look forward to.

***

The first day of January 1876, started out as a mist-filled day and although seasonably cold, at least it wasn't slippery underfoot as Cassie now feared falling so much. She had done well to keep both pregnancies safe inside her by resting up but she'd once known of a pregnant woman who had slipped on the icy cobbles outside her house and gone into labour straight afterwards. Thank-fully, her baby was born with no problems but Cassie didn't want to chance such things.

She was going into the tea room today, even though it wasn't open officially until tomorrow to help Polly clean the place up ready for a new year of trading. She glanced across at the book shop but all was in darkness and she figured that Harry had decided not to open today and she didn't blame him either. He'd gone away for the New Year to stay with some friends in London. Their home was fantastic by all accounts, and Walter, his friend, held a passion for hunting. There'd been a hunt planned for New Year's Day so she assumed Harry had stayed put for that. She couldn't abide the sport herself, all those nobs in red jackets hounding a poor little fox. Though Oliver had told her on more than one oc-casion when she'd protested at his participation in the sport that he was trying to keep that "poor little fox" away from their hen house. But no matter what he said she still thought hounding the fox for miles and then those selfsame hounds tearing it to pieces, extremely cruel in her book. She'd said nothing about her feelings about that to Harry though as she felt it was not her place to do so.

As she rinsed out a clean rag in a bowl of soapy water to wash down the tiles and paintwork she wondered what he was doing right now at this very moment.

***

Harry yawned. There had been too many late nights at Walter's house since he'd arrived and now he was expected to get dressed and go on a New Year's Day hunt with them all. Apparently, it had been a Winstanley tradition dating back to the days when Walter's great grandfather had occupied the house. Hunting wasn't something he was keen on himself but one of the male servants had laid out a red hunting jacket, stiff black hat, jodhpurs and leather boots for him in his bedroom. Now he stared at the items aghast. How was he to get out of this? He'd much rather be back at Wakeford checking on his mother's welfare and of course on Cassandra's too.

He'd never thought he'd be missing her like this, it was almost as though his heart yearned to be with hers. He was still deliberating about the situation when he almost collided with Walter, who was fully attired in hunting gear, outside his room.

'Ah, old chap, I thought I'd check you're ready to go but I can see you're not?' He raised a quizzical brow.

Drawing in a deep breath and exhaling, Harry said, 'The truth of it is, I don't much care for hunting...'

'It's not that though is it?' Walter looked him in the eye.

Harry shook his head. 'No, not just that. I've had a lovely time here, honestly, and you and Amelia have been the most wonderful hosts but I feel I need to return home to check on my mother.'

Walter chuckled. 'It's not just your mother either. It's that young widow you have designs on, isn't it? Oliver Bellingham's lady.'

Harry nodded, hardly daring to admit it. 'Yes, I have feelings for her.'

'And you always told me you're not the marrying kind!' He slapped Harry on his forearm with friendly affection.

'I know I did. And I kept Annabelle waiting long enough, but the feelings I have for Cassandra are much stronger than that.'

'I see,' said Walter, his face looking serious now. 'Then you must go to her then and tell her how you feel about her. Life is far too short. The love of a good woman is what you need, old fellow!'

Harry relaxed and smiled. 'Thank you, Walter!'

'I'll send one of my men up to pack for you and ask someone to get your coach ready, shall I?'

'Yes, please do that,' said Harry returning to his room with a big grin on his face.

Closing the door behind himself, he then threw himself on the bed yelling, *Home James and don't spare the horses!*

Chapter Nineteen

Darkness was falling fast when Harry's coach approached Wakeford. It was that time of day when shapes of buildings, trees and mountains became silhouetted against the clear sky as stars started to emerge like tiny diamonds on an ever-darkening sky. Something inside him had been niggling for a long time to unfold his feelings towards Cassandra. It wasn't something he'd normally do but then again, Cassandra was no normal woman, as indeed, she was exceptional in his book.

The street was quiet as if a hush had fallen over the place, almost as though the little village was holding its breath to hear and not to disturb what Harry had come to say. The coach drew up outside the tea room and after Harry alighted, he had a word with the driver telling him not to wait but to return to Rose Cottage with his luggage. He realised that the staff who had worked for his family up until now were in a state of shock about the fact a new owner was to take over and they must now fear losing their positions at Hewitt Hall if the owner didn't wish to take them on, but he'd already advised them to stay put for time being as until the reading of the will (which was to take place in two days' time), no one would be any the wiser. He had promised them that even if they were dismissed by the new owner that they would be paid up until that day. So for time being, everyone opted to stay put.

He smiled as he glanced in the tea room window, Cassie was alone and appeared to be stacking some crockery behind the counter. She looked breathtakingly beautiful, pregnancy obviously suited her.

The doorbell jangled as he entered the shop and removed his hat.

***

Cassie was alone in the tea room, having just dismissed Polly to return to the cottage and make the evening meal, while she tidied up the few pieces of crockery left behind by the last customers. There had been few customers all day as the tea room wasn't officially open, but Cassie felt she needed to keep busy, the idea being to keep her mind off the fact of how much she was missing Harry, even though he'd only been gone a few days.

The doorbell jangled and she was about to say, 'Sorry, but we're closed!' When she turned to see Harry approaching her with his top hat in his hand, looking astonishingly handsome. His eyes illuminated with warmth as he held both hands out to her and she took them in her own.

'You've returned,' she said breathlessly. He nodded and then laid his hat down on one of the tables. 'You're here to check on the book shop? I'm sorry to say but custom has been sparse today...'

He shook his head. His dark floppy fringe falling across his forehead, he removed his leather gloves from his hands and placed them inside his hat, then swept his fringe back off his face with his bare hand. 'No, it's you've I've come to check on.'

'Me?'

'Yes, Cassandra. It was while I was away from you that I realised I couldn't bear to be parted from you for a second longer.'

As much as she didn't like to admit it, the same had been true for her too. 'I know just what you mean, Harry,' she whispered.

Then he dropped to his knees and looked up at her with pleading, hopeful eyes. 'I don't have a ring to give you at the moment and I can't ask your father for your hand, but I hope he'd approve...' he swallowed hard. 'Cassandra, would you do me the honour of becoming my wife?'

Tears filled her eyes and she heard herself gasp, 'Yes, yes, Harry. I would love to become your wife, but one thing I must ask you first?'

He nodded towards her. 'Anything.'

'You're not proposing because you feel sorry for me and the predicament I'm in? You always said you're not the marrying kind...'

He shook his head and smiled, his eyes crinkling at the corners. 'No, not at all. I think I've loved you from the moment I first set eyes on you if I'm being blatantly honest. The day you walked into the book shop and took me to task as you feared I'd take your trade away from you!'

'And I think,' she replied, 'I loved you too from that moment you made me laugh with your quip about sticky jam buns!'

He pulled himself up onto his feet and drew her towards him, so that she felt secure against his chest and then he lifted her chin with his thumb and forefinger so they were gazing into one another's eyes, and what she saw there was pure love for her. He brought his lips to meet with hers and kissed her passionately as he held her in his embrace.

Outside the tea room window stood Jem and Clyde who had returned to the shop to drop off some furniture they'd purchased in Drisdale. Jem turned to his brother and said, 'See, what did I tell you, Clyde. I knew those two were meant for one another...'

Clyde nodded and grinned.

***

The following day, Cassie took Emily for her first day at the church school. Although her daughter had been looking forward to starting there, she became overwhelmingly shy when she arrived and saw all the other children, most of whom were older than herself, but a young classroom assistant reassured Cassie that she'd keep an eye on her daughter, and by the time she was to collect her that afternoon, she'd have settled in nicely.

Cassie had knelt to kiss Emily's cheek reassuring her that all would be well and she'd be back to collect her later, then she made her way to the tea room where Polly had things underway, as yet, she hadn't told a soul about Harry's marriage proposal.

When she entered the tea room, she untied the ribbons of her bonnet and removed her shawl and placed them on a shelf beneath the counter. She suddenly noticed Polly giving her sideways glances and Rose seemed to be smiling rather a lot. Although Cassie was helping out once again, she didn't tend to stay too long but rested up more as Rose took over her duties.

'Is there anything going on?' Cassie looked at Polly.

'I was about to ask you the same thing!' Polly chuckled.

'What do you mean?' Cassie raised her brow with puzzlement.

'According to Clyde, he and Jem saw Harry on his knees to you through the tea room window when I'd gone home last night?' Polly's eyes held a mischievous twinkle.

For a fleeting moment, Cassie felt annoyed but then she released the tension with a chuckle. 'I suppose you were all about to find out at some time anyhow...'

Rose approached the counter with interest, placing her elbows on top of it as she gazed at Cassie.

'Be off with you, girl!' Scolded Polly.

'It's all right, I don't mind,' Cassie said beaming. 'Yes, Clyde had got it right. Harry did propose.'

'And you said "Yes"?' Polly stared at her.

'I did!' Cassie nodded.

Rose almost swooned with the excitement of it all as her eyes glazed over. 'Ooh, he's ever so good looking,' she said.

Polly cast her a glance. 'As long as you're happy. I know I said about lionesses protecting their young a while back and that you need no man, but in this case, I think Harry will be good for you. He's strong and dependable and it's obvious he thinks the world of you.' She leaned over to peck Cassie on the cheek.

'Thank you, Polly. That means a lot coming from you.'

'What about Edna though?' Polly angled her head to one side.

'There's no real problem there as it was she who told me on New Year's Eve that Harry thought a lot of me and she hinted about marriage.'

'I see,' said Polly. 'So, you honestly hadn't considered it before now?'

'Not really...' she lowered her voice to say

something, but Polly realising she needed to speak in confidence looked at Rose and sent her to lay the tables. While the girl was out of ear-shot, Cassie whispered, 'After what happened with Jem, no, I hadn't considered it. I mean I knew Harry liked me as we have drawn close to one another, particularly on Christmas day when we danced together. It was while he was away though staying with a friend that we both missed one another madly.'

Polly laid a comforting hand on Cassie's shoulder. 'Then I think it is meant to be...'

***

The following morning, Harry was sat with his mother in the solicitors' office of Walker Brothers and Sons. It was twenty-five past ten in the morning. So far, only they were there and they wondered if the new owner of Hewitt Hall would arrive.

Harry glanced at Nathaniel who smiled at him. 'Would you both like a glass of sherry or a cup of tea?' he offered.

'Sherry, please,' said Edna, and Harry nodded in agreement.

The clerk was sent off to fetch the sherry and as the large wall clock ticked loudly, Harry's eyes were on the door. A couple of minutes later, it opened suddenly and he startled expecting Mrs Butterworth to emerge, but it was the clerk with a silver tray in his hand containing several schooners of sherry and he handed them a glass each, as he shot them a wry smile. Harry had never been keen on the fellow and felt like wiping that supercilious grin off his face but he was polite as they accepted the drinks.

As the clock chimed the half-hour, there was a knock on the door and the clerk went to open it. Harry looked on with surprise as as Tom Langstone, foreman of the pit, entered with his flat cap in his hand.

'Do take a seat,' said the clerk.

Harry and his mother exchanged glances. Surely this wasn't the new owner of Hewitt Hall?

Tom smiled nervously and took a seat which was set in a row of three behind the pair. Then there was a second knock and Clyde and Jem entered.

'Sorry,' apologised Jem. 'We received a letter just this morning that had been delivered to the wrong address and it requests that we attend here today.'

Harry stared in astonishment at the pair. Of course, it was fitting that Clyde attend here, but Jem had said "we" so maybe there was something for him in the will too.

The tray of sherry was offered around and everyone accepted a glass, and then Nathaniel took a seat at his desk with the clerk by his side. He shuffled some papers and then clearing his throat began, 'You are all aware as we have written to you to inform you that as beneficiaries you are welcome to attend the reading of "The Last

Will and Testament of William Montague Hewitt" who latterly resided at Hewitt Hall in the parish of Wakeford in the county of Marshfield.'

The attendees sat forward in their seats to listen with avid interest.

Nathaniel continued, 'There are one or two beneficiaries who have declined to attend today either due to the distance they would need to travel, ill-health or other reasons and that is their prerogative, as it is by no means law that any beneficiary has to attend the reading of a will.'

Harry guessed that some mentioned there would be his father's family, particularly his aunt from London. She had made it to his father's funeral but to make another journey would be too much for her advanced years within such a short space of time.

'Then I shall endeavour to begin the reading of the will,' said Nathaniel solemnly. *"I, the undersigned, William Montague of Hewitt Hall, am of sound mind on this day dated the sixth day of June in the year of our Lord, 1875. This is my only will to date..."*

There was something significant about that date sixth of June and Harry couldn't for the life of him recall what it was but he figured it would come back to him soon enough.

Nathaniel continued, *"To my wife, Edna Hewitt, I bequeath a two-bedroom cottage at Drisdale and a regular food and clothing allowance for her to live* on at a sum of two pounds a year for the remainder of her life..."

Harry cast a glance at his mother who sniffed but stared blankly ahead, it seemed to him she was now prepared to accept that her old life had gone for good.

"To my son, Harold Edgar Hewitt, I bequeath the shops at number 3 and 4 Rowan Road in the parish of Wakeford in the county of Marshfield, my coach and two horses, and shares in the lead mine at Hackingdale."

Harry gasped. He'd recently been informed that his father had been left money from the lead mine but not that he also owned shares in the place. From behind, he felt a comforting hand from Jem on his shoulder as if he was pleased for him. Edna glanced at her son and smiled.

"To my sister, Cynthia Methuen, I bequeath fifty pounds and two works of art classified as Artwork A and Artwork B from Hewitt Hall.' Nathaniel paused for a moment then he looked at Tom Langstone. 'To my faithful friend and foreman at the Marshfield Coal Pit, Tom Langstone, I bequeath Artworks C, D, E and F from Hewitt Hall with a view to him selling them to make money for himself and his family." Harry glanced over his shoulder to see Tom wipe away his tears with his handkerchief. He realised those pieces of artwork were worth a considerable sum but he didn't begrudge the man having them as the money would come in handy for him and his family. An auctioneer and maybe an art expert would need to be consulted so the man got the best price for them.

"*To Elizabeth Butterworth...' Harry noticed his mother hold her breath, 'I leave a sum of five pounds...'* His mother exhaled, so his father hadn't left the woman that much then, but Nathaniel continued, *"also Artworks G, H, I, J and K along with a set of solid silver jewellery pieces labelled as 1, 2, 3, 4 and 5 and a property at Wakefield known as "Grange House"..."* Harry watched as his mother's face crumpled and she extracted a lace handkerchief from her reticule and buried her face in it.

This was all too much for the woman and he wished they could leave but he knew he needed to stay. He took her hand and drawing near to her whispered, 'Would you like to leave, Mother?'

She vehemently shook her head.

"*Finally, to my second-born son, who is known locally as "Clitheroe Clement", I bequeath Hewitt Hall and everything else that remains in it along with a sum of one hundred pounds and a regular trust fund. I would also like it made known that I would hope that the man who was brought up as his brother, Jeremy Clement, should reside there also, though the deeds shall be in the name of Clitheroe Clement."*

Harry was shaking inside. He'd been convinced that Lizzie Butterworth would inherit Hewitt Hall but of course, it was Clyde and should be Clyde he figured as the young man had missed out on his real mother and father's love. Though what he despised most was the fact that it sounded as though Mother had no claim on her own jewellery and to add insult to injury, Mrs Butterworth would receive several pieces of solid silver jewellery along with property. Then it came to him, The Grange House was a fancy house quite near to the guest house. Why hadn't his father bequeathed that to his mother instead of a poky little run-down cottage in Drisdale?

He was still perplexed as they all stood to leave and then Jem called after him outside in the corridor.

Harry turned to meet his gaze. 'I'm so sorry, Harry,' he said. 'Clyde is concerned that you'll be angry with him for inheriting Hewitt Hall. He's all of a tremble with nerves. Harry then noticed Clyde standing in his brother's wake. He walked towards him and held out his hand to shake Clyde's. Clyde reciprocated by shaking Harry's hand.

'Now don't you go worrying,' Harry reassured. 'If I wanted that house to go to anyone it would be you.' Tears formed in Clyde's eyes as he nodded with understanding. 'Besides, now that I officially own the shops and shares in a lead mine, I'll be able to afford to buy a new house. Who knows, I might even build one for Cassandra and myself.'

'It's official then?' Jem said, slapping Harry on the back.

'Oh, yes,' said Edna, 'he's told me all about the proposal and how Cassandra accepted.' Her face softened as she spoke about the pair. 'To be honest with you, I think I had a feeling before they knew themselves.'

'I...I...f...feel terrible about pushing you out of your home,' Clyde said looking at Edna.

'Never you mind about that,' Edna reassured Clyde taking him by the arm, 'you're family now. Harry is another brother to you and I'd rather see you inherit the house rather than some others I know.'

Harry realised she was speaking about Clyde's mother but Clyde wasn't to know that. He supposed that the emotional pain ran too deep for his mother ever to forgive his father for taking up with Lizzie Butterworth and for the way he'd treated her with disdain when it came to his will. Harry consoled himself with the fact that at least once he, Jem and Clyde had worked on the cottage it would be liveable and she'd have a modest allowance for the future to live off. Many in the village now viewed his father as some sort of saint since the pit explosion but there were many other words he could choose for the man and saint wasn't one of them right now.

***

Cassie looked up as the bell jangled on the tea room door to see Harry and Edna enter.

She approached them and could see by the woman's puffy looking eyes that she'd been crying. 'Please take a seat, Edna,' Cassie reassured.

Edna nodded and smiled and Harry joined his mother at the table. 'Please sit with us for a while,' Harry said looking up at Cassie.

She bit her lip and nodded. 'I'll have Polly prepare a pot of coffee for us.'

Harry nodded gratefully, then after she'd given their order to Polly, Cassie sat opposite the pair. 'So, what happened in the end?' she asked.

Edna sighed. 'It was awful, truly awful, Cassandra. I mean I knew more or less what would be left to me but to add insult to injury it wasn't so much about Clyde inheriting Hewitt Hall that appalled me as, after all, the lad is William's son too, but was more the inheritance that will be going to his mother.'

'Oh dear,' Cassie shook her head.

'Yes,' explained Harry. 'Mrs Butterworth has gained a new property, a house known as The Grange near the guesthouse.'

'Yes, and she already has a big guest house,' Edna shook her head sadly. 'That's not all she is to inherit some expensive paintings and solid silver jewellery which I believe come from a set he purchased for me when we were first wed.'

'That's appalling,' said Cassie stretching her hand out to take Edna's across the table.

'And other expensive paintings will go to Tom Langstone, Foreman at the pit, which I don't mind too much and others to my auntie, but I detest the way my father has treated my mother.'

Harry slowly shook his head.

'I never realised he hated me so much.' Edna lowered her head and wept. Fortunately, the tea room was quiet as she was quite a private person.

Polly turned up at the table and left the tray of coffee there without speaking, it was obvious she could see Edna's distress.

'I don't know what to say,' said Cassie, she shot a sideways look at Harry, 'but Harry and I have discussed this and when we're married, we'd like to have you to live with us.'

Edna looked at her across the table, eyes shining with tears. 'You'd do that for me after all that I've done to you?'

Cassie nodded. 'Of course, I would. What do you say?'

'It's very nice of you to suggest but I think you'd be better off beginning off married life as a couple in that house, but if living at the cottage doesn't work out then I'll consider it. Thank you both.'

It was some consolation at least to think the woman would gain a daughter-in-law and a new family with Cassie and Emily, Aunt Bertha, Polly and even Jem and Clyde.

'You'll never be lonely with us,' said Polly suddenly as she showed up beside them. 'I got the gist of what you were saying but didn't like to disturb you. I've brought some brandy to put a tot in your coffee, as I think you could do with it right now?'

Edna nodded gratefully as Polly poured a generous tot of brandy into Edna's coffee cup.

'It's not the New Year you might have been expecting, Mother, but I promise you this, you still have a lot to look forward to.' Harry smiled at her and planted a kiss on her cheek.

Cassie and Polly nodded eagerly as Rose watched on from the counter, wondering what on earth was going on.

Epilogue

It was in the middle of the night that it came to Harry: the significance of the date of his father's will, *June the 6th of 1875*. He had awoken from a strange dream where his father was laughing maniacally at him and his mother from his coach window. Then it came to him, the date of the notice for him and his mother to quit Hewitt Hall was the same date that the will was dated. There had obviously been some planning going on there on behalf of his father. Also, the man had purchased the properties at Rowan Road just before Christmas which seemed strange to him. It made him wonder if "Madame Claudette", who his father referred to as Mrs Roberts and appeared to be the only person who knew her by that particular name, was more than an acquaintance towards him. Maybe his father had acquired a string of women with whom he'd had dalliances with over the years. One woman was enough to wound his mother deeply though so he had no cause to upset her further with his thoughts.

At the reading of the will, all the other beneficiaries who were not present were bequeathed modest sums of money or gifts. Harry had recognised all the names as they were family members—apart from Lizzie Butterworth, no other woman's name had been mentioned who wasn't a family member. Yet, it was puzzling to him why his father had suddenly bought those two shop properties in Rowan Road, maybe it was a way of paying Madame Claudette off for her services in a manner of speaking. Still, he didn't want to rake things up, so that was something he thought he ought to keep to himself for the rest of his life. Thankfully, he knew the woman did not have any children of her own. The thought of another brother or sister born out of wedlock would have been too much for him to take right now.

The next task, on Nathaniel's suggestion, was to take both Clyde and Jem to Hewitt Hall and introduce them to the staff there, explaining that from now on Clyde would be the new owner and the reason why. He realised they would be shocked but at the same time, hopefully, pleased that they were to carry on employed at the place.

Harry was glad that when Clyde inherited the property it would be under the supervision of Jem. He had a little chuckle to himself at the thought of Clyde taking over Hewitt Hall and what the villagers' reactions to that might possibly be. Imagine the likes of Artie Crabtree and May Malone knowing that from now on Clyde was a person of power as he lived life in fine style and had the money to do with what he wished. And the funny thing was he didn't begrudge his brother having all of that one tiny little bit. All that mattered now to Harry was his upcoming marriage to Cassandra and taking care of his mother. He counted his lucky stars that not only was it a pleasure being around Cassandra but Emily was a little treasure to behold and the sweetest little girl who had even won his mother's heart.

***

Preparations had been made for Harry to wed Cassandra at the village church. Edna Hewitt had changed her mind about attending there in the end even though she had sworn she'd not set another foot in that place after all that her husband had done to her. Cassie and Harry were pleased she'd finally relented as they didn't much fancy marrying anywhere else and Emily was so well settled at the school there. For time being, the pair were going to begin married life at Rose Cottage while Harry sorted out somewhere more permanent for them to reside. Emily, of course, would be moving there with Sammy too, she couldn't bear to be parted from him. Meanwhile, Polly, Aunt Bertha and Edna would remain living at Hawthorn Cottage. The plan was for them all to live together under the same roof someday soon. Clyde had offered them the opportunity to move in at Hewitt Hall but both Harry and Edna thought that just he and Jem should reside there, there were too many memories in that place for either of them to contend with. Yes, a fresh start was what was needed for everyone.

On the day of their wedding, Cassandra was dressed in one of her best satin gowns that she'd brought with her from Marshfield Manor. It was cerulean blue with white Belgian frilled lace around the neckline. The dress had cost an absolute fortune when Oliver had been throwing his money around, so she planned not to waste it as it had never even been worn. Polly had worked hard to let out some of the seams to facilitate Cassie's ever-increasing waistline. Thankfully, there'd been no further signs of any pregnancy problems; apart from the odd bout of tiredness; the nausea had ceased and now she felt in rude health. Although her wedding gown was one she hadn't had to purchase herself, she wanted to feel special for her big day, so she'd had a bonnet especially made for her at a couture hat shop in Hocklea. Madame Claudette had crossed her mind briefly at that time but she was thankful to have no more dealings with the woman after being previously duped about the tenancy of the tea room like that. Still, all had turned out well in the end. More than well in fact.

As she admired her reflection in the long freestanding mirror in her bedroom, she gazed out through the window towards Marshfield Manor. Her life there now seemed like some sort of distant dream. One of those bittersweet sorts: parts that you remembered all so well and others that you wished to forget.

Today was also a special day as it was Saint Valentine's Day, a day that embraced both love and fertility, and she had both of those she thought as she patted her stomach affectionately. Downstairs, she heard the murmur of voices as Polly, Aunt Bertha, Edna and Emily sat waiting for the coach Harry had ordered for them to arrive. Patiently, she waited for her escort to take her to the man she loved. Jem had insisted upon giving her away to Harry as she had no father to do so and she had been glad of that. Jem's proposal hadn't got in the way in the end, it had cleared her mind for what and who she really wanted in life. And what she wanted most of all was for them all to be happy.

Her stomach flipped over as Polly shouted up the stairs to say they were leaving for the church and she shouted back down that she'd see them all soon as "Mrs Hewitt". That had brought a tear to her eye.

Now, as she gazed at her bouquet which was composed of white tulips and blue hyacinths, tied neatly with a blue satin bow that matched her bridal gown, she glanced at her left hand. Soon there would be a gold ring placed upon it. A new ring. She was determined this marriage would be her final and finest of all because Harry loved her like no other man.

'Come on!' Jem shouted up the stairs, breaking her out of her reverie. 'The carriage Harry booked for us is ready and waiting to take us to the church! You want to see how many folk are lining the street to wave you off!'

Cassandra gasped in astonishment as she made her way slowly down the stairs and out through the open front door of the cottage to see so many warm, smiling faces—at long last, she felt welcome in Wakeford.

Copyright

The characters in this book are fictitious and have no existence outside the author's imagination. They have no relation to anyone bearing the same name or names and are pure invention. All rights reserved. The text of this publication or any part thereof may not be reprinted by any means without permission of the Author. The illustration on the cover of this book features model/s and bears no relation to the characters described within.

Books by Lynette Rees

<u>Historical</u>

The Seasons of Change Series

Black Diamonds

White Roses

Blue Skies

Red Poppies

Winds of Change Series

The Workhouse Waif

The Matchgirl

A Daughter's Promise

The Cobbler's Wife

Rags to Riches Series

The Ragged Urchin

The Christmas Locket

The Lily and the Flame

The Wakeford Chronicles

The Widow of Wakeford

A Distant Dream

Act of Remembrance

Printed in Great Britain
by Amazon